Newly Divorced; Cat Owner

eBook ISBN 978-0-6483653-3-4

Written by Angus Peter Chisholm

Edited by somebody inconsequential

Cover by Amazon

Author's Note:

I wrote this novel in 2021 but did not publish it until 2026. One of the main locations in this novel has subsequently changed branding. I lament its loss to the rich tapestry that is the Queensland Gold Coast. So, please think of this story as happening at an earlier moment in time to when you are reading it.

Table of Contents

Chapter 1

Divorce Equals Insecurity

Once there was a man who lived an unremarkable life. In fact, the only thing noteworthy that could be said of his life was that it was so completely devoid of note. His name was Joseph. He was born and grew up in Broadbeach Waters. He went to school in neighbouring Miami. In his final year he met the childhood sweetheart that would become his wife. Upon completion of their further studies Joseph and Isabella married. They had ten years of wedded bliss before they decided to have a family.

Twins were born one boy one girl. Austin and Karalee absorbed most of Isabella and Joseph's time and energy as children do. Nevertheless, they were raised, schooled in Broadbeach Waters of course, and then set about their own further education to find careers for themselves. However, neither of them was inspired enough by Joseph's career to follow in his footsteps. This perhaps should have been an early warning sign for Joseph that all was not well with course he had laid out for himself. But he did not see it. The twins now aged 21, had moved out of home. This is where our story about Joseph really begins. You see a new beginning can only come about if an existing way comes to an end. And Joseph's ordinary life was about to change in the most extraordinary way.

***

Joseph held the letter in his hand and read the contents once more. it was the notification of the successful divorce of Joseph and

Isabella. It was all at Isabella's request not his. Joseph would have remained happily married; at least his approximation of happily married; for the rest of his life. But Isabella had made her intention to dissolve the partnership excruciatingly clear. And Joseph simply could not come up with any adequate arguments to support the continuance of the marriage in the face of a very logically argued case against.

It was Friday night and Joseph had just arrived home from yet another hellish week in a job that he really could not stand. Instead of relaxing on a deckchair in the backyard with a gin and tonic, He was instead confronted with the legal ending of his marriage. This definitely was not a good week at all.

Although in her mid-fifties, Isabella was still a very attractive woman. Her long dark hair was elegantly styled. Deep earthen-brown eyes and flawless skin only managed to further accentuate her incredible figure. She regarded Joseph's expression and wondered how many times he planned to read the letter before making a comment, any comment? Eventually, she took pity on him and decided to start the conversation herself.

"Look at it this way" she said, "We simply grew apart; no one is to blame". Isabella waited for a response from her now, ex-husband.

Joseph seized upon the cliched statement. He lowered the letter from hiding his face so that Isabella could see him clearly.

"That is the equivalent of children in a playground, telling you that you stink!" He said.

His response was not in any way vitriolic, but Isabella could sense the tension in its delivery. She knew Joseph well enough to know exactly what was behind his mood.

"Another bad day at the office?" she queried.

Joseph almost rolled his eyes and managed a stiff nod. Isabella thought it best to get his usual complaints about his work and work-colleagues over and done with. Somewhat akin to ripping off a band aid in order to get through the pain as quickly as possible.

“What happened” She asked without any real conviction.

Joseph gathered his thoughts and then launched into his usual tirade about Big Lips Advertising; the digital advertising agency that he worked for. As their Accountant, he was charged with ensuring that billing was done, invoices were paid, and the budget was balanced each month.

“Fraulein Flick did it to me again” he said. “The management team are supposed to invent a brand-new product in order to create advertising for it, so that we can showcase our abilities in an online digital advertising symposium later in the month. Correct me if I’m wrong, but isn't that her job? Why am I even involved? It's so typical of her to flick one of her tasks to me and expect it to be done! What does she even do in that company? I'm not getting paid to be the Operations Manager she is. And of course, if I don't, I'll be branded as being ‘not a team player’. Oh, for goodness sake!”

Joseph's outburst had all of the aplomb of a child complaining about having to eat his Brussels sprouts before leaving the dinner table. Isabella waited a moment just to ensure that his complaining was done.

“I know you usually have a gin and tonic on a Friday night but how about a martini instead?” she offered.

“Aren't martinis a polite way of drinking pure spirits and not seeming like an alcoholic? I mean, a way of attempting to seem sophisticated, but actually needing intervention from Alcoholics Anonymous?” blurted-out Joseph.

“I’ll make mine a double” responded Isabella before moving out of the family room and toward the kitchen, where the drinks were kept. As she left the room, she reminded Joseph of an uncomfortable reality now facing him.

“You’ll need to find somewhere else to live. And don’t forget that you are taking the cat with you.”

‘Oh great’, Joseph thought to himself, ‘fifty-five and searching for rental accommodation’. He had assumed that those days were all behind him. It was a rude awakening to find himself on the lowest rung of the property ladder at his stage of life.

“I’ll start looking online tonight” he shouted after Isabella. He made a mental note that he would need a landlord amenable to pet ownership.

Joseph did not want to make the divorce any more painful than it already was. So, he had been quite compliant through the whole process. He moved out to the small backyard. It was enclosed with palm trees, as was the local style in the neighbourhood. The house was in Welby Street and suffered from the ignominy of being one of the few houses in Broadbeach Waters, that did not back on to the canals. It was a long-standing source of disappointment for Joseph, Isabella, Austin, and Karalee as well as family, friends and visitors.

The three-bedroom home had been built in the 1990’s and reflected its age perfectly. It was all that they could afford after they married and began their careers. Joseph in particular liked it, because it reminded him of his parent’s home, the one that he grew up in. That house however, was long since sold, so this was the only remaining connection to the area for him. Joseph and Isabella’s home had served them both through the early part of their marriage and carried through to raising the twins until they both decided to move out of home following the completion of high school. Now, it felt like the house was divorcing him too. As if it wasn’t bad enough to lose his wife, he had to lose the house, the car and his wife! But as a small consolation, he got to keep the family pet.

As if hearing his thoughts about her by telepathy, the medium-haired, golden-eyed black kitty appeared from beneath a nearby bush and plonked herself down at his feet. She looked up at Joseph and let out a single ‘meow’.

“At least you’re not divorcing me” he said to her in return.

The entire picture of the rest of his fifties was clear. Rental accommodation and public transport, and a job he absolutely deplored. How could his situation possibly get any worse? Joseph sighed and decided that his earlier derision of Martinis was perhaps misplaced. He took out his mobile phone from his pocket and proceeded to text Isabella, that he too would have a double Gin Martini.

Chapter 2

Fit into the Rental Mould

After two double Martinis ably prepared by Isabella, and following the feeding of the cat, Joseph decided to skip dinner and go straight to the study, log on to his computer and search for accommodation. Being particularly habitual with his choice of living areas, he naturally searched in Broadbeach Waters.

It was the first day of the first month of summer, and the heat and humidity were already making themselves known. He would have preferred his usual Friday night dinner on the back deck in a cooling breeze. But this had to take precedence.

The first thing that stuck him was the incredible specificity that some of the landlords required of their tenants. There was the usual ‘non-smoker required’ demands on most of the listings. But there were others that he simply could not measure up to. ‘Must be vegetarian so no meat cooking smells permeate the property’, demanded one. 'Must only practice tantric sex so that the neighbours are not disturbed', dictated another.

Joseph was somewhat embarrassed that he was in his fifties and had no idea what tantric sex was? But he thought that regardless of what it was, he most definitely did not want to live near such persnickety neighbours. Was it just that he viewed Broadbeach Waters through rose coloured glasses, or was the suburb full of difficult to please people?

Yet another, in complete defiance to the all-pervading non-smoker rule, absolutely insisted 'Must be a smoker – no self-righteous do-gooders welcome here!' Joseph rolled his eyes. The property looked otherwise quite inviting. But he didn't want to commit to taking up a habit like smoking at his age because it seemed like it would take up too much of his time. He was forced to expand his search beyond his preferred locale, to the neighbouring suburbs as well.

Eventually he managed to gather a small list of properties to view. Some were open for inspection tomorrow, a couple of the others were by appointment with the Realtor only. He wrote the details for all of them on a foolscap page. Then he noted which ones he would need to phone first thing on Saturday morning to try and arrange a viewing that could be worked into his schedule. However, only one of them was in Broadbeach Waters. The others were either north or south of his location, one, two, or more suburbs away.

This divorce may yet deal him another blow. He had lived in Broadbeach Waters his entire life. How would he respond to not being here anymore? He could only hope that the first property that he was due to see, the local one, would work out and this annoying task would be over before he was forced to go further afield.

With his head swimming in the plethora of demands that may yet be made of him in order to become a successful candidate for tenancy, he retired to bed. Joseph had been sleeping in Austin's old room during the proceedings, as it seemed the polite thing to do. He put on his customary t-shirt and boxers and climbed into the single bed.

Kitty decided to join him. He was always amazed at how much room the cat could take up on a bed for something that was so small.

"Good night, Molly-X" he said as she stretched out beside him. It occurred to him as he drifted off to sleep, that allowing the children to name the cat when they were at the height of their night clubbing teenage years, was probably a mistake. He did challenge them about the name that they had chosen at the time. To Joseph it sounded very much like two colloquial terms for an illicit party drug, joined together. Austin and Karalee had strenuously denied it then, but always managed to smirk at each other whenever the cat's name was spoken.

***

Isabella was nowhere to be found when Joseph awoke on Saturday morning. His thumping head reminded him of why he did not drink undiluted spirits. As he wandered into the kitchen to prepare the cat's morning meal, he recalled something Isabella said about taking up Pilates. This must have been one of the class times that she was now attending. It was odd, he though. She had always been careful about her figure. And even now, she still looked pretty hot, at least to him. Why put such energy into something designed for people to stop parts of them sagging, when they hadn't yet started to droop?

He dismissed his line of thinking. There must have been more to it, and most likely it was something that he was simply not comprehending. Checking the kitchen wall clock, he planned enough time to prepare and eat breakfast, shower, shave and drive to his first rental viewing.

"Oh No!" he said, startling Molly-X who was enjoying her kitty gruel. 'No car' he thought to himself, finishing the exclamation. That meant that he would have to catch the light-rail or the bus, or a combination of both to each of the locations. He quickly recalculated the time he would need to get ready and adjusted his preparations accordingly. Grumbling beneath his breath he proceeded according to his newly set timeline.

***

Joseph had pulled it all together in record time and arrived at the first property just as the Realtor was taking the 'Available to Rent' sign out of the boot of his car. Joseph was slightly out-of-breath after power-walking the distance from home to the townhouse. Although in the same suburb, it was on the far side of it, so the journey took a little longer than he had anticipated.

A few things struck Joseph immediately. Firstly, the real estate agent's car looked expensive. He wasn't entirely sure what make and model it was, but there was clearly more money in real estate leasing than there was in accountancy. The second thing was the number of good-looking young couples that were also waiting to inspect the property.

Was it his imagination or were they all regarding him with a good deal of either suspicion or naked animosity? One of the couples greeted the Realtor.

"Good morning, Bob" they both exclaimed in unison. The real estate agent looked up gave them a wave and responded.

“Hey Tom, Hey Martha”

‘They were on a first name basis’, thought Joseph? He was surprised, but that soon turned to incredulity when almost all of the other couples greeted the agent using his first name as well. Joseph immediately felt on the back-foot. The plethora of couples waiting to see the property, and the fact that they all seemed to know the Realtor was nothing short of disconcerting to say the very least.

Eventually Bob the agent, unlocked the door and stood at the ready with a clipboard and pen ready to gather the contact details of the visitors to the rental property. It was almost entirely unnecessary as he knew all the visitors, except of course for Joseph.

“Who do we have here?” he asked in a tone that sounded duplicitous with curiosity and suspicion rolled into one.

“Joseph Whynee; five Welby Street here in Broadbeach Waters” he replied.

“Ah yes, one of the homes without the canal frontage” came the reply which was a rather cutting and cynical summation of Joseph’s house. Or rather his former house. Joseph was immediately put off-side.

“I suppose so” was the only retort that he could think of under the circumstances.

“Looking to upgrade to something with a view?” asked Bob innocuously.

Joseph did not want to go into detail about his current situation, so decided that it would be best to offer the Real Estate agent a quick one-liner to summarise his situation. Joseph mustered all of the decorum that he could, as he delivered the abridged version of his reasons for looking for a rental property.

“Newly divorced; cat owner. Looking for a place to live.”

“Say no more,” said Bob.

Bob reached around the back of clipboard and handed Joseph a rental application form. Joseph took it with a quizzical look on his face.

"I had just assumed that all of this would be done online nowadays?" he said.

"We like to ensure that our tenants can actually read and write" replied Bob without a hint of satire.

"You're kidding?" asked Joseph almost breaking into laughter at the ludicrous regulation. He was met with an impassive stare from Bob which left Joseph in no doubt that the imperative was an nonnegotiable requirement.

"We don't want that tired old excuse from our tenants if we need to serve an eviction notice for any reason, that they can't read and therefore didn't know what it said!" stated Bob with a dour expression. He looked Joseph up and down as if sizing up his potential to be a troublesome tenant.

"Oh; Is that common?" Joseph inquired as he walked into the townhouse.

"More than you might think" replied Bob.

What greeted him was a table full of forms that had already been completed and were deposited on a central pedestal table in the small entrance foyer. Joseph looked at the pile of paperwork in amazement. How could anyone have possibly completed the lengthy four-page form in the time that he had his brief exchange with Bob? It just did not seem possible.

His wonderment clear on his face, one of the couples nearby solved the mystery for him.

"Always have a stash of forms ready to go, if you find a property that you're interested in." said the male of the couple.

"And Bob likes to collect the forms from any table that is closest to the front door." Interjected the female.

Joseph was stunned. He felt like a complete amateur surrounded by professionals. Clearly these people had been working with Bob so long that they knew his habits as well as his name. This did not give Joseph any confidence that his property search would be a short and fruitful one.

"How long have you been looking for a rental?" inquired Joseph.

The question was clearly not one that potential tenants asked of one another because both sets of eyes narrowed in suspicion.

"Why do you want to know?" came the rather terse reply from the fellow.

"Oh, um, I'm just starting. I mean, this is my first viewing. I've only just started to look for a rental today."

Joseph explained his situation, hoping to diffuse the misdemeanour that he had unwittingly committed. The couple nodded with indifference and moved out to chat with Bob the Realtor, leaving the question unanswered. This was the first time that Joseph had a chance to actually view the property that he had pinned such hopes on. If he could secure this one, then he would not have to leave the area. And he could at least have some semblance of the continuity of his life in Broadbeach Waters.

The townhouse was ineffably eighties. That is to say, it looked like something straight out of a ninety-eighties home decorating show. Glass bricks abounded to separate kitchen from dining and dining from living spaces. The tap wear in the kitchen and bathroom was faded gold. Overall, the entire thing looked tired and dated. Joseph could not help thinking that he and this townhouse would make a good match in this regard.

But time was ticking by. Joseph completed the form and by the time he was finished he looked up to find Bob glaring down at him with impatience.

"Times up!" he declared, indicating the end of the open for inspection viewing time.

"What do you think my chances are? You see, I already live here and getting this property would mean that not much would have to change…" Joseph was wasting his breath and he knew it.

"I'll let you know what the owner says when we've gone through the applicants together" said Bob the Realtor. It sounded very much like he was being fobbed-off whilst simultaneously being told to not hope for a favourable outcome.

"Well, at least you can see that I can write" offered Joseph. He hoped a little light humour would put him in better stead with Bob. It did not. Instead, Bob squinted at the form and the messy scrawl of Joseph's that covered the pages.

"Is that an 'S'?" queried Bob.

Joseph looked at where Bob was indicating and corrected him.

"It's a five" he replied.

"And is that an eight?" Bob continued.

"No, it's a B."

"What about that one?" Bob said indicating another entry on the form that looked exactly the same.

"Oh, that's an eight" he declared with a smile.

"I see" said Bob with more than a hint of annoyance.

"What about................" Bob began again and then summarily decided that it was an exercise in futility.

"You know what, don't worry. I'll figure it out, and I'll call you if you're successful."

Bob's tone left Joseph in no doubt that his property search scheduled for the rest of Saturday morning and part of the afternoon, had better proceed with more success than he had managed here. Otherwise, he would be remaining as a reluctant resident in Austin's room for a lot longer than either he or Isabella would prefer.

***

Joseph spent the rest of the morning darting off the light-rail and onto a bus and vice versa in order to accomplish his complete list of property inspections. He could not help the feeling that it would not result in anything resembling victory. He ran into several of the same couples at some of the other property viewings. The ones that he had first seen at the Broadbeach Waters townhouse. After reaching the end of his compiled list, he found himself in Surfer's Paradise and desperately in need of cheering up. He decided to have a coffee.

He was in the quieter part of the beach-fronted suburb when he found two cafes. Neither had a view of anything by the look of it, but Joseph did not care. All he wanted was a meal and a strong coffee to pep him up a bit.

He noticed something about the two cafes. They were directly opposite each other. Both were in older low-rise buildings that had somehow managed to make it this far into the twenty-first century, without being redeveloped into modern high-rise apartments. One of them was absolutely full of youngsters the guys sporting beards the girls looking like the image of 1950's housewives.

'What was it with those pretentious Hipsters?' he thought to himself. To him there was nothing separating the two cafes. They both looked of equal measure to satisfy his hunger and thirst. Yet one of them for reasons that would forever remain a mystery, had found favour with the millennials and was inundated with them. The other, ostracised through no fault of its own.

Joseph additionally pondered how his own twin children managed to avoid falling into the Hipster sub-culture within the millennial generation.

He decided upon principle, to patronise the quite café. Firstly, there was more chance of getting served in a reasonable time-frame. Secondly, he was sure that just about every barista nowadays could make a good coffee. Whatever the hipster-popular café was doing, Joseph was certain that the competitor could do just as well. He set off resolutely to affirm his belief.

Chapter 3

Choose Your Coffee Provider with Care

Joseph strolled into the café without taking note of its name and surveyed the scene. It was small, consisting of an inside section with rustic looking tables and chairs. There were a couple of tables out the front pavement section. And a courtyard could be seen through a single door, that led past the washroom. No doubt there was a kitchen somewhere at the back, possibly behind the washroom. A lone operator stood behind the coffee machine which formed part of the front counter. A sign could be seen clearly displaying the procedure for ordering in the café.

ORDER AND PAY AT THE COUNTER BEFORE BEING SEATED.

Dutifully, Joseph stepped forward and greeted the barista.

"Hello. May I have a strong café latte and.........." He trailed off now perusing the blackboard that was on the wall behind the man. He studied it and was left somewhat confounded by the descriptions of the food available.

It seemed to be a mishmash of Thai, and traditional café style food. But he was unsure of what some of the ingredients were. It all seemed to be very vegetarian. Not something that Joseph objected to, but he could really do with a burger, he thought.

"If you can't see anything there that takes your fancy, I can have our chef whip something up for you. He's a completely certified macro-biotic-vegan-practicing chef." Offered the barista.

"A what?" queried Joseph, confused by the number of the adjectives prior to the title of chef.

"What would you really like to have today?" asked the barista.

"How about a chicken burger?" answered Joseph.

"No problem. One TVP burger coming up!" exclaimed the barista.

"Tee,Vee, Pee?" said Joseph his inflection becoming higher as he progressed through the acronym.

"Textured Vegetable Protein" replied the barista "You won't be able to tell the difference between it and chicken. But no cute little bird must die in order to feed you. Isn't that fab?!"

The joy on the baristas face was a little infectious. It went some way toward ameliorating Joseph's concern about the meal that he had just ordered.

"What kind of milk would you like in your latte?" inquired the barista.

"Just regular milk please" replied Joseph.

The barista shook his head and gave Joseph a look like a teacher admonishing a pupil for bad behaviour. He pointed at the secondary board beside the food menu. This one listed all the different types of coffee and an even longer list of milk substitutes that could be used to make them. At the top of the list was a sign that left Joseph in no doubt that he could not simply have regular milk.

COW'S MILK IS FOR BABY COWS; DON'T STEAL IT FROM THEM!

Joseph was astounded at the length and complexity of the list. He looked at the barista with a mixture of amazement and confusion. Perhaps choosing this particular café may not result in the satisfying experience that he had assumed. He looked out the window across the road to the competition. From here he could see the barista serving a coffee to a waiting patron. The baristas in both cafes had the obligatory man-bun, sleeve tattooed forearm and lengthy beard. Yet Joseph had managed to find the one that was a militant vegan, through and through.

There was almond milk, rice milk, soy milk, and a plethora of others that he had not even heard of.

"Isn't calling all of these milk a furphy, though?" stated Joseph. "Afterall you can't milk a soybean? And how about the ethical objections to stealing milk from baby almonds? Am I right?"

His assertions had the opposite effect of amusing the barista, who gave him a snide, harrumph in reply.

"Tell you what" said the barista after a short pause. "If you can't decide, I can give you the closest approximation. Something to fool your tastebuds and not offend my vegan principles. What do you reckon?"

It seemed like a reasonable thing to do. There certainly was no specific objection that Joseph could think of that would get him out of the situation. So, he agreed.

"Good show!" Said the Barista.

As Joseph was paying for the meal, a rather mangy looking dog ambled into the café. It was medium sized and rather scrappy looking. Perhaps a cross between a blue-healer cattle dog and a Stafford-shire terrier.

"Hey there Joseph". Said the barista.

"How do you know my name?" Asked Joseph.

“I was speaking to the dog. He wanders around here. Spends some time in my café. Has a sleep in the courtyard and then disappears? I assume that he belongs to somebody around here. He has a collar and a nametag – Joseph.”

Joseph was enlightened by the explanation.

“Well, he’s got a good name” said Joseph of his canine counterpart.

He went to choose a table in the courtyard out back. The dog followed. The courtyard was completely enclosed with other 1950’s or 1960’s buildings to each side and the back. Blond brick structures with aluminium sliding windows. And exterior waste pipes coming through and down the walls, usually from the area below the frosted glassed windows, indicating that it must have been from the apartment’s bathrooms. Not exceptionally beautiful, as far as courtyards go, but nevertheless, it was shaded from the harsh summer sun. Joseph settled into a chair with a matching table. It looked to him like something cheap from a mass-market Swedish furniture manufacturer.

As he waited for his fake chicken burger and dubious café latte, Joseph browsed his phone hoping for any word from any of the leasing agents that he had met today. There was nothing via text nor email to give him a glimmer of hope that his housing crisis would be sorted anytime soon. The dog settled down at Joseph’s feet, contented to be with company.

It wasn’t long before the Barista delivered the café latte to Joseph’s table. The barista announcing proudly exactly the type of coffee that Joseph had ended up with.

“One thick rice milk café latte topped with an oat milk foam” he declared and waited for a reaction from Joseph.

“Sounds good” replied Joseph hoping desperately that he was getting away with his blatant lie.

“Excellent” said the barista and disappeared back inside.

Joseph gave the coffee a distrustful look and then elected to continue surfing the internet on his phone whilst the burger was prepared. Eventually, the barista then delivered the Textured Vegetable Protein 'chicken' burger.

"Let me know what you think" said the barista as he delivered the burger with a flourish before disappearing inside once more.

Joseph regarded the burger with some suspicion. He leaned forward and gave it a cursory sniff. There was nothing to indicate anything even resembling chicken in its neutral aroma. He decided to deconstruct the burger to see what its constituent components were.

There was the top and bottom of the bun. That seemed to be perfectly normal bread. It would not have any butter or egg in it owing to the vegan leanings of the proprietor. But that could be overlooked. Joseph comforted himself that it would simply be like eating gluten free bread, able to be done if there was nothing better available.

Coleslaw was present for sure. But of course, the mayonnaise would also not have any egg in it. Joseph wondered what vegans used in place of eggs. Perhaps it was something called T.E.S. Textured Egg Simulation. Joseph amused himself with his little parody.

Lettuce and cooked onions made up the remainder of the ingredients other than the TVP. Joseph mused that at least there was nothing in fried onions that a vegan could find offensive. A small victory for common sense, he thought. Lastly, there was a tomato-based relish of some description. Nothing offensive about that he decided.

He reassembled the burger and took a breath. How bad could it be? Scrunching it between his hands he lifted it to his mouth and gingerly took a small bite. It was enough to encompass a small taste of all the burger's ingredients. The moment his teeth crunched down after the initial bite, the TVP released some of its juice that rolled onto his tongue and then down the back of his throat.

Joseph almost gagged with disgust. It was absolutely VILE!

“Gaarrrgh!” he said as he nearly ejected the entire contents of his mouth onto the table in front of him. Either through instinct or revulsion he dropped the burger back onto the plate. It was taking all of his faculties to cope with not projectile vomiting. He needed something to wash down the hideous-tasting rubbery synthetic chicken patty that was assaulting his taste buds.

Without thinking he reached for the café latte and took a sizeable gulp. It was RANCID! If there was any flavour of coffee in the latte at all, it was totally obscured by the foreign invaders that had kept normal cow’s milk out of the mixture. Joseph felt the world around him shrink as he contemplated choking on the doubly disgusting mess that was in his mouth rather than swallowing it. With a huge effort, and with his eyes bulging out of their sockets, Joseph swallowed the contents in his mouth.

“Blahhhhhhh gggg hhhh ….whyyyy, meeeee!”

He said shaking his head, his tongue hanging out of his mouth in the vague hope that a passing seagull would shit in his mouth to disguise the putrescent taste. ‘How could ANYTHING taste that disgusting?’ he pondered whilst trying to compose himself.

The burger was completely inedible, and the latte undrinkable. What was he to do? What if the barista came out wanting to know how the meal was? He pictured the situation in his mind and contemplated pushing past the fellow and running as fast as he could for the exit. Joseph began to break out in perspiration beads on his forehead.

At least now he knew why meals had to be fully paid for before consumption. There would be no possible way that anybody with a sense of taste would pay good money to feast upon such flavour hideousness.

Looking around Joseph's mind raced. Maybe he could climb up one of the waste pipes and into a window. If he explained his sudden appearance, perhaps the resident would take pity on him and allow him to exit through their property? There simply was no other way out of the courtyard!

A rustling from below the table reminded him that there was the dog sleeping at his feet. Effectively it was another prisoner here in the courtyard with him. A thought began to solidify in Joseph's mind. It was just the patty that he could not bear the thought of eating. The bun and the other ingredients could be consumed without gagging for sure.

"Hey boy; want a *chicken* patty?" he asked of the dog.

Alerted to the potential of food, the dog stirred and sat up in a begging pose. Joseph separated the TVP from the rest of the burger and flipped it to the dog. He rubbed his fingers on the napkin trying desperately to remove any microbes of it from his fingers. The dog caught the 'treat' in his mouth and proceeded to gobble it down.

Perfect. Stage one of his plan was completed. The TVP was gone. There was no evidence that he was not the one that ate it. Anyone would rightly assume that he had consumed it. Time to enable stage two of his plan to escape from the café with his dignity intact. Joseph set about eating the palatable components of the Frankenstein chicken burger. He surprised himself with how quickly he got through it. He was really hungry after his day of property hunting.

This left the obvious remaining part of his exit plan staring back at him from the table. The poisonous caffe latte. What was he going to do with that?

He had lifted the noxious mixture to regard it with some further trepidation. Desperately searching the courtyard, he hoped to find a drain or something. He needed to dump the liquid, and quickly. There was nothing. It was concrete in all directions.

He was beginning to panic at the thought of attempting to swallow any more of it when, he heard footsteps coming from within the café. Without thinking, he tossed the entire contents of the glass over his right shoulder. He heard a muffled splash. Hopefully too dull for the approaching barista to register.

Joseph felt the panic begin to rise in him higher. The barista appeared and took note of the empty plate and latte glass sitting on the table before Joseph.

"Looks like you enjoyed those" he observed with a broad smile.

"Sure did" responded Joseph.

It was then that the barista caught sight of the brown liquid.

"What on earth is that?" he said looking behind Joseph.

Joseph turned and took in the sight that beheld him. The rancid coffee had managed to land completely on a sewer waste pipe extruding from one of the flats and was oozing down its length. It looked for all the world like the pipe structure had failed somehow and released the contents of it to the outside world.

"That sewer pipe must have backed-up and cracked somewhere?" said the barista incredulously.

"Oh, is that what that putrid stench is? I was wondering where it was coming from?" Joseph decided in an instant to support the incorrect assumption made by the barista.

And it was definitely in his best interests to enforce the improper recognition of the oozing fluid. Joseph stood up and seized upon the situation using it as an excuse to exit as quickly as possible.

He was about to make his brief goodbye, when a gagging-coughing could be heard coming from the dog. They both looked down to see what the matter was. The dog began vomiting on the concrete at their feet.

"Dog, what's the matter?" screeched the barista.

In reply the dog yacked up yet again.

"Must be something he ate" diagnosed Joseph. "I'd better go. Lots to do!"

Joseph said a quick 'goodbye' and 'thank you' and exited as quickly as he could without seeming like he was in a desperate hurry to get out of there. As he left the café, quickly grabbing a mouthful of water from the jug on the counter, he couldn't help looking around to take in its signage. Joseph could hardly believe his eyes when he finally registered the name of the establishment.

THE MILITANT VEGAN CAFÉ

It all became immediately and abundantly clear why the café across the road had all the business and this one did not. For the first time since the advent of hipsters, Joseph thought that maybe they could be used as a barometer for where to go and where to avoid.

He was busy contemplating this thought further when a bus could be seen approaching. It was displaying that it was a route toward Coolangatta. This suited Joseph perfectly. He decided to catch it to visit his father in the retirement home down there. Thankfully, he was near enough to the bus stop to wave the driver down.

Chapter 4

Old; Not Dead

Joseph managed to get through the entire public transport ride from Surfer's Paradise to Coolangatta worrying about his living arrangements. He was the kind of guy that internalised a lot. So, having something so critical to focus upon was perfect for his inherent sense of impending doom. As you can imagine, he was not exactly in the right frame of mind to visit his father in the retirement home in which his father voluntarily lived.

'Golden Years' was the name of the establishment. It always reminded Joseph of the title of the David Bowie song of the same name. He disembarked from the bus at the front door of the establishment. Some public servants had clearly planned the strategic position of this particular bus stop very carefully.

Joseph entered the double automatic smoked glass sliding doors and made his way to the concierge counter. It was manned by the ever-present Receptionist Fatima Forthright. Forthright by name, very forthright by nature, Joseph often thought.

"Hello there" said Joseph trying to sound as cheery as his current mood would allow.

Fatima looked up from whatever it was that she was doing and looked immediately annoyed at being disturbed.

"Ah, Harrington's boy" she stated as she recognised him.

Joseph always managed to feel like a schoolboy visiting his grandmother in a retirement home when *that* particular tone was used to describe him.

"He's in the smoking room" informed Fatima.

The nomenclature was of course a complete falsehood. There was no such thing as smoking in a retirement home of this calibre. It was just a name for one of the many common areas in which the residents could gather outside of their individual home units that were spread throughout the rather expansive, and expensive, establishment.

Joseph often wondered how Fatima always seemed to know exactly where his father was when he came to visit. And was so deftly able to direct him accordingly. He suspected that the electronic medical alert bracelets that all the residents wore, had some kind of tracking device in them and was linked to a screen just out of sight of visitors to the reception desk. But he could never prove it.

"Thanks, I know the way" he responded as he made off in the general direction.

Harrington Whynee was a retired Federal politician. After a lifetime of serving his country in either opposition, or in government, he was given a 'golden' handshake and retired from the service. His wife, Joseph's Mum had sadly died shortly thereafter following a brief illness. It was then that the 'family' home in Broadbeach Waters had been sold and Harrington basically liquidated his life in favour of the Golden Years aged care facility.

As far as old-age-homes go, this was the very cream of the crop. The exorbitant fees ensured that only the upper echelons of the retired were able to afford to live there. It kept out the riffraff, as Joseph's Dad liked to say. It also ensured that as an only child, Joseph was left in absolutely no doubt that any inheritance he may have hoped to gain at the end of his Father's life, would be for the most part already spent on accommodating Harrington throughout his twilight years.

Joseph entered the rather snootily named ‘smoking’ room. Harrington was sitting in a large chair having a lively discussion with one of the lady residents. Upon recognising his only-son he indicated that he should come over and join in the conversation.

“Hello Son!” said Harrington with all the diplomacy and finesse that you would expect of a retired politician.

“This is Cru-Ella” he added, introducing the lady sitting opposite him.

“I’m sorry” said Joseph immediately flummoxed. It sounded awfully like a fictitious character from a cartoon-movie that he and seen as a child. Perhaps he had miss-heard the name.

“Crooll-eella” she said with an indeterminable eastern European accent.

Joseph still did not quite comprehend the name and contemplated for a moment asking one of them to spell it out for him; but decided that he would rather live with the ambiguity.

“Do I smell egg salad? Is that what you had for lunch?” asked Joseph innocuously.

This had an immediate effect of raising a huge grin from both Cru-Ellah and Harrington.

“I’ll leave you to have a father-son discussion about *….lunch*” said Cru-Ellah before bidding them both goodbye.

“She seems nice” said Joseph trying to reignite the conversation once she had gone.

“It’s four p.m. Joseph. That means for a start, that we have all just had dinner. Lunch was at eleven a.m.” explained Harrington.

Joseph immediately had to readjust his thinking based upon his surroundings. He kept forgetting that time had to run according to what the residents wanted, and not what was generally acceptable to the rest of the population.

"Of course," he said apologetically.

"And that *egg-salad*, smell is one of two all-pervading odours that drift around the common areas. Along with *boiled-cabbage*, they both move like invisible pockets of fog. But in this instance, they are a stench that invades your olfactory sense, rather one that obscures your vision."

Harrington finished his explanation looking for all the world like he had just clearly, and succinctly explained everything that he needed to.

"I still don't understand, Dad. Where do the odours come from?" he asked innocently.

"Flatulence of course. This place is full of it!"

"What?" asked Joseph somewhat flummoxed.

"Residents here have a correlation to the amount of flatulence that they expel. Your number of close friends is directly proportional to the amount of gas that you exude. Less farts equals more friends!" Harrington made it all sound so normal.

"Errrr. Oh, that's nice" Joseph couldn't think of any other reply under the circumstances.

"Do you have lots of friends?" he inquired of his father.

"Plenty. What's on your mind? Or is this just a conscience-clearing visit?"

Joseph was a little offended. He liked to visit his dad and never felt that he needed to quell any feelings of guilt about him being here. After all Harrington had chosen this institution after the untimely death of his wife, Joseph's Mum, Betty.

This was the best of the best when it came to retirement homes. A cluster of common area buildings were surrounded by smaller one- and two-bedroom self-contained villas. All within the expansive and very nicely landscaped grounds. Which included a nine-hole golf course as well as a small lake, forested area, and an exquisitely manicured Japanese garden. Cleaning was done by the residential homeowner's association. Catering was provided, for lunch and dinner each day. Breakfast was the responsibility of the residents. But the higher-needs ones could have that done for them too if required. There was medical help close at hand, a hospital neighboured the retirement complex. All, up it was a very pleasant place to while away your time.

Upon retiring, and before Betty passed away, Harrington and Betty purchased a Winnebago and did a grand tour of the country. The mobile home was affectionately named 'Bago'. It came to be known as the Harrington Whynee Bago Winnebago. But also came to be called the Betty Whynee Bago Winnebago.

If it was a slow news day when they entered a township or city, they almost always made the local news. The name of the Winnebago changed dependent upon who was photographed or filmed driving it at the time. It had a great effect on the popularity of the retired Federal Politician. In fact, it made him more popular in retirement than when he was in office. Although, you could say that about any Politician really.

The only thing that could have possibly improved his public image more positively would be if he hosted a television series about travelling by train around his own country and others.

Now seventy-nine years of age, Harrington had elected a retirement home rather than living alone in the former family home in Broadbeach Waters. Which is why it was sold, much to Joseph's horror at the time.

“The divorce has come through,” said Joseph.

“Oh, I see. Feeling a little abandoned, are you?” asked Harrington.

Joseph had not considered exactly how he felt. He had tried to avoid thinking about the entire thing throughout the process.

“Feeling a little homeless actually” replied Joseph. “Isabella wants me to move out and today I’ve discovered that hunting for a rental is not an easy task.”

“I’d love to help you out Son, but I only have a one-bedroom villa.” Harrington said.

Joseph was put immediately off-guard. He hadn’t even considered moving in with his father in the interim whilst his housing crisis was sorted.

“No, really, that’s ok. I wasn’t looking for lounge to sleep on in the meantime. Besides what is the lower age limit for being able to be a resident here anyway? Surely I’m too young?!” Joseph said defensively.

“Fifty” came the rather sobering reply.

Joseph had qualified to move into a retirement home for the last five years but had never considered himself old, until now.

“Son, it’s like I told you throughout my entire career. You should have gone into Politics with me. Accountancy won’t get you a life like this in your twilight years. Politics is way to go! Pretend that you care about people and their pathetic little problems. Pick up your salary every month. And retire in luxury. Even if you suck at it, you are still looked after in the end. It’s a complete rort. I’m surprised more people don’t do it?”

Harrington’s rather cynical summation of his own entire career was well known to Joseph. He had had to endure it throughout his adult life.

"This is the life son! More sex than I ever had as a teenager. Nobody looking over your shoulder judging you. Let me tell you; old people can get away with a lot. It's fantastic!"

Harrington's revelation took Joseph by surprise.

"More…sex?" he gingerly inquired.

"Most people here are widows or widowers; what else are you going to do with your time; watch television?" Harrington shifted in his seat as if remembering some recent dalliance. He smiled and continued.

"Cru-Ellah, is an absolute devil in the sack" he said with a naughty glimmer in his eye.

This was more than Joseph wanted to know. As his own sex-life had completely disappeared long before Isabella had talked him into this divorce; he had little interest in anyone who was getting more lucky than he was. But something did intrigue Joseph. Enough for him to ask one follow up question of his dad.

"How many *girlfriends*, do you have here?"

Harrington looked at the ceiling and seemed to mentally gather the information for his son.

"Cru-Ellah, and Simone are my main roots. Then there are secondary roots, Sharmine, Jacinda, Alison, Frida and Fleur. And then there are the ones that you'd only do, if none of the others are available for some reason. Like, Chelsea, Cleo, Clarissa, Wendy,……….." Harrington went on to name at least ten other women's names, but Joseph had already stopped registering it. He was horrified. His father was a regular Casanova! Either that or a raving sex maniac?

"I'm sorry I asked!" he said with genuine regret.

"Lack of sex getting you down too?" suggested Harrington.

"You know what, I'd better get home and let Isabella know that this house-hunt may take more effort and a bit longer than anticipated."

Joseph decided to terminate his visit as quickly as possible. It was easier than imagining his father in the role of overly sexually active Grandfather. He briefly pondered if all the residents in the establishment were sexaholics?

"Well drop by anytime. I'm usually here" offered his father.

"I'd be afraid of what I'd walk in on!" replied Joseph.

Harrington did not get up to see Joseph to the door of the smoking room. It occurred to Joseph as he left that calling it the *smoking room* may be more apt than he first thought. His father was absolutely hot to trot!

Chapter 5

Is Bigger Better?

By the time that Joseph got home, or rather to Isabella's home, it was past six in the evening. The summer ensured that the sun was still shining though. He noted as he walked up the short driveway, that Isabella's lawyer was visiting. Joseph recognised the car driven by Mister Yarra Youngman, taking up far too much room on the driveway. 'Strange' he thought. 'Why visit on a Saturday evening?' He assumed that it must have something to do with their recently successful and finalised divorce.

He entered the house and made his way to the living room. Nobody there. He ventured into the dining room, then kitchen then family room and then outside to the rear garden. Other than being greeted by the cat, clearly making motions to be fed, Isabella and Yarra were nowhere to be found.

He decided to check the bedroom for no reason, other than he had not searched any of them yet. Out of habit rather than with any forethought, Joseph unceremoniously opened the door and walked into the main bedroom. The sight that greeted him defied description.

Isabella and Yarra were stark naked on the bed and intertwined in a love-making position that could only be described as one of the more obscure sexual positions of the Karma Sutra. In that split second Joseph felt his eyes bulge out of their sockets before blurting out a horrified scream.

"Aaaaarrrrrrrrrgggghhhh!" he exclaimed.

This was returned two-fold firstly by Isabella and then by Yarra. The chorus of hearty screaming with absolute surprise and abject horror, filled the room.

"What are you doing? Get OUT!" shouted Isabella.

This was all that Isabella could do under the circumstances, as the intricately complex interwoven position in which Joseph found the two lovers, would certainly take more than a few seconds to unravel.

For a split-second Joseph was about to demand an explanation of the shenanigans he had interrupted when the reality of his intrusion dawned on him. He was single now. Isabella was single now. And therefore, they were both free to engage in sexual relations with any other consenting and mutually agreeable adult that they so desired.

Joseph could actually feel his eyes retreating back into their sockets as he backed out and grabbed the door handle swinging it shut. He hurried down the hallway to the kitchen where he was greeted once more by the cat making her need very clear, that she simply had to be fed.

Joseph briefly wished for the first time since he was a teenager that he had a bigger penis. Certainly, the position that he had just witnessed made such an appendage a necessary prerequisite. And clearly, Yarra Youngman was a very well-endowed young man! But wait; there was something more. It was niggling at the back of his mind waiting for resolution. As the seconds ticked past, he came to the slow realisation that he felt completely inadequate.

Yarra Youngman, was well-hung, handsome, no-doubt earning a substantial salary, athletic, flexible and not even thirty! Joseph was none of these things. He could feel a deep spiral of self-pity beginning to open up before him. Thankfully, the cat having done her best to convince Joseph that she urgently needed to be fed, decided to up-the-ante.

Joseph pulled out a kitchen breakfast stool and took a seat. He was about to sink into a well of self-disappointment and recrimination for missed opportunities, but Molly-X poised herself and then jumped into his lap with claws extended.

"AAAAAAAAAHHHHHHH !" he said as he jumped out of the stool. All the thoughts he was about to wallow in, left him in an instant.

"Alright! I'll get your dinner!" he said sternly to the mischievous cat.

Joseph had managed to portion-out the exact amount of wet and dry food for the cat when Isabella appeared wearing a bathrobe. He looked at her and then down at Molly-X.

"Here you go girl" he said as he placed the bowl down to where the cat could get to it. The cat purring with delight at finally receiving her meal.

"Don't be upset Joseph; I'm just making use of my newfound sense of singularity." Isabella stated innocently.

It sounded all so perfectly reasonable. But Joseph could not help feeling hurt and abandoned. And then a further horrible thought occurred to him. He gave it voice.

"How long has this been going on?" He demanded.

"About a couple of hours. We've tried some pretty difficult positions. Ones that I've wanted to try for years but never had access to the right sized……………………sense of adventure!"

Isabella could see the growing horror on Joseph's Face.

She realised that she may have misunderstood the question. And strategically cut-off her explanation before making any denigration comments about the size of Joseph's manhood.

“Oh, you mean, have we been an item prior to the divorce? Good heavens no. I’ve only just seduced Yarra. It’s our first time…you know…together. I picked him up at Pilates. Turns out that we have a similar appetite for acrobatic sexual positions. Who knew!?”

Isabella’s explanation was said with a smile and was strangely comforting in the current situation. Although Joseph was not entirely sure why.

“Well, that’s good” replied Joseph.

Isabella could see that Joseph was doing his best to adapt to the situation. She decided to help him along a little.

“Tell you what” she said “I’ll give back the wedding and engagement rings. So, that you’ll have them handy should a new miss-right walk into your life. Would that help you feel more at ease with me exploring my new and reinvigorated sex life?”

Isabella was being a little crafty though. She believed in the old adage, that a divorced woman should always give back the ring; but keep the stone. She mentally made note that the diamond would need to be separated from the ring by a jeweller.

“I’ll have them cleaned and deliver the wedding band and the engagement ring, hopefully to your new home?”

Isabella’s reference to the fact that Joseph had been house hunting all day reminded him of exactly how completely unsuccessful he had been.

“Oh, yeah. About that…” he said.

“Yes?”

“I think that it could take a bit longer than I first thought. But I’ll keep trying. I had no idea that the competition would be so fierce.” He said and then added as an afterthought.

"Where's Yarra?"

"He's having a shower and then making a discrete exit. I get the feeling that he doesn't want to say hello." She explained.

"How old is he exactly?" Joseph inadvertently touched a nerve with Isabella.

"He is twenty-seven my dear! What of it!?" she replied defensively.

Joseph knew that he had irritated Isabella from her tone.

"No reason" he said. "Just curious."

She sniffed and giving Joseph a warning glance to never bring up the age difference again, left the kitchen.

"Dad says hello" he said as she left the room.

Isabella answered as she walked down the hallway toward the main bedroom and no-doubt the adjoining bathroom.

"Went to visit him did you. That's nice. I hope he is keeping busy?"

Joseph answered beneath his breath now that Isabella was out of earshot.

"As busy as you; apparently!"

He then briefly wondered if he too should join an online hook-up app of some description. But then immediately dismissed it. He could not bear the thought of stumbling across Isabella's profile. He could only imagine what it was like.

***

Joseph retired for the evening early that night. It was barely 8pm. But the day had proven itself to be so arduous that bed seemed to be a refuge from the many hurdles that he had faced. He ruminated that this had been a particularly unpleasant Saturday. Was he now relegated to having a hideous Monday to Friday at his job, and then a terrible Saturday as well? There would surely be further Saturdays wasted by house-hunting and competing with the other renters for a decent property.

'What if tomorrow was no better than today?' He pondered that thought for a while. But then decided that short of a meteorite entering the Earth's atmosphere and striking him in the head, he was sure that Sunday could not be any worse than today.

Joseph's thoughts turned to the assignment that he had received from work. That was nothing but another weight on his already over-burdened mind. He did not realise it at the time but thinking about work, would overnight, do him a great disservice. How could he come up with a pretend product that his company could then market at the forthcoming symposium?

Molly-X joined him on the bed once more. Her purring was always welcomed by Joseph. It had a hypnotic effect upon him. When he heard it, it always managed to lull him gently off to sleep. Molly-X began her melodic purring, and before long Joseph was fast asleep.

Chapter 6

The Dream

Joseph had entered rapid eye movement sleep quite quickly in the normal cycle of his slumber. But he was unaware of it.

'Everybody is getting laid except me?'

Joseph heard his own voice but was sure that he had not spoken the words. It seemed to come from all around him. He was in a dark corridor.

'Even Dad is getting lucky and he's in his seventies'.

The simple process of walking down this dimly lit passageway seemed to be able to pluck his thoughts and amplify them back to him. Being completely ensconced in the dream, Joseph did not question this new reality.

'What did I do so wrong in my life, that I've ended up divorced and looking for a place to live?'

The gloom surrounding Joseph seemed to darken even more with the prevailing mood that he was falling prey to.

'Isabella has already moved on with her life, just one day after the official notification of our divorce. When will I be able to move on? Leave behind everything that I thought I was supposed to strive for?'

The questions that Joseph was posing for himself were becoming increasingly distressed. It was an accurate reflection of where he found himself in his waking life. Of course, that thought did not occur to him yet. It was something that only the reflection of a fully aware consciousness could do.

Gradually Joseph became aware that something was pursuing him. He turned around but the prevailing light did not allow for clear vision beyond a very short range. He strained his eyesight to see what it was that was approaching. Gradually the vision became resolved. There were multiple small blobs approaching. He wondered what they were.

Closer and closer they came. There were about five, maybe seven of them. Each the size of an orange. But the colour was obscure for the moment, as was the final resolution of their shape. Alarm began to rise within Joseph. What were these things that were hunting him? Were they predators of some description?

He was frozen to the spot. His legs made of lead. He was unable to move. Panic began to grip him as tightly as a pair of hands strangling his throat. Then without warning the multiple objects revealed themselves. They were disembodied floating vaginas!

Joseph's initial terror was immediately replaced with wonderment. What on earth were these vaginas doing here? What did they want? Who did they belong to? And how did they become separated from their owners? These were the pointless questions that Joseph was pondering when they suddenly became aggressive.

Each of the vaginas grew a differing set of teeth. One was vampiric in design. One was hideous and could only be described as 'English' teeth; you know; *before* they discovered orthodontics.

Another set was so completely and unbelievably perfect that they had to be veneers of some kind. The rest, well it did not matter. They were vaginas with teeth! And all of them were snapping their vertical teeth at him, wanting to take a bite out of his flesh.

Suddenly, Joseph realised that he was naked! He was naked before an aggressive set of vaginas with sharp teeth; what was he going to do? How could he defend himself from these hideous things?

Joseph turned and ran as fast as he could, the snapping vaginas following trying their best to take a piece out of his flesh. He screamed in terror. They were catching up with him. Joseph ran and ran but the further that he ran, the faster that he ran, the more the gnashing vaginas gained on him. It was hopeless!

He was about to give up and shout a final scream of surrender and allow the predators to devour him. He turned in resignation of his fate but something extraordinary happened. All the vaginas began to lose their teeth. They all fell out like pieces of chewing gum from a packet. It was as if they were almost spitting their teeth out and becoming 'normal' disembodied floating vaginas.

One by one the now toothless vaginas began to merge. Two became one. Then a third melded into that one. Each time a vagina blended into the group the receiving vagina became bigger. Not by a factor of one, but by many.

From the logical standpoint taken by Joseph, two vaginas together should make a vagina twice as big. Three vaginas, a vagina three times as big. But the mathematical constraints of multiplication did not seem to apply here. Or maybe it was by a factor that he simply could not calculate without more accurate measurements.

Soon enough the last vagina made itself part of the gestalt. The resultant vagina was a bit as a car! It moved upwards and floated above Joseph. Terror was replaced with astonishment. Who did this huge floating vagina belong to?

But just as quickly the emotion of the event turned about. The vagina began to sink down and threatened to envelope him. Once again Joseph was running for his life. The dimly lit corridor that he was running down served to thwart him. The floor became gooey, and his feet began to stick to the ground. It became increasingly difficult to move. Bit by excruciating bit he was unable to escape from the massive floating vagina.

Eventually the floor became so viscous that he was unable to move. He turned to see the great vagina catch up with him. It hovered above him almost teasing him with the ultimate doom that it was about to inflict upon him. Slowly

Sluggishly, the vagina descended. Joseph screamed out, but nobody was around to hear is cry for help. The huge vagina enveloped his head, shoulders, torso, waist, thighs, knees, calves, shins and finally his feet. Joseph was completely absorbed by the huge vagina. It was suffocating him to death! The moist enclosure should have been a rapture for him, having been deprived of sex for so long. But the opposite was true. Joseph was wracked in absolute terror.

***

Joseph woke up in a cold sweat. He cried out as he sat up in bed, disturbing the pussy cat as he did so. It took him a moment or two to realise that the absorbing of his entire body by the enormous vagina had been only a bad dream.

“What the hell was that?” he said aloud, with only the cat to hear him.

As if sensing that his question required an answer, Molly-X let out one simple ‘meow’.

“Life is becoming increasingly difficult Mollly-X” he said to her. “At a time in my life when it should be becoming simpler”. He paused for a while before completing the thought.

“What am I going to do?”

There was of course, no immediate answer for Joseph, either from his cat, or from the universe in general. But an answer, of sorts, would come sooner than he thought. All he had to do was persevere a little while longer.

***

Thankfully for Joseph, Sunday passed without incident. He was unable to property search as real estate agents never worked on Sundays. Although, in this world of being able to access most things twenty-four hours a day, and seven days a week, Joseph could not understand why that was. Nevertheless, he was grateful for the break.

He enjoyed a gin and tonic on the garden chairs along with a piece of grilled Salmon for his lunch. He watched some sports on the television in the afternoon. But Sunday has a way of disappearing faster than most days, and soon enough he found himself retiring for the night.

'Oh no!' he thought to himself; another week at Big Lips Advertising, where his will to live would be further diminished. He pleaded with the world around him to give him a sign that all was not doom and gloom.

Chapter 7

Doing the Same Thing Gets the Same Result

The Big Lips Advertising offices are in a low-rise commercial tower in Surfer's Paradise. Just up one suburb from Broadbeach. It was situated there for the sole purpose of having a Surfer's Paradise address. The building itself was ineffably from the 1980's but had been given a face-lift a couple of times to try and redress its obvious architectural shortcomings. The latest of these had seen the peach and powder blue colour pallet altered to be various shades of white. None of it was successfully bringing the building into the new century, however.

It had a name that almost nobody knew. The Forum Building at 3173 Surfer's Paradise Boulevard had a circular atrium with twin hydraulic elevators to cover its mediocre three floors of height. Hydraulic lifts were all the range back in the 1980's for a reason that nobody in the current century could understand. They were painfully slow. And walking up the stairs was a speedier way to get to your floor and exit from the building rather than waiting for the elevator and enduring a ride so slow that you could knit a scarf on the way up or down.

The building itself had a way of rubbing Joseph the wrong way, just because of what it was. He secretly longed for a more modern office in which to work. But that was simply not on the cards for this organisation. Big Lips Advertising occupied the entire top floor of the building. So, at least, Joseph rarely had to put up with any other tenants on the excruciating elevator ride to the top level. He always chose to ride the elevator up, because it delayed the start to his working day. Upon leaving each day he hurried down the stairs to speed up his exit from work.

And then there was the company name itself. Big Lips Advertising. What genius thought up that one he had often wondered? The primary focus of the company was women. Which was completely and utterly ironic as most of the senior management positions were inhabited by men. Including that of the original founder.

He had in the past inquired about the origins of the name. Apparently, the title of 'Digital Advertising Agency' had been floated at the workshop done at the formation of the company. But the name had been dismissed as too boring. They wanted something more edgy. Something that reflected the values and the thrust of the company. So, Big Lips Advertising was born about ten years ago.

Joseph had speculated that if the company had called itself 'Male Media' and then purported to support the cause of women, that it may have looked a little too insincere. In the end the connotations of having Male Media champion the plight of women in the modern world would seem even more detrimental than the potential offence caused by calling it Big Lips Advertising. The staff in general had managed to abbreviate the company name to BL Advertising. Which was a little easier for Joseph to say to clients when he rang them chasing up an unpaid bill or the like.

But it was not just the Forum building that got on Joseph's nerves. Several the staff also managed to irk Joseph quite a bit. As Joseph arrived by the slow elevator, he had to contend with one of them. Dolby Doowright, the head of customer experience was in his mid-forties and had an exotic national heritage. Canadian mother and Vietnamese father. But he had a dumpy figure and strangely divergent eyes. Joseph could never figure out if one of them was dominant and the other lazy, or if it were simply the case that Dolby had the ability to look both left and right simultaneously. Either way, it was one of the plethora of things that Joseph found immediately infuriating.

Dolby was too close to the elevator for Joseph to not run into him. Dolby was busy with his overly loud and fraudulently happy, "Good Morning" aimed at each person that he saw. Unless he was instantly rewarded with a response the 'offending' person would be subject to a follow-up "Good Morning!" at an even closer range. His divergent eyes and pudgy face pushed way too close into the personal space of the person to be able to ignore.

Joseph groaned as he realised that he was next in line for the greeting. Dolby tended to wear leather sandals around the office. They slapped against his feet in the most aurally disturbing manner. It was a sure-fire way to extinguish any peace and quiet that Joseph hoped for in order to ease his way into the working week.

"Good Morning, Joseph!" he said a huge grin covering the man's face.

"Hi there Dolby" Joseph answered hoping that would be the end of it.

"Good weekend?!" Dolby further inquired.

Without thinking Joseph began to let out exactly what he was thinking, which was 'oh no I was hoping for no follow-up question'. But all that came out were the first two words before Joseph brought himself into check.

"Oh No"

"Really? That's no good! What was so bad about it?" Dolby asked.

Joseph had to think quickly to divert a catastrophe! That is, further conversation with Dolby Doowright.

"Oh No, it was nothing worth mentioning, that's all I meant. Weekends come and go with such rapidity".

Joseph hoped that his reply would not garner any further conversation from the man.

“I know that feeling!” replied Dolby before moving off, his sandals slapping the soles of his feet in the most maddening way.

Joseph thanked his good fortune for cutting short the exchange. He hurried to his office in order to take refuge from any further assaults. Settling himself down in front of his PC he switched it on and waited for the age-old relic to go through the motions.

It was then that he saw the note that he had written for himself on his notepad before departing on Friday evening of the week before.

‘Organise a meeting with Dolby to discuss the new client.’

The ten words were like a dagger in Joseph’s heart. He had just managed to extract himself from the bore. Now he had to ruin any hope he had of having a bearable Monday by meeting with him. Joseph groaned audibly. He muttered underneath his breath ‘why me?’

One of the other many shortcomings of Dolby Doowright, that aggravated Joseph intensely, was Dolby’s meeting calendar. It was always full. Every single day and all hours in the office. When Joseph viewed Dolby’s schedule through Outlook, it was impossible to get a meeting with the man. On the face of it, one could think that he was incredibly busy. But Joseph knew better. He had become suspicious long ago and made a point of sneaking a look over Dolby’s shoulder when his calendar was opened. All the meetings were completely false. What the head of customer experience was doing was booking up his day with petty things in order to look busy to the rest of the staff. He spent most of his day shopping online from what Joseph could tell.

Already Joseph’s week was lurching toward tragedy. The ignominy of having to come up with an invented product for the team was bad enough. Now, he had to do this as well. Joseph knew it from the get-go this was going to be a bad week (as usual).

***

Joseph's working days were beginning to blur into one. The mindlessness of doing a job he did not have a particular affinity with, combined with working for a management team that seemed bereft of direction and proper leadership was taking its toll on him. He did not like to admit it, but this was just another dreary week in a dead-end job. Another week of sleeping in his son's former bedroom at the house that he used to call his own. Isabella had been strangely absent during the nights. He guessed that she had become so enamoured with Pilates that she was immersing herself in it. Either that or she was drinking from the fountain of Yarra Youngman's youth. At any rate, he was grateful for not having Isabella around to remind him that he had to find a place and move out.

On a particular morning when he had exited the building for a mid-morning coffee, Joseph had returned and did his usual thing of catching the elevator up to the third floor rather than walk. He was surprised to find his boss in the elevator when it reached the ground floor. She must have come up from the basement car-parking level. Some other of the younger creatives from the office had managed to catch the elevator doors before they closed. It was a long and painful ride up to the offices of Big Lips Advertising.

His boss, Jeva Jungfer, or as he liked to refer to her Frauline Flick was carrying a white ceramic mug filled with golden coloured fluid. Joseph felt obliged to make small talk.

"What's that you're drinking?" he asked innocently.

"Chamomile tea" came the typically efficient Germanic response from Jeva.

Joseph leaned over and caught a whiff of the aroma being emitted from the cup.

"It smells like wine?" he stated.

All eyes turned to Jeva for a response.

"It's Pinot Grigio" she said in an earnest reply of the actual contents of the mug.

There was an awkward silence from everyone in the elevator. Sensing (rightly) that she was being judged for her choice of liquid consumption, Jeva made to justify the reason for consuming wine in her mug.

"I've had a hard week" she said with just a hint of menace.

"It's Wednesday morning." Stated Joseph.

The look that Jeva shot Joseph left him in no doubt that he was in very thin ice indeed. And should he say another word, he was in danger of breaking through and sinking into the frigid waters below without a hope of rescue. Joseph groaned internally. When it came to his boss, he did not even seem to be able to successfully make small talk without getting on her bad side.

"I'm sure that we are all looking forward to your presentation tomorrow, Joseph. You don't want to disappoint the advertising team with anything sub-standard, do you!?"

Jeva left Joseph in no doubt that he was the man in the current spotlight, and not her. Nor was her bizarre wine drinking schedule. Thankfully by then, the elevator doors opened, and the two younger staff members bolted as if they had been scaled by steam.

Joseph indicated that Jeva should exit first. He was nothing if not polite. She strode from the elevator taking a generous gulp from the cup of wine as if to spite him.

'Why me?' Joseph thought as he made his way to take refuge once more in his office. 'What am I going to do?' he added to his cascade of self-pitying pondering.

"What is it that I can invent that the advertisers can really get their teeth into?"

Joseph was alone, so his posed question would not have an answer from anyone. But then something ignited in the back of his head. 'Teeth'. He looked out the window hoping for the glimmer of a memory to become a spark of inspiration.

"What is it that women have, use or do, that has never been invented before?"

Once more Joseph was only verbalising his questions in order to help his own thought making processes. Then like a flash of lightening he joined the two thoughts together. In an instant he knew exactly what Big Lips Advertising should be displaying at the symposium.

He set about creating a PowerPoint presentation to reveal his inspirational thought to the management team tomorrow. For the first time in a long time, Joseph felt that he had come up with the goods. He was sure that he had absolutely nailed the brief that he was given. Big Lips Advertising would think that this was the best idea to come their way, ever! A sense of both pride and accomplishment began to fill Joseph. What could possibly go wrong?

Chapter 8

It is Called Lipstick, Not Lip's Stick, Nor Lips' Stick

The rest of that day and night were a blur for Joseph because he was so excited to show the company his idea for the advertising symposium. He was absolutely certain that the creatives would have a fantastic time coming up with inventive ways of advertising his new 'product'. The morning dragged on until the inevitable management meeting, of which he was always a part, convened in the boardroom of the Big Lips Advertising offices.

It began with his presentation of the financials of the company. As per usual, in his eyes of course, the presentation was impeccable. Thanks entirely to him, the company was in good financial stead. The entire, mostly male, management team nodded in approval at the thought of being in a company flush with money. Between the 12 of them, there were various self-congratulatory messaged bandied back and forth.

Oliver Opplesham, fifty years of age, original founder of the company stood up. He saw himself as another Bill Gates or Steve Jobs, but clearly did not have the talent to create an empire the size of theirs. Nevertheless, in his own eyes, Oliver was their equal in stamina, charisma, and intelligence.

"Time for us to talk about the forthcoming advertising symposium".

His words were spoken as if he were Caesar addressing the senate. Joseph had often wondered how Oliver hoped to emulate the success of his tech-wizard heroes. BL Advertising after all was just a digital advertising agency. It was not a technology start up as Microsoft and Apple were, with their visionary leaders at their helms. Oliver however was so self-deluded that he put more time into dreaming about his forthcoming empire, rather than doing any actual work to get his company and his employees to where he aspired them to be.

"I believe that Jeva has something for us" he concluded and handed deftly over to the head of operations.

Jeva Jungfer stood up and address the male contingent.

"One of the great pleasures of managing people is seeing them develop and grow. To this end I have managed downwards and have tasked Joseph with inventing the new *product* that we will be advertising at this year's symposium. To that end I will once more hand over to Joseph to show us the next big thing. Over to you Joe!"

She was so adept at flicking her work to him that it had become something that she could now boast about in the management meetings. Joseph would have been more upset, but he was so full of enthusiasm for this presentation that he put aside his normal grievances about his alcoholic boss. His PC was already hooked up to the big screen for his financial presentation, so all he had to do was begin the new presentation.

A large image of a lipstick appeared on the high-resolution large screen monitor.

"Did you know that lipstick is the single highest selling beauty condiment that women worldwide purchase regularly. In fact, a Gartnor-Symes study has found that a high percentage of women will purchase lipstick in favour of any other beauty product available."

Joseph clicked the 'next-slide' button and the figures that he had alluded to, appeared on the screen in a typically accountant's favourite, pie chart format.

"This is the kind of repeat purchase that we can now maximise with our new product. One that is sure to not only grow the lipstick market by a significant margin, but one that with the correct advertising, the correct *BL Advertising*-advertising, is a market that could easily be doubled in size!"

His grandiose claim garnered sharp inhales of breath from the group. Joseph looked around the room. He had everybody completely in his thrall. It was all going exactly has he had imagined that it would.

He brought up the next slide. It was another image of lipstick, this time gold in colour with embedded glitter particles. There was a simple phrase accompanying the image, 'Two Times'.

"What we need is a product that is twice the size of the one used by women for their lips".

The viewers all began to look at each other in confusion. But Joseph was ready for this and circumvented the obvious questions before they could drag down the flow of his masterful performance.

"No no no my friends. I am not proposing that we increase the size of women's lipstick!"

This however did nothing to clear up the misunderstanding that was happening all around him.

"What I am proposing is a new type of lipstick that is twice as big and used on an entirely different part of a woman's body. This newly created product will be used-more, depleted-more and therefore causing the need for women to buy-more of it!"

With a flick he brought up the crescendo of his presentation. The words appeared in their own.

"Presenting 'Lip's Stick'. A new kind of lipstick used on a woman's *other* lips! A lipstick twice the size, so that the femininity of a woman can be visibly enhanced with multiple colours. Bright, sheen, satin, glitter, extroverted or muted. It's all up to the confidence of a woman and how she wants to display her larger set of lips to those privileged enough to see them!"

There was what could only be called a horrified silence. Joseph looked at the faces of the managers around him. They were completely, utterly and totally aghast. It was Jeva that broke the awkward silence.

"Are you seriously telling us to advertise Lipstick for a woman's labia majora!"

Jeva's sudden reference to the medically correct name of the part of a woman's genitals that Joseph's *product* was referring to, was a bit jarring at first. But he realised that it was indeed what he was trying to express to the group.

"Why yes, of course. If a woman takes to using lipstick, or rather Lip's Stick on her labia, then more will be used, more sold, more advertising needed. It's a win; win situation. BL Advertising will be at the forefront of an entirely new wave of feminine beauty product. It will be our i-Pod, our Windows operating system. We simply cannot fail to succeed. We will be able to take a *fake* product from the symposium and out into the real world! And WE will be responsible for creating it."

Joseph used the Apple and Microsoft comparisons to his product because he knew that it would surely resonate with Oliver.

It took a few more moments for the other managers to compose themselves before the objections began to cascade forth like an avalanche down a steep mountainside.

"Are you absolutely MAD!" said one.

"It couldn't BE anymore offensive!" came another.

"We'll be vilified by women the world over! this is corporate suicide!" said someone else.

"How would you even portray that in our advertising, with extreme close-up photography!?" came another vitriolic retort.

There was at least one objection from each of the managers present. Some had two or three to spew at Joseph. The cacophony that filled the room was deafening.

Joseph was both perplexed and mortified that everyone did not absolutely love his idea. He sprang to its defence immediately upon hearing so much criticism.

“It’s no more offensive than naming a company Big Lips Advertising!” he insisted.

“You just don’t understand the meaning behind our branding; the power of Big Lips!” said someone.

“The power of Big Lips is that It’s empowering” stated another as if it were an obvious fact that Joseph had somehow missed.

The objections continued for a while. Eventually, Oliver and Jeva between them managed to wrest back control of the room.

“Joseph” said Jeva in her most scathing voice.

“I gave you a SIMPLE brief to give us a new product that nobody has seen before, and THIS is what you give us? It’s monstrous! What were you thinking?”

Joseph was crushed. He could not understand why everybody was not as enthusiastic about his new product as he was.

“And another thing” said the head of marketing, “The apostrophe is in the wrong place. If it is a noun concluding with the letter S, then the apostrophe should come after the S and not between the P and the S. To denote ownership”. It should be Lips’ Stick!”

This caused a smaller outbreak of arguing within the group.

“No, that is not right at all. He at least has the apostrophe in the correct place if nothing more”. Someone said coming to Joseph’s aid.

The ensuing argument about the correct placement of the apostrophe was completely lost on Joseph. He sank down into his chair with the weight of the world around crushing him. He was unsure how long the ensuing arguments about the value, or lack thereof, of his product went on. But he was left in no doubt that he was the only person in the management team that thought his idea had any value whatsoever.

This was not the first time that BL Advertising had argued about the correct way to present a simple English word. One of the former advertising campaigns that they were commissioned was about the number of fatalities suffered from electrocution. The campaign itself was excellently orchestrated. It concluded with a swathe of stickers that were surreptitiously stuck on power poles all around the city to remind people that electricity can be fatal. However, whoever signed-off on the sticker printing clearly could not spell correctly, because they were printed with the word Fatel. Which isn't a word at all.

The rest of the meeting was devoted to the management team trying their best to remedy the situation and invent something for the advertising symposium themselves. It was ironic thought Joseph; this was their collective job in the first place. His idea may not have been received with the vigour that he had anticipated. But in the end the effect was that he managed to manage the management team into managing the situation themselves.

His non-victorious idea suddenly did not feel as bitter as he would have thought. In fact, Joseph was feeling somewhat managerial.

Chapter 9

Retrenchment Hurts

Joseph had to bite his tongue when he arrived home that evening. He knew that Isabella would not want to know anything about the machinations of the office. It was in reality, one of her pet hates about his job. The fact that he despised it so much and the people that he worked with. And rarely missed an opportunity to complain about them to her. However, he clearly was not completely and utterly dissatisfied with BL Advertising. That is, not enough to go and find himself another job with a less objectionable crew. Or maybe he was just too lazy to up-stakes and start again elsewhere. She was not sure which, and he knew it.

"Oh just another day at the office" he replied when Isabella politely asked about his day.

***

Mercifully, Friday came around to help soon relieve Joseph of his work suffering. That is to say, that it would soon be replaced on Saturday with another kind of suffering, house hunting. Joseph had endured Dolby Doowright's hideously cheerful 'Good

Morning', accompanied by a symphony of slapping sandals against his bare feet as he paraded around the office pretending to be busy.

Joseph had had to persevere through the morning stand-up where Dolby read out what seemed to be an impossible to achieve list of things that simply had to be done today. But Joseph knew that when he returned to his office, Dolby would be right back online and doing some internet shopping.

The morning stand-up itself was a complete farce. Somebody had heard about stand-up meetings as an integral part of agile methodology project delivery. And although Big Lips Advertising did not actually implement any information technology projects, they had collectively liked the sound of it. So, it was adopted, just because it was the 'now' and 'happening' thing. Not because they actually needed to tell each other what they did yesterday, what was planned for today and if they had encountered any 'blockers'?

Following the morning stand-up meeting, Joseph was getting some financial statements in order when Jeva caught his eye through the various layers of glass offices between him and her. It was if he could feel her staring at him. He gave her a quizzical look and she responded with a motion of her hand. She wanted him to join her in her office. He audibly groaned knowing that nobody would hear it. He was skilled enough with this to ensure that his mouth did not move when he emitted the cry of pain.

He left his office and contemplated exactly why Frauline Flick would want to see him? Probably, to flick some more of her responsibilities his way prior to the weekend, just to satisfy her own ego. He sat without any of the customary small talk. There was silence for a short time before she said

"We will be joined by Iris".

It was a simple enough statement, but one filled with menace. Iris Ironside was the humourless head of Human resources. Austere and skinny, she was someone to avoid, even at the best of times. Joseph's mind raced. Was he in trouble for his grandiose but ill received, vaginal lipstick idea? What else could it be? Perhaps that twit Dolby Doowright had complained about him not responding in an equally overtly happy tone to a 'good morning'? They were the only two things that he could think of that could have possibly rubbed Human Resources the wrong way.

The skinny frame of Iris Ironside appeared at the door. She was carrying a manilla folder full of papers. She nodded politely to them both and took a seat next to Joseph.

"You're probably wondering what this is all about?" said Jeva

"Ahh, well, yes, actually" he replied.

"Big Lips no longer needs you Joseph" she said in a brief but all too confusing sentence.

Joseph looked at Jeva and then and Iris and back again.

"I'm sorry" he said bewildered by the statement.

"Accounts receivable and payable is not really the creative core business of Big Lips Advertising. So, the management team have decided to axe your function from the company."

Jeva seemed pleased with her simple and to-the-point explanation. Joseph however was left more confused than ever.

"I bring money into the company. What could be more important than staying in business?" he said pleading for common sense to prevail.

"Oh, for goodness' sake Joseph. Don't overestimate your value to Big Lips, please!" she retorted.

"We have found a specialist company in the Philippines that will do your job for us at less than half the cost. It makes great economic sense for us. And will allow you to pursue new challenges in your life."

Jeva finished her explanatory speech and waited for Joseph to react. He was mortified beyond belief and could barely gather his thoughts.

"Is this because of the Lip's Stick presentation?" he asked, trying to grapple with the reasons behind his sudden demise.

"No, not at all. We've had this in mind for the last couple of months. Now is just the right time to hand over to the new incumbent; remotely of course and cut you from our team."

Jeva was so matter-of-fact with her tone and rhetoric that Joseph could scarcely believe that it was *his* retrenchment that they were discussing. Iris picked that moment to pipe up and support Jeva's statements thus far.

"Let's face it Joseph, Big Lips just doesn't want nor need you. It's time to face facts. It's nothing personal".

"But I want Big Lips!" he replied in desperation.

This situation, he thought, was a metaphor for his life since the age of Forty. It was then that he noticed that he failed to turn any heads as he did in his youth. It was as if he had rubbed an invisible and odourless sexual repellent all over his body. This only escalated through his Fifties and now his unseen and unwanted sexual repellent was working to make him unattractive to his place of work too.

"And then of course there is the endless complaining. It has really irritated your fellow colleagues" added Jeva.

"Complaining? Me?!" Joseph was horrified.

"Oh yes; behind your back you are called 'Whingey Whiney Whynee', and 'Why Me Whynee."

Jeva's information was a sour revelation for Joseph who thought (mistakenly) that he had always managed to hide his dissatisfaction with the job and the general staff within Big Lips Advertising.

"Sometimes it is 'Why Me Whingey Whiney Whynee" she added.

"And other times it is 'Whingey Whiney Why Me Whynee". She further explained.

"I get the picture; thank you" he said rather curtly.

The rest of the meeting was a blur for Joseph. Iris took him through his redundancy payout and how that figure was arrived at. It did not seem to justify the years that he had put in. But he knew the legislation behind the calculation and figured that it was the best he was going to get as a parting pay packet from Big Lips Advertising.

It was barely nine-thirty on a Friday morning and suddenly, he was unemployed. Part of the final payout was that he would have to spend the following week handing over his current workload to the new overseas outsourcer.

Iris and Jeva told him to take the rest of the day off, to let the news sink in. And that they would see him bright and early on Monday morning for his final week with Big Lips Advertising. Joseph did not return to his office. There was nothing in there that he needed. He walked out of the front doors and made his way down the flights of stairs to the lobby. He arrived at the front doors to the building and looked through the heavily tinted glass for a short time.

"No marriage, no place to live and now, no more Big Lips" he said to himself.

Chapter 10

A Phone Call Can Change Your Fortunes

Joseph had nowhere in particular to go. Nobody that he felt he could confide in at this time in his life. He was down and out in every way. No home, no job, no wife. He walked away from the Forum building taking no direction in particular. He wanted to put some space between him and the office. That was his only plan at the time. He glanced at his watch; it was ten o'clock in the morning. Knowing that did not help him in any way.

What was he to do? He pondered the question whilst he walked aimlessly. Perhaps if he sat on the beach for a while and watched the waves rolling in, he would feel better. It wasn't much of a plan, but it was all he could think of to do. So, that is what he did.

By the time Joseph arrived at Surfer's Paradise Beach it was about twenty minutes past ten. He sat on the sand and looked at the perfect blue sky and sea before him. His plan was having a desired effect. It began to mesmerise him. The sound of the surf, the seagulls in the sky, it was beautiful. He almost failed to notice that his phone was ringing.

Abruptly brought back from the illusion of perfection that he had enjoyed for a brief time he answered the phone.

"Hello, is this Joseph Whynee?" said a rather strong male voice.

“Yes speaking” he affirmed.

“This is John Strauchn, the President of the Returned Soldiers League. Normally our head of marketing would be making this call, but she is away sick today, so I have the pleasure of speaking with you.”

Joseph was a little perplexed. But managed to pick up on the organisation that was calling him. The RSL and he had also heard the word marketing and put the pair of facts together before responding.

“Have I forgotten to renew a subscription or something. I do apologise, I’ve been very distracted” he said offering some solace for his perceived lapse in attending to them.

“No, no, no, Joseph. It’s nothing like that. As far as I know your subscription to our lottery is running perfectly. Just as well for you. Thank you very much for your support over the years. I can see from our database that you have supported the RSL for the two decades.”

Joseph was always happy to support the Returned Soldiers League. He believed in the programs that they had for our returned troops and was happy to help out by buying a lottery ticket in each of their prize draws throughout the year. He vaguely recalled that there were ten major prizes giveaways every twelve months. And then sundry other draws.

“You’re very welcome. But I’m unsure of why you are calling me?” he said, rather perplexed.

“I think that there is normally a script for this kind of thing, but I don’t have it so, I’m just winging it. Joseph I am ringing today with the best possible news.” John said.

This could not have come at a better time for Joseph. But his suspicions were now raised. How could anybody possibly be ringing with good news after he had suffered so many setbacks recently.

"What is the good news that you have for me?" he asked with some trepidation.

"Joseph I'm ringing to tell you that you have won first prize in our latest lottery. The major prize draw number four-two-two that consists of a luxury residence and a yacht" he replied.

Joseph was immediately dumbstruck. The stunned silence lasted long enough for John to ask if he was still on the line.

"Are you there?"

"Are you joking with me?" blurted out Joseph, unable to come up with anything else intelligent to say under the circumstances.

"This is no joke, Joseph. As you can see from your phone, I have not masked my number. What you are seeing is the direct line to my office. But if you need absolute proof, what we should do is end the call. I want you to phone directory assistance for the RSL headquarters phone number in Fortitude Valley and then ask for me. Tell reception who you are and believe me, they will put you straight through".

"John Strauchn" said Joseph reconfirming the man's name,

"Correct. Talk to you again soon".

With that John terminated the call. Joseph was shaking his head in utter disbelief and shock at what had just happened. It was so sunny that he was having trouble seeing the screen of his phone. But he persevered and managed to get through to his carrier's directory assistance number.

"May I have the phone number for the RSL in Fortitude Valley please" he asked.

"Shall I text that through to you or connect you directly" came the speedy response.

"Please put me through, and then text the number too, if that is ok?" he asked.

"Certainly, sir" said the operator.

The phone felt like it rang at the other end for an age before it was answered.

"RSL Head Office, Miranda speaking, came the greeting.

"This is Joseph Whynee, may I speak with John Strauchn please" he asked.

"Of course, Joseph, I'll put you right through. And, congratulations, you are a very lucky man indeed" she said.

Before long he was once more in conversation with the president of the RSL.

"I don't believe it. I mean, I DO believe, it! But I just don't believe it. If you know what I mean?" he blubbered.

"From what I'm told this is a very common reaction, Joseph. Put aside your doubts and tell me how you feel about winning this major prize from the RSL?" inquired John.

It was then that Joseph realised that he did not have a firm understanding of the details of the prize in this case. He had long ago stopped looking at the brochures that they sent him through the mail. In fact, now that he thought about it, he had agreed to emailed brochures instead of printed ones, a number of years ago to save them on the cost of printing and postage.

"I'm rather ashamed to admit this but I am not very familiar with this particular prize. I seem to have got rather caught up in some goings on in my life and must have overlooked the email". He said hoping that his explanation did not draw any further queries about his lack of knowledge of the prize he had just secured.

"No worries, Joseph; allow me to take you through it. You have won a three-bedroom condominium at Palazzo Versace on Main Beach. It has its own plunge pool. Access to all of the facilities of the five-star hotel that it adjoins. There is a full Versace furniture package included. You will be one of the privileged owners that make up the residential section of the complex. Current market value is two point seven million dollars "

John's explanation was giving Joseph a light head, he was so happy.

"In addition, your condominium comes with its own marina berth in the Palazzo Versace Marina. Moored there is your forty-foot sailing boat, an Elan Impression monohull yacht for your sailing pleasure. She's a real beauty and named rather appropriately 'Beat the Odds'. Valued at four hundred thousand dollars. Do you sail at all Joseph?"

John's question put Joseph off-guard completely.

"Well, no....but there's' nothing stopping me from learning right!?" he said with a chipper tone in his voice.

"That's the spirit," said John.

"Total prize value when we factor in the Palazzo Versace Homeowner's Association fees and marina berth fees for the first year brings the figure to three point one seven five million dollars. Joseph, you are now an instant multi-millionaire. I'll be sending you a detailed email about the next steps. That is, getting the title of property transferred into your name, and the ownership of the boat...... So, who is the first person that your going to tell the wonderful news too?" John inquired,

Joseph was once more flummoxed.

"Oh, my kids I suppose" he said.

"And how will you be celebrating?" John asked.

Once more Joseph had no idea but came up with a predictable response for the occasion.

“With the largest bottle of champagne that I can find!” he exclaimed.

“Wonderful. It has been a pleasure breaking the good news to you Joseph. Congratulations on your good luck, and once more, thank you for supporting the RSL”.

“Thank you, Goodbye!” said Joseph earnestly.

John hung up. Joseph was still on the beach. He had not realised it, but he was now standing up. His heart was racing. He looked about him. The world somehow seemed brighter than it did when he arrived on the beach. He felt like he should make good on his promise to celebrate. So, he headed toward the main shopping street to find a bar in which he could toast his unusual good fortune. And phone his loved ones to tell them the amazing news.

He began his search and unwittingly found himself in front of ‘THE MILITANT VEGAN CAFÉ’. It was closed and had an officious looking sign on the door. Joseph approached it and read it aloud,

“Closed by order of the City Council due to effluent contamination. Remediation works in progress”.

Joseph was horrified. What had he done? The coffee he threw over his shoulder had been mistaken by the Council as a sewerage pipe leak. And, he had had a lot to do with that mistaken belief being pawned off to the café barista. He must have in turn pointed it out to someone that had gone on to report it to the local council. It was amazing how his unbridled happiness had suddenly turned into all-encompassing guilt.

He was about to give some thought to how he could possibly correct the mishap when the news of his amazing win seemed to reassert itself within Joseph’s psyche. It pushed itself back into his brain. It was as if, it had been suppressed by the feelings of guilt, but it did not want to be. The incredible luck he had received, wanted to be the sole thought in his head right now. And it wasn't going to give in to something as petty as guilt. So, Joseph gave into the feeling. It was easier than suffering remorse for his earlier actions at the cafe. He fleetingly promised himself that he would solve this problem some other time.

Chapter 11

Bar Tenders are the new Priests

Joseph floated around the main strip for a while. He managed to wander around without remembering that he was looking for a bar in which he could sit and celebrate and phone his good news to the world. Eventually without even realising it he stumbled upon a bar on Cavill Avenue called 'Swipe Rite'. He had heard of this bar. Over the weekend it became a singles pick-up joint. But apparently through the daylight hours, it was full of tourists and quite respectable.

This would do perfectly Joseph decided. He would order a glass of champagne and phone his family about the news. Then he stopped to rethink his tact. He didn't have a car anymore. He did not need to drive anywhere in particular. He would instead, order a *bottle* of champagne and have his family join him here to celebrate. It was a great plan.

Joseph entered the bar. And predictably as it was only around eleven o'clock in the morning, it was empty except for the barman that he could see at the far end of a rather long, marble topped bar. A broad window allowed a view out to the avenue below. Sunlight streamed in through it giving the bar a glittering quality. Or maybe it was just Joseph's elevated mood that was doing it. But either way it looked a pleasant enough place from which to begin his celebrations.

The barman waved and indicated that as the bar was otherwise empty but for the two of them, that Joseph should sit anywhere that he desired. Joseph elected to take a rather large and imposing booth that looked as if it could seat ten or twelve people. Good he thought. This will be his throne from where he delivered the news to everyone.

The barman approached carrying what looked to be an extensive beverage menu. As he got closer Joseph had the feeling that he knew the fellow. He certainly was well tanned. It gave his face a weather-beaten textured look. He still had a full head of hair. Joseph guessed that the barman too must have been in his mid-fifties.

"Well bless my soul, if it isn't Joseph Whynee" said the man as he arrived at the table to present the drinks menu.

Joseph was surprised that the barman recognised him. It took a moment for him to piece everything together before he was able to adequately return the acknowledgement.

"Gavin Grosvenor? Is that you?" he asked.

"It sure is old school buddy. It's been absolutely ages since I've seen you. How are you Joe?"

It was indeed classroom chum from the old days in Miami school. Gavin and Joe were something that could best be described as second-tier friends. That is to say, they were not a part of each other's inner circle of friends. But there was always a lot of crossover whenever there were outings, or gatherings of some description. And they had cause to develop a friendship that never necessitated regular communications with each other, as you would with first-tier friends.

"I'm good. Actually, better than good. I'm absolutely fantastic. Celebrating in fact". He managed to say.

"That's fantastic. What are we celebrating today?" asked Gavin.

Joseph was not quite ready to talk about his amazing situation just yet. He had the idea that his family should be the first to know. So, instead he pulled out of his head the only other news item of note that had happened today.

"I've been made redundant from my job" he said with a wry smile.

"Oh, I see. You absolutely hated the job, and now you are free! Hopefully with a huge golden handshake to see you out the door?" inquired Gavin.

"Something like that" Joseph replied.

"That's fantastic. I'll give you the two liner of my life since we last saw each other, back in the eighties. Divorced a few years ago. Two kids that have their own lives now. Been waiting bars ever since I can remember. This is my latest gig. How about you?" Gavin said.

Joseph gave it a little thought and replied along the same lines.

"Newly divorced. Moving out of the house in Broadbeach Waters soon and going up to Main Beach to my new pad. Taking the cat with me. Two kids, both happily living their own lives nowadays. Oh, and the previously mentioned retrenchment. So, I think I'd better find something else to do with the rest of my life." Joseph smiled as he concluded his summary.

"I have just the thing Joe; check this out". Gavin moved to sit in the booth with Joseph and produced his phone. He opened an app and showed Joseph a photograph.

"What is it?" Joseph asked.

"A dating app. Time for you to get back on the horse Joe. This is how people get laid nowadays. Bars like this one are just a place to meet without needing to give out your home address. You connect with someone online. Arrange to meet them here. If there's a spark, then it's on for young and old. It was never this easy when we were teenagers!"

Gavin made it all sound so normal. But it was not something that Joseph had even contemplated, until now.

"Well, I have been wondering exactly how to celebrate my good fortune? I mean my redundancy and payout. If you know what I mean?"

"I think that I have just the one for you. She's a bit of a cougar. Had a different youngster in here every night this week. I'm sure that I saved her profile here somewhere in my favourites."

Gavin was madly flicking through what looked to be quite an extensive list of favourites. Eventually he arrived at the one he was searching for.

"Here she is, what a looker eh?" he asked Joseph as he held up a headless torso photograph of the woman. She was barely wearing some black lingerie. Her body was definitely a turn-on. Her profile name was listed as 'Minimum 10 Positions'.

"What does the writing mean below the picture?" asked Joseph innocently.

"That is the profile name. A nom de plume if you will. In this case she is advertising that in a one night stand she wants at least ten sexual positions from her lovers". Gavin's short explanation left no further doubt in Joseph's mind as to the voracious sexual appetite of the woman.

"Why no face?" Joseph inquired.

"You don't want the world to know your sexual preferences Joe. The face pictures are kept in the private album that is shared with you if you get along online, chatting, you know?" he explained.

"Oh, I see," said Joseph.

"Wait a minute be I have this horny woman's face picture here somewhere in an earlier chat. We swapped pix but didn't manage to get together. Then, I saw her in here a few hours later with some young buck. She's got quite the reputation already. A real wild woman in the sack. And she's new on the app. Exactly what you need, to *celebrate,* you know, eh, eh!" Gavin gave Joseph a knowing wink.

"Here she is" he said holding up a clear facial photograph of the nymphomaniac.

"ISABELLA!" Joseph was horrified.

"What?" Gavin looked vexed.

"That's my ex-wife! The divorce only came through last WEEK! I thought that she was out to Pilates every night!"

"Well, I'm sure that she's been bending and stretching quite a lot, Joe. Does that count as Pilates?"

"Oh my GOD! She just couldn't wait to get the chains off and sow her wild oats". Joseph was genuinely upset. He buried his head in his hands.

"Was that it all along?" he asked Gavin, who of course, would have no hope of answering such a complicated query.

"Was I just absolutely no good in bed? Is that why she pushed for the divorce?"

Gavin thought that it best that he answered Joseph in his best barman's 'sympathetic ear' tone of voice.

"Sounds like your ex-wife is making the most of her newfound freedom and is living it up. Good for her! What are *you* going to do to live *your* best life now that you are a single man about town?"

Gavin's summation of the current situation actually made Joseph feel better. He nodded and gave an affirming 'huh' sound.

"How about a drink?" Gavin asked.

Joseph thought about and gave a very definite reply.

"HELL YES!" he exclaimed.

"What'll it be?" inquired Gavin.

Joseph began to answer.

"Champ..........Whisk.............Gin.........." he trailed off before continuing.

"What sort of drink do you order when you've been retrenched and just found out that your ex-wife of only one week ago has been practising the Karma Sutra with anyone that will help her explore its hundreds of POSITIONS?!"

Gavin replied.

"An Orgasm?"

Gavin waited for a response and got a cold glare instead.

"A cock-sucking cowboy?"

Joseph was not amused. He shot Gavin a death-stare.

"How about a Cosmopolitan? Because that my friend, is what you are going to *be* from now on! A cosmopolitan gentleman around town!".

It was bizarre, but Gavin's infantile consolation somehow managed to offer Joseph some small glimpse into a new, desirable future. After contemplating it for a few moments he responded.

"Yes; that will do nicely thank you".

***

After enjoying two rather strong Cosmopolitans, Joseph was feeling a little less upset by his ex-wife's sexual proclivities. After all, she was a free agent. It's not as if she needed to be celibate nun now that they were no longer married to each other. And besides, he was still harbouring a fantastic secret. He was the winner of a luxury home and yacht. And he had still not managed to ring anybody and tell them of his good fortune.

Joseph picked out "Austin Whynee" from the contacts and pushed the 'call' button. After the usual amount of time, Austin answered the call.

"Dad; what's up!?" he asked.

"I have some brilliant news son. You simply WILL NOT believe it when I tell you".

Joseph hoped that the mysterious hook would elicit some curiosity and maybe even a little excitement from Austin. He was wrong.

"I'm just out of a lecture Dad and about to go into another one. Can it wait?" he asked.

Joseph was horrified. He had the most amazing news to tell Austin, and his son seemed to be more concerned with getting to his next university lecture on time rather than hearing it.

"Well, I suppose……" Joseph replied rather tentatively.

"Thanks; call you later!" said Austin.

And with that he hung up. Joseph looked at the phone. 'Call Ended' was displayed on the screen.

"Hmmm" he said to himself.

Joseph knew that Austin was in the third year of five, studying his medical degree. Maybe it was better to let him be. There was no such encumbrance with Karilee though. She had finished her Master of Business Administration and was now gainfully employed by a local surfboard manufacturer. He selected her from the contact list and pushed the 'call' button. She answered in due course.

"Dad; what's up!?" she asked.

Joseph pondered for a second that Karilee and Austin were not just fraternal twins, but identical twins in their greeting to him as well.

"Hello luv. I have fantastic news..........."

"Oh my GOD; WHAT DO YOU THINK YOU ARE DOING. Are you trying to get yourself killed!?" she shouted.

"Um, No" he said, rather confused at her response.

"Not you Dad; this intern. He simply doesn't KNOW the meaning of occupational health and safety AND duty of CARE! And of course, HUMAN FACTOR ERGONOMICS!"

"Neither do I?" he proclaimed honestly before adding "is everything alright?"

"Dad, can I call you back tonight while I get this mess sorted out please?"

Joseph was deflated, but as usual, compliant.

"ok" he said meekly.

“Thank you, Dad; talk to you tonight” she said as a rather abbreviated goodbye.

Before he could answer the screen was showing ‘call ended’.

Joseph put down the phone. He pondered for a moment calling Isabella but decided that she may be tangled up with some hapless twenty-year-old, or two. The next person on his list was his father. Maybe another visit to ‘Golden Years’ was in order? Then another thought occurred to him. He could drop by Big Lips Advertising to proclaim his good fortune. Joseph thought about it for about two seconds before concluding that there was nobody in the company that he cared enough about to tell. Golden Years it was then.

He stood up and swayed a little from the alcoholic beverages that he had consumed.

“Gavin; My good man!” he said in a loud voice.

Gavin looked up from behind the bar where he was cleaning some glasses.

“I’m off to visit my Dad. What’s the damage?” Joseph asked.

“I’d say your brain, liver and kidneys Joseph; but other than that, twenty dollars. We’re in tourist- hour cheap cocktails until seven o’clock tonight. Bargain!” he said with his usual winning smile.

Chapter 12

The Old-Age Daily Drug Routine

Joseph arrived at 'Golden Years' around 1pm. His head was still swimming from a combination of the cosmopolitans and the news that he was suddenly a multi-million-dollar property owner at Palazzo Versace.

Joseph entered the main double doors and immediately noticed that David Bowie's Golden Years was playing softly as the background music. 'How appropriate' he thought. Fatima Forthright was sitting behind her desk as per usual giving rise to the musing that she never seemed to take time off. He was puzzled by the fact that he never seemed to encounter any other reception worker when he visited.

"He's in his villa" she said as he came to within earshot.

It only solidified his suspicion that all of the residents were being surreptitiously electronically tracked.

"Thanks you" replied Joseph.

He realised immediately that he had slurred the response and erroneously made it a plural when it was not meant to be. But rather than correcting himself and potentially giving away that he was a little tipsy, he elected to simply continue through reception and out to the capacious gardens.

Taking the familiar pathway to his father's tucked away villa, he arrived at the front door and rang the bell. Best not to just barge in just in case the old man was otherwise occupied with one of his *regulars*.

Harrington answered the door in due course and was delighted to see his son standing there.

"Son! Come in!" he exclaimed with a huge smile.

"What's happening?" he further inquired.

This was the opportunity that Joseph had been waiting for.

"Dad something amazing, let's sit down".

Joseph almost herded his father toward the sofas in the living room. There on the central coffee table was a compendium of pills that was open. The day of Friday was full of various pills of differing shapes and colours. Joseph was alarmed and distracted at the same time.

"What on earth are those?" he asked with some horror in his tone.

"My daily drug routine designed to stave-off death for another twenty-four hours". Harrington's answer could have easily been taken either way, as humorous or deadly serious. Joseph could not tell which it was.

"Is this normal?" he asked feeling a little guilty that he had not kept abreast of his father's pharmacological interventions.

"Of course, it is. You should see poor old party-boy-Pete next door. A life of debauchery has left him with a drug regime that makes mine look pallid by comparison."

Harrington's comparative explanation did little to ease Joseph's concern at the amount of pills that his father was taking on a daily basis.

“If you shook him; he’d rattle!” joked Joseph trying to ease his own feelings with a little lighthearted humour.

“More to the point, son, if he would sell his pills on the dark web he’d make way more per pill than he pays for the complete bottles with his pensioner’s discount. It would be a terrific secret revenue stream”.

Harrington gave Joseph a wink. Joseph was horrified.

“You can’t be serious?” he said with genuine disbelief.

“Of course, I’m not serious son. Why would anybody that can afford to live here want to become a pensioner drug dealer!”

“To save them dying of boredom?” Joseph was too quick with his retort before he realised that he had fallen completely for his father’s joke.

“Oh, right, sorry, should have seen that one coming” he said by way of apology for being so completely fooled by this father. It was then that he noticed the laptop open, there was a document showing on the screen.

“What are you doing? Other than taking your ‘Friday’ set of pills?” he asked.

“I’m writing an article for the national paper. It’s about a travesty that has befallen one of our greatest rugby league football players. I was asked my opinion and with my connections my point of view made it to the editor of the paper. And they have agreed to publish it. Sometime next month I think”. Harrington finished his explanation.

“That’s fantastic news Dad. Good on you. But now to my news. You are not going to believe this!”

Joseph’s tone was bristling with excitement. He leaned forward and looked his father directly in the eyes.

“I have just won first prize in the RSL lottery. A fully furnished three bedroom condominium with private Marina berth and 40 foot yacht at Palazzo Versace in Main Beach”.

Joseph concluded the summary of his extraordinary news and waited for his father's reaction. Harrington regarded his son with a look of disbelief. He stroked his chin with his fingers before seeming to come to a decision.

“Are you serious?” he asked.

Joseph was beaming a smile so large that it became evident to Harrington that the news was indeed true.

“Yes! It’s true!” Joseph said and stood up with excitement without even realising it. He waited for his father’s reaction. Harrington stood up so that he could look Joseph in the eyes.

“That is fantastic news son!” He said with genuine enthusiasm.

“It means that you won’t be sleeping on my couch while you look for a place to live!” he added.

Joseph’s initial joy at his father’s reaction came crumbling down to earth with a bang.

“Is that all you can say about this once in a lifetime piece of news?” he asked incredulously.

Harrington looked at the ceiling for a moment, and then back at Joseph.

“If you’re going to own a boat, then you’d better learn to swim”.

Harrington was nothing if not practical when it came to planning matters. It came from years as the shadow and actual Minister of planning. One of his many portfolios over the decades of his federal political career.

It was as much irony as it was unbelievable that Joseph had never managed to learn to swim, in spite of being raised so close to the coast, and with access to so many beautiful beaches. Much like his (former) home at Broadbeach Waters, not having a canal view or access. Harrington liked to point out any such perceived deficiencies of his only child whenever and wherever possible.

Joseph rolled his eyes and let out an exasperated sigh. Would there be nobody that was as happy as him about his fantastic news?

Joseph pointed to the compendium of pills that was yet, not taken.

"You don't have a pill that could make you less critical of me, do you?" he asked.

"Most of this is just to keep my hair from falling out". Harrington replied.

"I think that I'll have an early gin and tonic on the back deck" Joseph proclaimed.

"On your back deck that has a view of nothing?"

Harrington's jibe was not lost on Joseph. So, he decided to retort appropriately.

"My new back deck at Palazzo Versace has a view of my very own plunge pool". Joseph proclaimed.

Sensing that his reaction to the news may not be exactly what his son was expecting, Harrington reiterated how glad he was of the luck that had come along.

"Son, it's great news…and not just for me; for you too!" he said hoping that his affirmation would appease Joseph's need for approval.

Realising that he was not going to get the kind of reaction from his father that he was hoping to see in everyone he told, Joseph decided it was time to retreat.

"I'll leave you to your writing Dad". He said.

Chapter 13

The Interim Chapter

By the time Joseph arrived back at Isabella's home in Broadbeach Waters it was around 3pm. The effects of the earlier Cosmopolitans had all but dissipated by now. He entered the house and listened carefully for any sounds of frenetic activity. Hearing none he ventured into the kitchen. Isabella was there. She turned around surprised at his early arrival home.

"Good day?" she inquired politely.

"Actually, yes and no" he responded rather mysteriously.

"Oh?" Isabella's curiosity was aroused. Joseph was glad that that was the only thing that was aroused at the moment.

"I was retrenched today; my job is being outsourced to a business in Manilla".

Joseph waited for a reaction. Isabella was horrified.

"Joe, that's terrible. I am so sorry. How could they do that? After all the years that you've given them, it's callous and uncaring". Isabella was genuinely shocked and taken aback by the news.

"It's not all bad. I've managed to get a place to live up in Main Beach. So, that softened the blow, considerably". He explained, before adding.

“I have one more week to put in and hand over to the company taking over my job, then they pay me a retrenchment package and I’m free. I think that I’ll take some time off before looking for another job. How about a gin and tonic on the back deck with me?” He concluded.

“Of course, I would love to, Joe thank you. You poor thing”. She replied.

“I don’t feel particularly poor but thank you. It certainly has been a very different day to the one that I thought I was going to have. I’ll get those drinks now”. Joseph began to bring together the necessary items in order to mix the drinks.

“I’ll put together a cheese platter”. Offered Isabella.

They moved as one would expect of a couple that had lived together for so many years. Each performing their tasks without interrupting the flow of the other. Before long they were sitting on the rear deck enjoying the afternoon. They spoke of the old days when they first met. The hunt for and purchasing of the house, and the birth of the twins. It was a very pleasant walk down memory lane.

By six in the evening, Isabella had offered to make them both dinner, but Joseph declined.

“Let’s go out to that local Italian place instead; my shout,” he offered.

“That would be lovely, thank you. But why does it feel like a celebration rather than a commiseration about your job?” she asked.

“I think that it can be both. I can drown my sorrows about the job with a great Lasagne. And celebrate the next stage of my life in Main Beach, with a decadent Tiramisu”. Joseph explained.

“Perfect. I’m really proud of you Joseph. You’ve taken a lot on the chin recently and you can still find a positive side to it all. Am I seeing the beginning of a new Joseph Whynee?” Isabella looked happy but a little vexed at her ex-husbands lack of incessant complaining.

"I think you are," he replied with a big smile.

There was of course Molly X and her dinner to take care of before they left. As Joseph prepared the shredded chicken in jelly and the hard biscuits to ensure that her teeth were well cared for, he told her a secret.

"Soon we will be living in the lap of luxury Molly X" he said as he placed the bowl of food down for her to eat.

For her part, Molly X did something very unusual. Instead of gobbling down the food, she looked at Joseph with an expression that could easily have been interpreted as 'What is *that* supposed to mean?' Following the brief interlude, she proceeded to eat her dinner with all of the enthusiasm that he had come to expect from her.

The restaurant was within walking distance. So, as there was no need to drive, Joseph was planning to buy the most expensive bottle of wine available and drink, surreptitiously, to his good fortune and his forthcoming new life.

Neither of the twins promised returned calls eventuated, thus giving Isabella and Joseph and uninterrupted dinner.

***

Dinner was as wonderful as Joseph and Isabella had anticipated. Upon returning home, Isabella retired to bed, full of sumptuous Italian food and ready for a long sleep. Joseph went to the study and opened his emails. He homed-in on the one from the RSL. He opened it and read the contents. In summary it seemed, that he could sign the papers onsite in his new abode. All he had to do was arrange a time and day with them.

He was very excited about the prospect of being a homeowner in one of the world's first 'branded' hotel residences. For the next hour Joseph poured over the electronic literature that was available on the prize. The condominium itself looked opulent. The furniture, decorative to the point of being over-the-top.

'Beat the Odds' was a beautiful yacht. It had a small swimming deck at the rear that could be lowered when anchored so that one could simply slip into the water from the polished wooden surface. Images of his new life appeared before him. He would learn how to sail (and how to swim) and take paying passengers on tours of the surrounding waterways and out into the ocean too.

An entirely new life opened-up before him. No more, the pain of dealing with obstinate and unhelpful colleagues. He would now be the master of his own destiny. And that destiny was a bright, bright one indeed.

***

Saturday and Sunday were equally as blissful. There was time to reflect on the life that was coming, rather than the one that had somehow left him behind. He managed to perform the usual gardening maintenance and other household chores knowing that this would be the last time. Soon, Broadbeach Waters would be just the place that he used to live.

But then it was the end of the weekend. Joseph's thoughts turned to what it would be like being in the office tomorrow. News of his retrenchment would have spread through the company by now. How would they react to him when he arrived? How would he react to them? Did he even care?

After contemplating that thought for a few seconds, he decided that the answer was no. 'Bring on Monday' he said to himself. 'I'm ready to shed the old Joseph Whynee and start my new perfect life in Palazzo Versace'.

***

Monday was not the usual for Joseph. He decided, for a start, to sleep in. There was no need to be in the office by 8am? Why bother? When he did arrive, he noticed that people were reticent to look him in the eye. Even Dolby Doowright failed to give him the customary annoyingly happy greeting. Which for Joseph, was a blessing. But in general, there was a sense from his colleagues that he was the 'dead man walking'; or rather the 'retrenched man working (his last days)'.

Joseph got down to work. He opened his emails and found the details of how to contact the company that was to replace him. Jeva had been efficient and supplied it whilst he was out 'commiserating' after receiving the news of his retrenchment. If only she knew what had happened, he thought.

Looking around the office Joseph couldn't find a single person that he wanted to tell his good news to. More of a reason to get through this week and get it over and done with. He set up an online meeting with the contact that he had been given. The meeting invitation was accepted withing minutes. As there was still twenty or so minutes before it began, Joseph used the time to phone the RSL and arrange for a time to sign the paperwork. His pulse was racing as he dialled the number.

The President of the RSL answered the phone.

“John Strauchn”

“John, this is Joseph Whynee; how are you?” Joseph tried to keep his voice low for fear of being overheard.

“Hello Joseph. I’m all the better for hearing from you. Did you have a chance to go through the material that I sent?” he inquired.

“I did indeed. In fact, that is why I am calling you. Would it be alright to sign all of the paperwork sometime this week?” Joseph was barely able to contain his excitement.

“Why not. And to save you a trip up here to Brisbane, how about we do it onsite at the condominium so that I can show you around personally”. John offered, before adding, “I’m available Thursday and Friday of this week if that suits?”

Joseph was just a little disappointed. He would have preferred sooner. But if that was what was on offer, he would take it.

“Thursday would be great. What time works for you?” Joseph asked.

“Midday. I’ll be waiting for you in the main lobby”. John answered.

They exchanged the usual pleasantries and ended the call. Joseph knew what John looked like from the website. There was a message on it from the RSL president about the work that they do with the funds raised from the major prize lotteries. Suddenly, Thursday seemed too far away.

He had to put thoughts about the future on hold as his calendar reminded him that it was time for the video call with Manilla.

"First things, first" he said to himself and proceeded to initiate the video call.

Chapter 14

Farewell Lunches Are Customary

Tuesday and Wednesday were of a similar ilk to Monday. The staff were distant and even when Oliver Opplesham or Jeva Jungfer were in the office, they somehow managed to avoid Joseph completely. Joseph, however, did not care. He was so buoyant from the forthcoming tour of his new home that nothing could drag his mood down.

Thursday eventually arrived and Joseph was a picture of brightness as he entered the office. He even made an extra effort to creep up on Dolby Doowright and surprise him with a huge toothy smile and an exaggerated greeting.

"GOOD MORNING DOLBY; HOW ON EARTH ARE YOU TODAY!?"

Dolby nearly jumped out of his skin; he was so surprised by the verbal attack. Instead of the overtly happy demeanour, Dolby cringed away and managed to stumble through a reply of sorts.

"Oh, yes. I suppose so, I think, good, maybe….yes good thanks" Dolby replied feebly

"EXCELLENT!" bellowed Joseph, and with a smile that would not have looked out of place on a psychopathic killer, he retreated to his office to waste time before he could leave for lunch. Leaving behind him a very rattled Dolby Doowright. Joseph ensured that he had Dolby's favourite online shopping site clearly visible on his screen as he whittled-away the morning hours.

Eventually it became time to make his way up to Main Beach. Joseph left the building but instead of catching the light-rail and walking the rest of the distance, he ordered an online ride. More than that; he ensured that it was something that exuded class. An impressive looking black Mercedes Benz arrived to pick him up. Joseph wanted to arrive at Palazzo Versace in style.

The black car pulled up and he climbed into the back, thinking that it would look more regal if he emerged at the other end of the journey, from the rear of the car rather than the passenger's side. He did not have to give any instructions to the driver but did offer a customary polite hello.

"Hello Joseph, we meet again," said the man.

Joseph was stunned he looked more carefully at the suited and chauffeur hatted man. He did look familiar but for the like of him, could not quite place where from?

"The Militant Vegan Café" said the driver, rightly assuming that Joseph was struggling with recognising the man. For his part, Joseph was shocked. It was indeed the barista from the café that had tried to poison him with a putrid coffee and inedible vegetable substitute *chicken* burger.

"Good heavens! What are you doing here? Driving a car, I mean?" asked Joseph.

"The city shut me down. Effluent leak. You remember, you were there" the ex-café owner explained.

Joseph was struck with a pang of guilt that felt like a knot in his stomach. Attempting to ignore it he tried to give the impression that he was recalling and hoped that he did not have a guilty look on his face.

"Oh, yeah, that's right. I'd forgotten" Joseph lied in response.

“Well, until the source of the problem is found, and remediation works can be done, I have to make ends meet driving for a hire-car company. Sucks eh?” he shrugged as if such bad luck could happen to anyone.

“Off to Palazzo Versace I see. We had better get going.” Said the man. He put the car into drive and pulled nicely into the traffic and proceeded north toward Main Beach. Making further conversation the chauffeur offered a morsel of information that he thought would be relevant to the situation.

“You know that the RSL gave away one of the Condominiums up there recently? I heard that it was won by a family man of some description. Apparently lost his entire family in a hideous accident of some kind and now ekes out a maudlin and solitary existence. All that money and all alone in the world. Pretty sad eh?” he said.

Joseph was both stung by the words and confused at how such rumours get started and spread.

“No, I hadn’t heard that”.

“Poor bastard” added the chauffeur.

Feeling that he needed to add to the conversation, even though he did not want to, Joseph ventured with a nonsensical promise.

“I’ll let you know if I see him when I’m there”.

“Of course the whole thing is never publicised by the RSL. So, I guess we’ll never know the full story”. There was a small pause from the driver before he further inquired.

“Business Lunch, or something like that?” inquired the driver.

“Yes, that’s exactly it” responded Joseph, hoping that the chauffeur did not seek further clarification.

Thankfully, the remainder of the journey was concluded in silence. Perhaps the driver was contemplating the fate of the purported winner of the prize. Either that or, how much longer he would be driving cars instead of tending to his coffee machine.

***

It was incredible to contemplate, but in all the years that Palazzo Versace had been there, Joseph had not once visited it. He had in the meantime though, familiarised himself with it. Opened in the year 2000, the hotel has 200 rooms and suites and 72 neighbouring condominiums. Its own 90 berth marina, 3 restaurants, and a lagoon pool with a white sandy beach that looked too pristine to be real.

Joseph had, in the last weekend, become an expert in the Palazzo Versace. He was aware of the newer one in Dubai, but that would always be second to the original. And apparently there was another one coming in Macau. Something for him to explore at a future time.

The Mercedes pulled up in the circular colonnade driveway. The centre of the driveway itself containing an intricate mosaic of the head of Medusa. The Queen and one of the three Gorgon Sisters from Greek Mythology. It was a fitting symbol of the Italian Fashion House because both the Greeks and the Italians had had great empires in the past. And both empires were smart enough to incorporate the mythos of the other into their own.

Joseph was still mesmerised by the beauty of the place when one of the doormen opened the car door for him. He instinctively unfastened his seatbelt and exited the car with a customary thank you to the driver.

The doorman ushered him inside the glass doors into the main lobby of the hotel, which was an atrium of chandeliers, tall white Corinthian columns, intricate marble floor design, opulent furniture with extravagant fabrics and serene piano music. Joseph was captivated and stood there looking up and down, left and right. At the far end the expanses of glass on the roof and the rear wall overlooking the lagoon pool, gave the impression of even more largess. He was overpowered by the magnificence of what was by far the most impressive lobby he had ever been in.

He would have stood there mesmerised for much longer, but he detected that somebody was moving towards him. He looked at the man approaching him, it was the president of the Returned Soldiers League.

"Joseph!" said the man greeting him with a large smile and an extended hand.

Joseph took John's hand and shook it with vigour.

"Hello, hello" was all that he could manage to say at this point.

"Beautiful, isn't it?" he asked. Clearly appreciating Joseph's overwhelmed demeanour.

"Yes; yes, it is. It really is!" he managed to reply.

John indicated that Joseph should follow him.

"I'll show you around the facilities later. Right now, I want to give you a tour of your new home. Ok?" he inquired.

"Sure". Replied Joseph.

They moved to the side of the reception area. Staff looked curiously at Joseph but were unerringly polite and did not motion to prevent their ingress.

“There is lots of curiosity about the new resident Joseph; let me tell you. I had hoped that Ismail Islington would be here to meet you too. But circumstances have seen that he is unavailable. He is the residential care manager. The interface between the hotel and the residents. You’ll meet him in good time I’m sure”. John explained.

But Joseph was still so enraptured by the surroundings that he barely heard a word that John had spoken. He was led into outside to the lagoon pool area. The residences were separated from the hotel.

“The residences are all in their own wing of the complex” explained John. Just a short way across from the white sandy lagoon pool's edge there was a door with the customary intercom controls to contact the people inside. John opened the door and indicated that Joseph should go in and move to the left slightly.

“This is it! Condominium number four”.

The gold door handle had a card-key entry mechanism. John produced the card and unlocked the door. Joseph’s heart began to race. John opened the door and indicated that Joseph should enter first.

He stepped through the entrance and took in the scene. There was a mirrored lobby leading on to a raised dining room and kitchen beyond. The living room was surrounded by Corinthian columns and sunken. The marble marquetry in the floor design was simply exquisite. It was echoed by an intricately patterned plaster ceiling. Through the sliding glass doors, the patio could be seen and the raised plunge pool beyond.

All around there was furniture and wall hangings either of framed pictures or plaster work circles that wreaked of expense and difficulty to produce.

“The look itself is called ‘Barocco” by Versace. I think that it looks very apt in the setting, don’t you?” John inquired.

Joseph realised that he had been walking into the condominium one step at a time and with his mouth hanging open.

"Yes, it is absolutely amazing" he managed to reply and hoped that he sounded somewhat coherent in the process.

They moved to the top of the step leading down to the living room to take in the view from there.

"Three bedrooms, the master is the farthest on the left down that hallway. Two other bedrooms of equal size. But let's go outside to the patio and look at the view, shall we?"

Joseph was without the ability to argue or guide their tour at this point. So, he simply nodded in agreement.

The outside was a feast of light, the sound of water and blue sky. Planter boxes full of lush tropical plants ensured privacy from the neighbouring condominiums. The elevated and enclosed in frame-less glass fences, plunge pool was a backdrop for the extensive water feature that lay beyond. Sensing Joseph's wonder, John put into words what Joseph was viewing.

"The water garden lies beyond your patio and plunge pool. And beyond that the boardwalk leading to the Versace Marina. Complete privacy is yours thanks to the clever way that it has been planned. What do you think so far?"

Joseph was aware that he needed to answer John's question, so he gathered his thoughts and managed a rudimentary reply.

"It's just perfect, John, absolutely perfect".

John seemed pleased and motioned that they should go inside. There he was shown the laundry room, the main bathroom, and then the master suite. It was by both definition and execution a suite of lavish design. Not overly large, but impeccably formed. The entire tour took on the form of a dream.

Joseph had already planned to set up Molly X's scratching and climbing post and kitty litter tray in the laundry. It would be perfect.

With the tour of this part of the prize complete. John once more led Joseph out into the hallway and past the pool. Somehow, they were now approaching the before mentioned boardwalk.

They walked the marina out to one of the berths and there waiting for them was 'Beat the Odds' a beautiful forty-foot sailing yacht moored securely in its place. Visions of carefree days sailing from place to place and only stopping to jump into the pristine ocean for a swim began to dance before Joseph's eyes.

Joseph was aware that John was saying something to him, but he was so enraptured that he could not interpret what it was. He eventually managed a reply that he hoped would please his tour guide. It did.

"What a beauty!"

Without realising exactly what was happening, Joseph was given a quick tour of the boat, its beautifully sculptured cabins, galley, head, and masterfully crafted deck before they once more returned to the air-conditioned comfort of the main building. Before long Joseph and John were back in Condominium number four and seated at the dining table. There was a manilla folder full of papers waiting for them.

"Time to sign up for a life of luxury and privilege!" John tempted Joseph.

"Will you be moving in with your family?" John asked.

"No, no, just myself and Molly" Joseph replied.

"Your daughter I take it?" he inquired with a quizzical expression on his face. Before Joseph could answer John added.

"Because pets are forbidden in the building, I'm afraid".

Joseph froze. He was about to confirm that Molly was indeed his beloved pet but in the magic of the moment could not bring himself to ruin it with the news.

"My daughter. But she has her own life now. And will more than likely leave home soon enough!" he lied.

John nodded and gave various affirmations before taking Joseph through the paperwork that would transfer ownership of the condominium and the yacht to him. John explained about the two car spaces, which were redundant as Joseph no longer owned an automobile. The storage space in the basement that was part of the package. There were discounts in the spa, and three restaurants for the residents. And something called the 'welcome party' that he was supposed to throw for the other residents so that they could meet him.

"Vanitas, the main restaurant will cater it for you, but it is an additional cost of thirty thousand dollars, which is not covered by the prize inclusions". John explained.

The magical moment was broken like an expensive crystal glass on the patterned marble floor.

"HOW MUCH!" he yelped.

"It's a fairly standard cost for the 'new residents welcome party' or so I hear" explained John.

Joseph was taken aback. Although he was going to get a handsome payout from his company by tomorrow, he couldn't bring himself to part with such a huge amount of money just to meet the new neighbours. Sensing his thoughts John was able to throw him a lifeline.

"You are able to simply cater it yourself. But I think that it is something that you should discuss with Ismail Islington when you finally do get to meet him. I hear that the residents are rather particular about this meet-and-greet aspect when it comes to the new owners".

John’s explanation was seized upon immediately by Joseph as a potential money-saver.

“I’ll do just that”. He promised.

“You’ve chosen the ‘not for publication’ option when purchasing the ticket. So, your real name will be obscured from all of the publicity about the prize draw”. John explained.

“Yes, my ride here was telling me about never knowing the full story of who has actually won”. Joseph responded.

It was then that he noticed a couple of expenses mentioned at the bottom of the list of outgoings that he could not account for. The wording explained that although the first year of outgoings was covered as part of the prize, the successive years would not.

“These ongoing costs that I will be responsible for John, what are they for?” Joseph’s accountancy instinct was in full swing.

“It’s two halves really. One side are the homeowner’s association fees for gardening, water feature maintenance, elevator maintenance, security guards and monitoring, common area cleaning. And the second are costs associated with services to your boat whilst it is in its berth. Water, waste extraction, power, security for the marina. So, think of them as covenant fees, or strata fees. I’ve forgotten the exact wording that they prescribe to it here, but it all amounts to about six hundred dollars”.

John’s explanation left Joseph in a slight state of shock.

“Six hundred dollars to cover all of that?” Joseph said in wonderment.

“Six hundred dollars *each* for the two main components Joseph. Six hundred for the residence *and* six hundred for the marina and boat”. John’s shocking revelation cut through Joseph like a knife.

“Oh, my goodness. Twelve hundred dollars a month to support the condominium and boat?” Joseph was truly flabbergasted. John then corrected him in the worst possibly way imaginable.

“Twelve hundred dollars a *week* to support the condominium and boat Joseph”.

Joseph felt his heart skip a beat. He stood bolt upright.

“What!?” Are you JOKING with me!?” he said his voice rising in alarm.

John was conciliatory. He motioned with his hands for Joseph to calm himself.

“Nothing you need to worry about for the next twelve months Joseph. All taken care of until this time next year. Don’t let it detract from your moment of triumph. Sign there on the line and all of this will be yours. You can move in any time after that”.

John’s logic, and the reality that he did indeed not have to make provisions for the outgoings until then, did in fact, help Joseph calm down. He thought about it for a little while and then agreed.

“You’re right. This is still the best thing that has happened to me in years”. Joseph affirmed.

Joseph signed in all the places that he was meant to and felt a slight tingling through his body. He had just entered the world of the branded designer home. An owner in Australia's only Versace hotel and residences. This would help to reinvent himself. He did not want the divorce but equally, did not want to refuse Isabella what she wanted. He did not want to get made redundant from his job, but also did not have a choice.

But somehow, fate had picked him up and wrapped him in a secure blanket. It was a sign. He needed to move on with his life and living at Palazzo Versace was going to be a very big and important part of the brand-new Joseph Whynee (maybe one that won’t be so whiney?).

***

John had very kindly given Joseph a lift back to the Forum Building in Surfer`s Paradise. Joseph bounded up the steps, not waiting for his usual customary overly slow elevator ride up to the BL Advertising offices. When he walked in the main doors the first person that he ran into was Frauline Flick herself, Jeva Jungfer. Joseph groaned internally. She was the last person that he wanted to deal with.

"Back from lunch?" she asked.

"Yes" he replied without giving any further detail.

"Where did you go?" she asked.

It was then that Joseph noticed that she was slurring her words slightly. He figured that she must have had a three-martini lunch or something similar. There was no getting away from her trivial conversation when she was in this condition.

"Versace" he said. Immediately cursing himself for letting on where he had been.

"Lovely!" she said with a big smile before adding "What was the occasion?"

Joseph needed a good excuse for going to such an extravagant place for lunch.

"Celebrating my new life after BL Advertising" he said hoping that it would suffice.

"You know, the RSL gave away one of those Versace Condominiums recently. Apparently, the guy who won was an ex special forces soldier suffering from post-traumatic stress disorder. The residents are scared-stiff that he will snap one day, run wild and cause injury!"

Jeva's eyes widened, and she leaned forward as she delivered her alarming news. Joseph was busy recoiling from the vodka fumes exuding from her mouth. He had to really try to not wave his hand in front of his nose to waft away the smell.

"That is horribly stereotypical of a returned soldier suffering from PTSD. It's much more likely that the poor fellow will suffer in silence. And another thing, how on earth did you find *that* out anyway. Surely it's all private?" He asked with a serious note of incredulity in his tone.

She responded by holding her finger to the side of her nose.

"I find out things that others cannot".

Her mysterious reply was in danger of provoking an eye-roll from Joseph. He elected to change the subject as quickly as he could.

"Speaking of lunches. Where's my farewell lunch going to be tomorrow? I was expecting an email about it by now. You know to gather together the people that want to see me off".

Joseph for all the world, looked like an eager puppy ready to be picked up and cuddled.

"Farewell Lunch?" parroted Jeva, as if she had never before heard the phrase. Her expression turned to one of being completely vexed.

"You have organised a lunch to bid me goodbye, surely?" Joseph asked his tone now slightly alarmed.

"No"

Came her simple response. Then she looked at him as if he was crazy man ready for the forced application of a strait jacket.

"You do know that you're not the most popular person here, right?" she asked.

Joseph was horrified. He responded in a higher and louder pitch than normal.

"But I'm not Adolf Hitler either surely!?" he squawked.

Jeva looked around as if hoping to find something or someone to extract her from this awkward situation. Finding nothing she turned to him and gathered her thoughts.

"Perhaps you can think of your lunch at Versace today as your official farewell lunch from Big Lips Advertising?" she said with a small self-satisfied smile.

"But nobody from the office was there!" he growled.

"Even better from our point of view; we didn't have to pay for it!" She responded smugly.

Feeling that she had brilliantly handled the uncomfortable subject, Jeva flicked her short hair with one hand and made to move away from Joseph. She stopped as if remembering something important and turned back to him.

"How's the handover going with the outsourcing company?"

Joseph was mortified that she could be so dismissive of a custom throughout the entire workforce. There was *always* supposed to be a farewell lunch for long-term employees. Absolutely nobody on the management team had even considered that he should receive that honour. As for the foreign company that was to replace him, Joseph did not care whether they were fully briefed by this point or not. His reply was dripping with vitriol; all of it lost on Jeva.

"I think that they have everything they need to be as effective *as* they can be for you".

Joseph's explanation pleased Jeva enormously. Once more in her mind, she had triumphed. Was there anything that she couldn't handle she thought to herself.

"Perfect" she said before marching away from him.

Joseph looked around the office. The people that he could see, were not meeting his gaze. All those years looking after the balance-sheet for them. Ensuring that money was coming in so that business could continue, and this is how they thanked him.

He could have sunk into a self-pitying spiral, but he snapped himself out of it. He was about to start living a life that these people could only dream of. In that instant he elected to pack the few personal possessions that he had at his desk, and leave quietly, stopping only at the office of the Human Resources manager to ensure that his final payment would be received tomorrow. A better use of his Friday would be to make the move into his new residence.

Chapter 15

Cat out of the bag

Friday morning dawned. Joseph awoke with Molly X beside him purring in the way that meant 'feed me'. He looked at her and started to formulate a plan to smuggle her into his new residence without anybody knowing. The condominium was so private that there was no chance of people seeing her from the boardwalk. It was so far beyond the 'water garden' that you would need binoculars to see in the large glass sliding doors.

Even then, you would have to be deliberately looking for her. Nobody in the hotel residence knew that he owned a cat. So, there should be no problem. Even the neighbours would have to contend with the oversized planter boxes separating their patios. Without one of them climbing a ladder to peek over the plants, there would be no chance of them seeing Molly X by accident. She was not a particularly noisy cat; hardly ever meowing. It should all contribute to ensure that he could keep her presence undisclosed to everyone.

"Time for breakfast Molly X. We have a big day ahead of us".

Molly X clearly recognising some words in the sentence leapt off the bed and made her way toward the kitchen. She turned around a couple of times during the journey to ensure that Joseph was obediently following her.

Arriving in the kitchen he came across Isabella eating some sliced avocado on a small, toasted slice of sourdough bread. Her favourite breakfast.

"Good morning, Dear. Moving day today for me. Time that I started packing whatever it is I'm taking with me." He then moved to prepare the cat's meal for her.

"You've got the lease sorted already? That's wonderful. Up at Main Beach somewhere, isn't it?" she asked.

Joseph nodded in affirmation.

"Fully furnished too! Including crockery, cutlery, bed linen, the bathroom even has bathrobes. It's got the lot. All I need to do is pack my clothes, and Molly X's accoutrements and move in. Simple as that." He was very pleased with himself.

"Joseph, I'm thrilled. That is excellent news. I'd give you a hand, but I have a women's support lunch today up at Southport" Isabella explained.

"Support?" Joseph was somewhat vexed.

"Yes, I'm sorry, I thought that I told you about it. I have joined a women's support group for those of us that have gone through or are still undergoing a divorce. We've met a couple of times already. They're a great bunch of ladies and this is a rather major get-together for all of us. I simply have to be there. Please say you understand?"

Isabella's explanation raised more questions than it answered for Joseph. He thought that he had been a picture of conciliation throughout the entire proceedings. The fact that Isabella now somehow needed a support group was both a complete surprise and a censure. What had he done wrong to warrant this?

Realising that he was taking too long to answer he hurriedly put together the best response he could under the circumstances.

"Of course, I understand. It's important that you do what you *need* to. And I am just moving my clothes and Molly X's stuff. It shouldn't take long. No need for a helping hand, I can knock this over on my own."

Joseph's answer pleased Isabella immensely.

"Thank you darling, I knew that you'd understand. I want to get in a Pilates session before then, so I'd better get moving" she quipped.

"If you're having a cocktail or wine with lunch maybe I can drop you off at lunch and you can get the light rail back. It will save you having to worry about how much your drinking".

Joseph's characteristically logical offer was seized upon by Isabella.

"You know, you're right. I'm doing a local class around the corner, then I can catch the tram up and back to Southport. Would you like to use the car for your move? It will save you hiring one. And you don't have that much. It should all fit in the boot and the back seat. No need to drop me off at lunch first. You can use the time to get everything together for yourself instead".

Today was shaping up to be a good day for Joseph.

"Thanks; that would be terrific" he said.

In the meantime, Molly X had become quite irate at not receiving her breakfast. She walked up to Joseph and extended a paw placing it directly on his ankle. Feeling the touch, he looked down and immediately realised his tardiness. He hurriedly got the wet and dry foods together in her ceramic bowl and placed it down for her. She began to eat with her normal ferocity.

Isabella got up from her seat and gave Joseph a peck on the forehead as she exited the kitchen. After she was gone Joseph addressed Molly X.

“Today is the first day of the rest of our lives Molly X”.

The cat stopped eating. Looked directly at Joseph for a moment and then resumed her breakfast.

From somewhere in the house Isabella shouted out.

“Don’t forget to leave me your new address Joseph!”

Obligingly Joseph got up from leaning over the cat and wrote his new address on the magnetised notepad attached to the front of the refrigerator door.

4/94 Seaworld Drive

Main Beach QLD 4217

There was no other hint nor nomenclature as to the name of the hotel. For all intents and purposes, unless you knew any better, it was just another generic address within Main Beach. No need to give away any pertinent information just yet. It was time for him to begin packing.

***

One of the advantages of going through a move of abodes when you’ve been stagnant for such a long time, is that it gives you the opportunity to shed the unnecessary items that you had amassed over the years. Much to Joseph’s amazement, now that he owned a luxurious condominium in a fabulous hotel, he began to look down-his-nose at the trinkets and holiday purchases that he had accumulated.

Every time he picked up something that had previously given his much mirth, like a snow-dome of Waikiki beach in Hawaii, he judged it far to pedestrian, kitsch or just plain low brow to sit beside his beautifully curated furniture, fixtures and fittings. Even the artwork on the walls of his new home was so far removed from his framed print of the Mona Lisa holding an iPhone; that he could not bring himself to take it with him.

Eventually he settled upon his toiletries and his clothes, including his rather meagre shoe collection. Given that the main wardrobe in the master bedroom at Palazzo Versace had copious amounts of shoe-specific storage, Joseph pondered that it may be time to invest in a few more pairs of shoes.

He packed everything into the rear seat of the car and then turned his attentions to the cat's paraphernalia. He would have to work out how to get the scratching post, kitty litter tray and all of her associated supplies, along with the kitty carrier past everyone and into the condominium without being noticed. Joseph rummaged through the various cupboards that had become full of stuff, since the twins had moved out. Then he saw his deliverance.

Karalee had left a set of luggage with them, as it was too large to fit in her meagre apartment shared with her flatmates. One extra-large suitcase would easily hold the kitty carrier and scratching post. The rest of the stuff would fit into the other two medium sized suitcases. It was perfect. He could unload in full view of the security people, cameras and hotel staff, and nobody would know any different. He set about packing everything carefully into them.

***

Joseph made good time from Broadbeach Waters up to Main Beach. It was so much easier in the car he thought to himself as he passed the light rail. Something occurred to him as he approached the hotel. He did not know how to enter the underground car park. Nor did he know which car spaces were allocated to his condominium. He knew that he had two spaces; but beyond that, he was clueless.

First things first, though. He needed to secret Molly X into the largest of the suitcases. He had left her kitty carrier in the foot well of the passenger's side front seat for the journey up until now. There was a soft shoulder on the road that he pulled onto. As he walked around to the other side of the car and lifted the kitty carrier out, he assured her that she would not be in the suitcase for very long.

"Only a few minutes Molly X. You'll be the very first thing that I move into the condo."

For her part Molly X gave a resounding meow. Joseph took it that she was agreeing with his plan with her vocal response. He carefully put her carrier into the capacious suitcase and gingerly closed it up. Now it was a race to ensure that she did not suffer any discomfort at being enclosed for too long. He hurriedly took the driver's seat once more and resumed his Journey.

He decided to drive into the circular colonnaded portico and ask a doorman for directions. One of the many advantages of having hotel staff available for your convenience. As he approached on Seaworld Drive and turned into the hotel, Joseph was filled with awe once more. He could scarcely believe that this was his new home. It was so far removed from anything that he had ever dreamt of before, that it barely seemed real.

As he approached the main doors, a dutiful doorman stepped forward and opened the car door for Joseph.

"Hello, I am Joseph Whynee, I am moving into condominium number four today" he said by way of introduction.

This seemed to jolt the man into action. He hurriedly began to talk into a discretely positioned walkie-talkie before turning his attentions back to Joseph.

"Of course, Mister Whynee. We did not know quite when to expect you. But we are very happy to welcome you to Palazzo Versace. Mister Ismail Islington, the residential care Manager is looking forward to meeting you. If you'll allow me, I'll pilot us to your designated car spaces in the underground parking station?"

The offer was too good to refuse, and so politely delivered that Joseph would not have refused even if he had wanted to. Joseph obligingly gave up his driver's seat and shuffled over to the passenger's seat to enjoy the ride.

"Thank you so much" said Joseph trying to read the man's name badge as he did.

It was obscured enough for him to not be able to clearly read the name; but decided that he could take his time to learn the who's who of the staff in due course. The doorman expertly navigated them out of the circular portico and to the entrance to the parking lot. As he should have expected, even the parking spaces were incredibly clean and somehow up-market looking. The plethora of exclusive cars was nothing short of a concourse de elegance of expensive looking classics, the usual European marques and interspersed with exotic high-end sports cars. Some he had never before seen outside of a magazine.

Maybe it was a good thing that Isabella was keeping the rather ordinary car. It would look a bit pallid by comparison to its neighbours if left in this company.

By the time that Joseph and the doorman arrived at the car space. There was a small group of people awaiting them. Joseph was a little taken aback. He wasn't expecting a welcoming committee. The car pulled in and he dutifully exited.

A man in a pristine black suit stepped forward. He was perhaps in his mid-thirties. Dark hair, and a slightly middle eastern appearance. But that first visual impression was juxtaposed by the very prim and proper English accent that came forth when he spoke.

“Mister Whynee, I am Ismail Islington, the Versace Hotel resident’s relationship manager. I apologise for being unable to greet you the other day, but I was unavoidably detained with a personal matter”.

Joseph listened to the introduction and apology with some pithy. The fellow really didn’t have anything to apologise about.

“No need to concern yourself mister Islington. I’m here now and ready to move in.”

Joseph gave Ismail his best smile as he delivered his reply.

“Please call me Ismail, all of the residents do” Ismail explained.

“Ok then, I shall, thank you, Ismail”. Joseph said.

“The porters will help you with your luggage, if you would pop the boot we can begin.”

Ismail and the staff were an unexpected fly in the ointment of Joseph’s plan to surreptitiously move into his new home. But now, he had to roll with punches, as it were. He obediently opened the boot with the car’s remote. Two of the staff moved forward thinking that they would find boxes or suitcases in there, but were a little flummoxed to find clothing, all still on hangers (and cheap looking wire hangers at that!) piled into the boot space.

They were too well trained to show their disapproval and obediently began to sort through the pile and organise it into categories of clothing. Ismail opened the rear door of the car and saw the large suitcase.

“I’ll take that one!” said Joseph with a mild note of alarm.

“Nonsense, I wouldn’t hear of it” replied Ismail as he lifted it out and set it down on the concrete upon the case wheels.

“It’s not at all as heavy as it would seem upon first impression” he said. Judging the case to be nowhere near full, by the feel of it.

Joseph began to break out in a sweat on his forehead. One sound from Molly X and the game would be over! The cat would be both figuratively and literally out of the bag! The other items were divided up between the staff and with Ismail in the lead they headed for the elevator that would take them from the basement up to the ground floor.

As they walked Ismail took it upon himself to explain more about his role to Joseph.

“If there is anything that you need to know about the rules and regulations or the services that you may avail yourself of, please just give me a call. My phone number is in your condominium. You will find it in a folder marked ‘Resident’s Handbook’. Oh, and another thing, we would like to know about the welcome party? You will need to choose a date to host it in your condominium”.

Molly X chose that moment to let out a meow of disapproval at being enclosed in a suitcase and being wheeled somewhere that she could not see. Ismail had been looking forward rather than at Joseph when the meow erupted. He turned to Joseph.

Joseph thought quickly and then did his best impersonation of his cat.

“Meow!” he said to Ismail with a huge smile. One that he hoped would cover up the fact that he was turning red with embarrassment.

“I beg your pardon?” queried Ismail.

“Oh, it’s just a sound I make when I hear about something that I’m really looking forward to. That welcome party sounds like a real hoot!" he said hoping that the flimsy explanation did not sound as ridiculous as he thought.

"You like to meow, like a cat?" Ismail asked, attempting to confirm the odd behaviour.

"Yes" responded Joseph with as much authenticity as he could muster.

"I see". Ismail's tone indicated the exact opposite, but he was clearly not going to push the point.

"How about we give me a month to settle in and schedule the party for some day around then. My time is my own at the moment. Does that work for you?" Joseph asked.

"Of, mister Whynee, whatever suits. The other residents are understandably curious about their new neighbour. I imagine that there will be quite a large turnout."

Ismail called the elevator. It must have been one dedicated to freight because it was very large. All the group were able to fit in it with room to spare. Once they had piled in and the doors closed. Ismail was about to continue with the verbal induction to the hotel with Joseph when Molly X let out another meow.

Everybody looked at Joseph.

"That wasn't me that time. It was my phone. I have it set to make that sound when I receive a text message". He beamed a huge smile to everybody, hoping that it would help make the flimsy lie more believable.

"Your phone makes cat noises too?" asked Ismail, attempting to confirm that he had heard correctly what Joseph was saying.

"Yes" replied Joseph, showing his best 'innocent' expression.

“I seeeee”. Ismail’s tone waivered up and down as he stretched out the word.

His eyes narrowing slightly as he regarded Joseph with a little bemusement. The elevator seemed to take forever to go up just one floor. Eventually after a torturous journey the gleaming mirrored doors opened, and the group exited.

“This way” Ismail directed.

They marched as a troop down the beautifully carpeted corridor to Condominium number 4. Joseph obligingly took out his key and opened the door. Everybody moved inside settling just between the small foyer and the dining room.

Ismail addressed Joseph.

“Now you must let us unpack for you; it’s the least that we can do for our newest resident”.

Joseph was horrified at the thought. He was working on a polite way to say no thank you when Molly X once more decided to make a noise.

This time Molly X let out a rather odd sound. It wasn’t a meow; it was hard to tell exactly what sound it was. The large suitcase was behind Joseph at the time. Joseph had to find a way to empty the room of the intruders before anything else went wrong.

“Was that another text message alert?” inquired Joseph.

“Um…Noooooo” responded Joseph.

Ismail gave Joseph a look as if to ask, ‘well, what was it then?’ Obligingly, Joseph provided an explanation.

“I had baked beans and black pudding for breakfast” he said to clarify the origin of the noise that they had all heard.

It was like he had suddenly asked the entire team for a donation to some spurious pseudo religious movement because they all developed expressions of people that desperately wanted to exit the condo as quickly as possible.

"But of course, if you'd rather do that yourself, we will understand perfectly. Wouldn't we everyone?" Ismail asked the porters.

There was a resounding chorus of approval, and a desperate look to Joseph to allow them permission to leave.

"Thanks for your help, I can manage from here" he said much to the relief of all involved.

He had barely finished his sentence when they all moved as one to the front door, almost pushing each other out of the way to be the first to exit the premises. Within a few seconds the door was shut, and Joseph was alone.

"Phew!" he said aloud.

Unbeknown to Joseph, Ismail who had been the last to leave and shut the door behind him managed to hear the word, muffled through the thickness of the wood. He misinterpreted it as "Pew!" and thanked his lucky stars that they had escaped the fallout of Joseph Whynee's explosive breakfast. He hurried down the corridor away from the danger zone.

Inside condominium number four, Joseph was opening the large suitcase. Lifting out the kitty carrier, he opened the front cage and Molly X marched out with as much dignity as she could muster. She gave him a glare at being incarcerated for so long and settled into some self-preening.

Joseph picked up some of the clothes deposited on the dining room table and made his way toward the master bedroom to put them in the walk-in wardrobe. Molly X followed, curious about her new surroundings.

***

Returning from the bedroom, Joseph looked around at the mess of clothes, and suitcases. He noticed something on the coffee table in the living room and moved down the two steps into the sunken area to investigate. It was a small basket with a bottle of champagne in it and some cards. The first card that he opened had a proclamation from the staff

'Welcome to your new home. We are very happy to have you join the Palazzo Versace family'.

That was nice, thought Joseph. He picked up one of the other cards. It contained a gift card to the hotel Spa. Good for a $500 treatment. Joseph was very impressed. The next was a gift card for the hotel's signature restaurant 'Vanitas' also for the value of $500. Joseph was even more taken with surprise. The final was a similar gift card for, you guessed it, $500 for the Versace boutique that was onsite.

"Amazing. I can afford a really swish meal and maybe a Versace outfit, right before I get a facial or something like that?"

He said to Molly X who had joined him in the living room. The gift basket welcome was a very nice touch indeed. But first he had to get his new home in order.

It wasn't long before Joseph had his clothing sorted. He next set up the kitty litter in the laundry, along with the scratching post. Unless there was a deliberate search nobody would see them. He would have to keep her water and food bowls in his bathroom, he decided, as she was not going to be happy with having food and water near her kitty litter. It was perfect. He was going to succeed in hiding his cat here in the hotel and nobody would ever be the wiser.

Molly X had wandered around, looking at the living room, kitchen, both spare bedrooms and the main bathroom and caught up with Joseph just as he was taking a seat on his bed to wallow in the luxurious comfort of his new living situation.

Then came the voice. It was clear. It was female. It had a definite superior air to it, and it most definitely came from the cat, even though her mouth did not move when the words were delivered.

"*Pussy is very pleased with her new abode!"*

Joseph froze. He looked closer at the cat.

"Did you just say something?" he asked, completely unsure of exactly what he had heard.

" *Pussy is very pleased with her new abode. You have done well primary servant. Very well indeed".*

Joseph shook his head. He must be hallucinating or something? Maybe the stress of losing his job and losing his marriage and losing his home and finding out his father is a sex maniac had finally got to him? He pondered the question for a while before dismissing it completely. He has had greater stresses in his life than this? And it never resulted in a talking cat before. No, this was something that was very definitely different to his normal life.

"*Nothing to say to Pussy, primary servant?"* asked the cat.

As he was being pushed for a response, Joseph felt obliged to give one.

"I'm glad that you like it. I have a question though; why do you keep calling yourself Pussy? Your name is Molly X".

This had quite a negative effect on Pussy, and her tone reflected it.

"Does Pussy look like a tablet of ecstasy or a capsule of MDMA to you!? What were you thinking letting your drug-addled children choose a name for Pussy?!"

Joseph seized upon the reference.

"I knew it! But I could never get them to admit it! Those cheeky buggers". He said ruminating about how Pussy came to be named four years ago.

Her indignation still apparent, Pussy continued the explanation of her name.

"Pussy's name is Pussy. It is a regal name. There is only one Pussy, and Pussy is she! Get used to it".

At that moment Joseph felt that there was suddenly an entirely new world opening up to him that he would need to become accustomed to. Not just the sumptuous one surrounding him, but an entirely new way of perceiving his relationship with his cat.

Chapter 16

What's in a name?

"I suppose it could be fatigue, or a fever, or something like that"?

Joseph tried to verbalise the reasons that could be causing him to imagine that his cat was talking to him. She, of course, seized upon the implication of doubt and made her displeasure known to Joseph immediately.

"It's a good thing that primary servant is finally listening to Pussy. Pussy can achieve a greater state of calm and relaxation, knowing that Pussy's commands are being carried out as intended".

This did not help Joseph's situation at all. He squinted and leaned forward to stroke the head of the kitty. He did so. She blinked and purred in agreement to the touch. And Joseph was convinced that the cat was real, and he was not dreaming. But he couldn't comprehend why the pet he had owned for four years could communicate verbally now, when she had never done so before.

"Cats cannot talk. It's a fact. There is no record anywhere in human history of a cat striking up a conversation with a human being".

Joseph decided to fall back on simple facts. If cats could talk, then it would have been recorded somewhere. And he would have heard about it. Pussy, however, was less than impressed with the basic premise of his point of view.

"*Well, there's your problem to begin with primary servant. Humans are not the best at hearing cat's instructions to them. You know what we cats say? Humans are un-trainable. Some are more un-trainable than others".*

Joseph couldn't believe what he was hearing. And not just because it was coming from a cat.

"I'm pretty sure that's what we humans say about cats?"

He hoped that his correction of the adage would put Pussy's thinking on the subject back to the accepted normal. He was wrong. Pussy had lost interest in the conversation and had begun to saunter out of the bedroom.

Joseph jumped up from the bed and followed her. She made her way back into the living room and chose the three seat sofa to jump into and begin kneading the soft, and detailed fabric.

"Why have you never spoken to me before?" He asked.

"*Pussy has been speaking to you the entire time. You've just never heard Pussy before!"*

Pussy finished kneading the fabric and did a half circle before settling down in her classic croissant shaped sleeping position. Joseph asked a further question but was rebuked by Pussy.

"*It's Pussy's time to sleep now".*

"Wait, just before you do that, I have to know something".

"*What is it?"*

"Why do you call me Primary Servant instead of by my name?"

"Because that is what you are, Pussy's primary servant. It's funny that you ask Pussy that though. Pussy has associated names with other people before, just not you for some reason".

Joseph was mortified.

"Like who?" He asked genuinely intrigued by the situation.

"Isabella, that grizzly ex-wife of yours. Karalee, your bland daughter. Austin, your porno-addicted son. Pussy just never noticed that you have a name".

"Why ever not? You've lived with me for the last four years! All this time, other than Primary Servant, what have you called me?"

"Hey you"!

Pussy's tone left Joseph in absolutely no doubt that his name was of very little concern to her. Joseph was crest fallen. He was genuinely hurt by the lack of interest in him. Sensing his displeasure, Pussy did a good impersonation of rolling her eyes.

"Well, Pussy is asking now. Please regale Pussy with the munificence of your name, primary servant. What is it?"

Joseph could have sworn that her tone sounded somewhat insincere but elected to answer anyway.

"Joseph" he said simply.

Pussy blinked a few times, and gave a dramatic pause, as if contemplating the name.

"Now that you say it to Pussy, Pussy does seem to recall that it is a name Pussy has heard before. Somewhere?"

It was the best that Joseph could hope for under the circumstances. He was about to respond when he noticed that Pussy had closed her eyes. He had always admired his cat's ability to fall asleep in an instant.

Feeling a little more alone than normal, when in the company of a sleeping cat, Joseph decided to return the car to Isabella. He looked at his watch. She would probably be home from her lunch by now. Before leaving he ensured that there was some dry food in the food bowl, and fresh water in the water bowl. If Pussy awoke whilst he was gone, she would probably want a prior to dinner, snack.

***

Joseph was indeed correct. He had returned the car and entered the house to find Isabella having a snooze on the sofa in the living room. She awoke has he came into the room.

"All moved in?" she inquired as she struggled to get up. More than likely from the effects of too much alcohol served with lunch.

"Yes; yes. All done. The car is in the driveway. I'll leave the keys in the kitchen".

Joseph paused as if there was something more on his mind. Isabella sensed that he wanted to say something and attempted to preempt him with what she thought it may be.

"I know what's on your mind. It's taken longer than expected to get the ring separated from the diamond. But the jeweller has left a message on my phone saying that it is now done. I'll have Austin pick it up and drop it over to you this evening. He should be here sometime soon. You're on Seaworld Drive, right?"

Isabella had managed to not guess what was actually on Joseph's mind at all. But to be fair, who could guess that your ex-husband would want to engage you in a conversation about a talking cat? At this stage Joseph was still under the mistaken impression that he was getting the diamond from the ring and Isabella was retaining the ring. This was not concerning him at all. So, he was left with no alternative but to try and approach the subject as carefully as he could.

"Oh, yes, thank you very much. That would be great. Austin can see my new digs. The address is in the kitchen".

Joseph was unsure of how to approach the subject of Pussy.

"I've renamed Molly X" he said.

"Good heavens; why?" inquired Isabella genuinely confused at the minor revelation.

"It seemed the right thing to do. It's almost as if she whispered her new name to me".

Joseph hoped that the reference would evoke a response from Isabella. Something like how close pets can actually be with their owners; and how they can communicate across the chasm of coming from different species. Instead, Isabella seized upon the subject matter and relayed something that she had heard whilst lunching with the ladies.

"Maryanne told me that her dotty old father started to hear his pet dog talking to him".

Perfect! This was exactly what Joseph wanted to hear.

"Really?" he said with a smile and look of intense interest on his face.

"He had to be sectioned and spend some time in a mental institution! A power of attorney was appointed, so he lost the ability to make financial decisions for himself. There was no history in the family of mental illness, no schizophrenia and no Alzheimer's. It's all really very sad".

Isabella concluded her retelling of the woeful tale, her eyes wide.

“That’s terrible” said Joseph, deflated at the turn of events against his hope to approach the very subject of a talking pet with his ex-wife.

“So, what’s her new name?” She asked.

Joseph paused for a moment as if he was thinking entirely of something else and then shook himself out of his thoughts.

“Pussy………..the…….errr….cat” he said, stumbling his way through the announcement.

“You’re kidding?” Isabella looked very unimpressed. She rolled her eyes and tried to make sense of the new double entendre name.

“Is this some form of belated reaction to being made redundant from Big Lips Advertising?” she asked.

Joseph shook his head in denial.

“It’s nothing like that. I just think that Pussy is a rather regal name for a cat. Don’t you?”

“No” Isabella replied in a deadpan tone.

“Is it because you haven’t been getting any, and are missing ………well…..pussy?” she inquired.

“NO!” Joseph exclaimed, genuinely offended at the presumption.

“Are you sure Joe. It sounds like a cry for help to me”.

Isabella was unconvinced that she had not indeed, hit the nail on the head with her analysis of the situation. Feeling that he had better count his losses and get out whilst he could, Joseph made an excuse to leave.

"Still a lot of tiding up to do back at the new place. I'd better go. Much on for the weekend?" Joseph hoped that the change of subject would help. He was luckily, correct.

"Pilates. And rearranging the furniture. Karalee and I are going to feminise the house now that there are no men living here. Something a bit more 'Barbara Barry' if you know what I mean?"

Isabella's brief explanation of how she wanted to remodel the house left Joseph no clearer as to what she was hoping to achieve.

"Who?" he asked in earnest.

"Joseph you are such a philistine! A famous interior designer of international repute".

"I'm more of an interior designer luddite than a philistine" said Joseph in his defence.

Isabella decided to put an end to the conversational topic, as it was sure to go nowhere with her ex-husband.

"I'll phone Austin and remind him to pick up the ring and drop it over" she said. And then as an afterthought.

"A letter arrived for you today. Don't forget to set up a redirect with the Post Office to your new address. It's on the kitchen table" Isabella said.

"I'll go and get it now" he replied.

With their goodbyes exchanged, Joseph made his way to the light rail stop. He knew that he could catch it up to Main Beach. But was unsure of exactly how far away the stop was from Palazzo Versace. He would find out soon enough he thought to himself.

Chapter 17

The Fly

Joseph arrived back at Palazzo Versace and was greeted by the staff as he entered and regaled at the fabulous lobby once more whilst walking through it. This was the first time that upon entering the residential wing, he noticed that there was in fact a security door. It should have occurred to him that the residents would be well protected from the Hoi Polloi. He dutifully got out his security card and slotted it into the reader beside the glass door, which obediently made a sound that gave Joseph the assurance that it was now unlocked and able to be opened.

Safely ensconced once more in his luxury condominium, he set about getting Pussy her dinner.

"*It's about time primary servant*" she said as he fumbled with the lid of the cat food can.

"I'll thank you to call me by my name Pussy" he retorted in a semi-stern voice.

"*Hurry up with the meal.....um....urrrr......Darren*" she said.

Joseph was genuinely annoyed. Pussy had failed to remember his name.

"It's Joseph!"

"Oh yes, Pussy knew it was something insipid".

Joseph gave a rather gruff harumph sound and finished serving up the food for his impatient feline.

Whilst Pussy made a complete pig of herself gulping down the food, Joseph moved into the living room. He opened the large glass sliding door. The sun was setting. A cool breeze was blowing. The sound of the water feature, as well as the flowing water in his plunge pool, emanated from outside. The peace and serenity of the scene was palpable.

He reversed into the living room and accurately guessed where the main lounge suite was without looking back. Sinking down into it, Joseph was entranced with the setting, his new home, and the prospects of an entirely new chapter in his life opening before him. Thoughts about how he would run a successful boat charter business drifted before his mind's eye. The future was going to be very perfect for him indeed!

He would have happily sat there bathing in the joy of the moment for the next few hours, but then came the fly. Not just an ordinary housefly; a large blowfly. It buzzed into the room with such ferocity that it snapped Joseph out of his joyous trance and back into the moment.

Giving the fly an annoyed look, as if that would somehow rid him of it, Joseph tried to go back into the peace and serenity of the visions that he was just having. There was no hope of that happening though with the constant noise from the irritating blowfly. Following a random course around the living room, it managed to collide with Joseph's forehead at one stage further raising his ire.

He brushed the air slowly at first, hoping to send a message to the noise-making insect that it was unwelcome in his home. Each time however, he only managed to vaguely scrape the air where the fly had been, but never where it was at the time. The ferocity of his air swipes began to increase along with the anger he was feeling toward the unwelcome invader.

Eventually he was waving his hands in the air with all of the aplomb of a chimpanzee swinging from a branch in a jungle.

"AAAARRRRGGGHHHH !" he yelled at the blowfly.

Maddingly, it seemed to detect his attempts to shoo it away and it increased its overall flying height. Now it was just out of range of his hands. This had a twofold effect upon Joseph. Firstly, he was insulted by the insect that it had somehow managed to thwart his (unsuccessful) attempts to get rid of it. Secondly his level of annoyance with the buzzing intruder more than doubled within seconds.

He began to jump up repeatedly, hoping to increase his overall height to impact the little bugger and knock it to kingdom-come! But each time the blowfly either skilfully or out of blind luck, evaded his frantic waving hand.

There was nothing to it. He would have to launch himself off the sofa in order to get the upper hand on the interloper. Mistakenly thinking that nothing could possibly go wrong with such a logical course of action he stood on the three-seat-lounge. Carefully judging the random course of the blowfly, Joseph somehow managed to convince himself that he had worked out the pattern that the trespasser was using. He projected in his mind exactly where he assumed the fly would be and hurled himself off the lounge, whilst simultaneously giving a forceful downward swipe with his hand.

He missed the fly, and landed with a thud just short of the intricately carved wooden coffee table.

"Right; I'm going to get you mister!" he proclaimed at the blowfly.

Joseph marched into the kitchen and opened the utensils draw. Picking out the egg-flipper he raced back into the living room. Now he was appropriately armed for this conflict. The blowfly seemed blissfully unaware of its own impending doom at the hands of a kitchen utensil. So much the better, though Joseph. But let's be big about this and give the assailant a chance to escape.

“Coming up! One dead blowfly!” he announced to the trespasser, as if that would be enough to get the aggressor to fly away fearing for its own mortality.

The blowfly of course had no idea what was happening and continued to buzz loudly and irritatingly as it zipped around the airspace of the living room. With the extra height afforded by the stainless-steel flipper, Joseph was confident of imminent victory in this battle of wits.

He made a trial swipe at the offender but to no avail. Once more mounting the sofa he felt he was in a more commanding position. He took a breath and studied the erratic movements of the fly before reaching back and with a huge sweep of his arm he made to slice the miscreant in half mid-flight. Instead, the steel of the flipper intersected the glass and metal central light fitting splitting a rather large shard of glass from its formerly, perfect shape.

“DAMN IT!” Joseph shouted at the top of his voice.

This was entirely the fault of that bloody fly; he was certain of it. Angered and even more focused on killing the blowfly. Joseph once more considered the movements of the fly, attempting to make sense of the chaotic flight pattern. His eyes narrowed in anticipation. Time seemed to slow down as he willed the fly to come once more within his reach.

By complete happenstance, it did just that.

“I have you now” he said to the blowfly.

The fly had made the mistake that Joseph had been waiting for. It came down from its lofty altitude and began a new zigzag pattern more around the height of Joseph, elevated as he was, on the lounge suite. This was perfect. Joseph could now really get some swing and force into the final chop that would end the war he had waged upon the lilliputian insect.

Moments seemed to stretch into minutes as he gathered his strength and waited for the perfect opportunity to present itself.

Without quite knowing that he had decided upon that very moment, Joseph reached back and gave an almighty swipe at the fly, once more missing. Even the laws of averages had deserted Joseph. With all of the hysterical and somewhat uncoordinated and definitely uncouth antics that he had been exhibiting, the fly should have been at least grazed by now. But no; not so much as a near miss could be claimed by Joseph at this stage.

Instead, the oomph that he had put into the thrust, that missed, caused him to become quite unbalanced (literally not figuratively) and he swung around unceremoniously on the sofa. Finding absolutely nothing to grip onto to prevent his fall, Joseph elected in that microsecond to jump for his life. This time not missing the coffee table by a whisker as he did before. But instead, landing directly on top of it with a loud thump. By some miracle, he somehow managed to maintain his upright position.

"Phew!" he said aloud.

He looked down and was grateful for the expensive looking coffee table to break what could have been a very nasty fall. However, fate was only playing a brief waiting game with Joseph before pulling out its trump card and playing it.

Like a scene from silent slapstick movie, the entire four (medusa head carved) legs of the coffee table sprang off simultaneously. The platform of the table crashed to the marble floor with a crash that could have awakened the dead (well, obviously not the blowfly, because it was still very much alive).

Joseph was so shocked at the proceedings that he flung his arms up and the steel egg flipper flew out of his hand and across the room. It impacted a rather expensive looking glass framed print on the other side of the living room. Which upon smashing, also broke free from its hanging hook and crashed to the ground.

Joseph decided to be very still in case anything else he did would result in calamity. Above him, he became aware of the very noise that had driven him to begin his battle campaign. He looked up at the victor in the war of the living room serenity (or rather lack of it). The blowfly continued buzzing away as if nothing had happened.

Pussy had been watching the proceedings from the dining room with some amusement. She chose this point to enter the living room, making sure to avoid the various areas of smashed glass. Sitting on the marble floor she watched the blowfly with her keen eyes. The pupils dilated and her concentration on the object of her desire grew. Unfortunately for the blowfly, it chose that moment to do some low-level reconnaissance. Without very much effort whatsoever, and in a graceful show of athletic ability, Pussy jumped up and clasped the blowfly between her front paws. Bringing it successfully to the ground she trapped it beneath one paw.

From where Joseph was standing, he heard and almost imperceptible click.

Pussy removed her paw, expecting the buzzing toy to provide her some more amusement and attempt to escape. But it lay there mortally wounded. And the lone soldier, buzzed its last in the vast landscape of the battle of condominium number four's living room. Silence was restored to the apartment.

Bored with the lifeless thing, Pussy made her way to the sliding door so that she could enjoy the final moments of the setting sun. Joseph surveyed the damage that he had done to the light fitting, the framed print and the coffee table.

"This is going to cost me" he said.

And then thinking beyond the fiduciary costs, he wondered exactly how he was going to explain the vandalism to Ismail?

He still had the rather generous redundancy package from BL Advertising. So, replacing the broken items would be an inconvenience, but one that he could more than bear. He decided to sit in one of the tub chairs and try to come up with a plausible explanation that could be used for the raucous first evening in his new home.

He put his hands in his pockets and sat down. There was something in the left pocket. A paper that was not supposed to be there. He pulled it out. It was the letter that Isabella had directed him to take with him. Opening it by force of habit rather than by any pressing need to find out the contents, he pulled out the paper and unfolded it.

The letter was in fact, the final bill from his solicitor for managing the divorce proceedings for him. Joseph was horrified. The cost was nothing short of astronomical.

"WHAT!" he shouted as he saw the figure that he owed his retained legal firm. A sizeable chunk of his money was just about to walk out the door. Joseph began to break out in a sweat. Getting divorced is expensive, he thought. Imagine what it would have cost if things had not been so amicable.

"Maybe I should count my lucky stars" he said to himself.

"At least I have Pussy on my team, eh Pussy" Joseph waited for a response but got none.

He contemplated cleaning up the mess but decided to wait for the final vestiges of the sunset to disappear before doing anything. It was a good decision. In spite of the shock of the bill, the damage he had done to the apartment, he began to feel at peace once more.

It lasted for at least another full minute before he was alerted to a really irritating whining sound. A mosquito buzzed somewhere near his ear. He angrily brushed it away; unsuccessfully. It returned and buzzed near to his ear a second time.

"Oh my GOD !, What do I have to do to get some peace and quiet?" he shouted.

"Pussy. There's a mosquito over here, can you please come and kill it for me?"

Pussy turned her head around, whilst remaining seated and gave what Joseph thought was an impassive stare. As it turned out, her stare that was one of being particularly unimpressed with his plea.

"*Mosquitoes don't interest Pussy, Alan. It's your problem*" she proclaimed.

"My name is JOSEPH!" he yelled.

"*You're the only one who cares about that*" she retorted.

Chapter 18

Millicent Williams

Joseph decided that there was nothing to it but to clean up the mess that he had made. He busied himself hiding the evidence of the broken coffee table and the smashed print in its frame in the laundry. Amongst the glass he found the shard of glass that he had cleanly shaved from the living room central light fitting. He disposed of the rest of the broken glass into the glass recycling bin that was neatly secreted in one of the kitchen cabinets.

He was pondering if the light fitting shard could be super-glued back into place when there was a knock at his front door. He put the glass shard down on a side table and let Pussy know that she should make herself scarce.

"Pussy, there is someone at the door. If you're found here there will be trouble. Would you please go to the bedroom and wait until they are gone?"

Thankfully for Joseph, Pussy needed no motivation. She was not particularly enamoured with people that were not her direct servants. So, without responding she trotted off toward the master bedroom.

Joseph gave the condominium a cursory look over. Everything seemed perfectly normal now. He also checked himself in the hall mirror near the front door. He managed to convince himself that he looked absolutely without guilt or culpability. He opened the door, unsure of what to expect.

Standing patiently, was an old lady. She was immaculately dressed in a white outfit that although it looked simple, also managed to impart an air of somehow being rather expensive. Her short grey hair was tied back into a neat small bun. Joseph guessed that she would perhaps be in her mid-seventies.

"Hello" she said with a disarmingly pleasant smile.

"I felt that I should introduce myself. My name is Millicent Williams. I am your neighbour".

Joseph was relieved that it was not the security guards wanting to know what all of the noise was about. He visibly relaxed.

"Hello. My name is Joseph Whynee. Please come in".

He motioned that Millicent should go through to the living room. He shut the door and followed her down the two steps. She turned and asked in a plain voice, that did not sound accusatory but nevertheless disarmed Joseph considerably.

"What was all of that unholy racket earlier? I assumed that you were either watching a sports game of some description, or you were hosting a convention for terrorists!"

Millicent gave Joseph a look that made him feel like he was back in school and was being admonished by the principal for being naughty in class.

"Oh, Ahhh, errr, That?!" Joseph fumbled for a believable explanation.

"Please have a seat, Millicent. May I call you that?" he said hoping to deflect the original question.

Millicent nodded her thanks and took a seat on the sofa. Joseph sat in one of the tub chairs. Millicent now comfortable gave

Joseph a look as if to say 'well?' Realising that he would have to come up with some explanation decided that honesty was the best policy. It was something about his memories of attempting to lie his way out of trouble at school that never yielded results in his favour that swayed Joseph toward the truth.

"I was chasing a blowfly with an egg flipper" he said, laying the truth before her.

"I hope you got it" she said in earnest.

"Eventually" he said, hoping that she did not notice that he could not hold her gaze for the incorrect admission.

"So, how long have you lived here in Palazzo Versace"? inquired Joseph. He was genuinely intrigued as this was the first actual resident that he had met.

Millicent must have been satisfied with Joseph's explanation of the blowfly battle because she did not press the issue. Or exactly why it had been such a noisy battle with such a minuscule opponent.

"Ever since the death of my lovely husband four years ago. I wanted to get out of that large house we owned and live a simpler life. And, I must say, it has worked out beautifully. The staff are lovely. And the hotel guests don't know if I am one of them or a resident. It's only the staff and other residents that know the difference. So, it becomes a collective secret that we all share".

Millicent was certainly an engaging individual. Joseph hadn't had time to consider what the residents may actually be like. He just assumed that they were all wealthy. But beyond that, nothing.

"That's lovely" he said.

"Of course, we have been very curious about the winner of the RSL prize moving in. A rumour began to circulate that you were a homeless man that scrounged together the price of the ticket by begging on the street".

There was no malice in Millicent's retelling of the incorrect rumour. Joseph was amused at the misinformation that had spread about him before his arrival

"I've heard a few since I got here. But, just for the record. Newly divorced. Newly retrenched from my accountancy job and looking to start a new chapter in my life. I guess that just about sums up the situation".

Then he thought of something and hurried to ask Millicent.

"What are the other residents like? I know that I must host a party to meeting them. But I'd appreciate a heads-up. What can I expect? It has been weighing on my mind. I want to make a good impression". He smiled hoping to get some insights.

Millicent raised her finger and waggled it in the air.

"You're in luck Joseph. There are surprisingly few that you will see on an ongoing basis. The numbers of permanent residents are actually quite small. Most of the owners are fie-foes"

Millicent's explanation did nothing to clear up the mystery.

"As in; fee fi foe fum. Like Jack and the beanstalk?" he asked innocently.

Millicent laughed aloud.

"No, Joseph. F.I.F.O. Fly in; fly out residents. You'll only see them when it is winter in the northern hemisphere. So, what is left are the ones like me; anchored here because it is comfortable and there is nowhere else that we would rather be. Which is a good thing. We are therefore all of a very similar ilk. I'm sure you'll get along with all of them."

Then as if she had a sudden thought, she added a caveat.

"Except of course for Charles Carver. Have you heard of him?"

Joseph had heard the name. He was somewhat of a celebrity, not just in Queensland, but throughout Australia.

"The eminent neurosurgeon?" Asked Joseph attempting to confirm his understanding.

Millicent shook her head, almost in disgust.

"There is absolutely nothing eminent about that pompous ass" replied Millicent.

Joseph smelled some gossip and was surprised at how much he was interested in gleaning more details.

"Really?" he said and leaned forward in anticipation of further clarification.

"Oh, I'm sure that he will show up to your welcome party, just to criticise your foie-gras or tell you that the Maison of champagne you've chosen isn't one that he would normally drink. The man is completely infuriating. I simply cannot abide him at all."

This was juicy stuff thought Joseph. But then as if realising that she may have gone a bit too far with her criticism Millicent tried to regain some moral high ground.

"Well, if all we have to put up with is one bad egg, then life here is still marvellous. The others will be simply fine Joseph. You have nothing to worry about".

"That is good news" responded Joseph. He was about to make further light-conversation when Millicent said something that could have easily doubled as a backhand across his face.

"Hiding a cat here could get you in trouble though. Just make sure that none of the other residents see it. Especially Charles Carver. He is absolutely humourless when it comes to enforcing the rules and regulations of the establishment".

Joseph was stunned. What should he do? His first thought was to deny all knowledge of a cat. He was fumbling for a sentence to form in his mouth when Millicent held up some fine black strands. Pussy's fur.

"I take it the cat has black fur. And it is sticking to the legs of my white Versace suit." She explained.

Realising that he had nowhere to go but forward, Joseph gulped and admitted to his crime.

"I couldn't move anywhere without my pussycat. My ex-wife never really got along with her. I simply had no choice but to bring her with me".

Joseph hoped that his plea did not sound as pathetic to Millicent as it did to his own ears.

Millicent needed no further pleading from him though.

"Divorced and retrenched. I think that you've had your share of rejection Joseph. Your secret is safe with me. In fact, I'll aid and abet you in this endeavour. Just to spite Mister Charles Carver!"

Millicent had a look of mischievousness on her face.

"Oh?" said Joseph innocently, wondering what she had in mind.

"Whenever you need to give her shelter, like when the party is on, your pussycat can take refuge in my condominium. There is no need for anyone else to know. And I'm quite a pet lover. In fact, I had a small dog of my own hidden here in my condominium, before Charles Carver set the owner's corporation lawyers on me and I had to give her up for adoption. It nearly broke my heart".

Joseph could now see the reason behind the vitriol for the neurosurgeon. He sounded like quite a piece of work. One to be avoided.

"I see. That must have been horrible. Oh, thank you Millicent very much indeed. That would be wonderful. And, I will take every precaution that I can to keep secret my little lady. And keep her here with me". Joseph said with unmasked feeling.

"I should be going. It was lovely to meet you Joseph" she said as she rose from the sofa, dusting the cat fur from her trouser legs.

"Likewise, you too Millicent. Thank you for dropping by and thank you very much for helping me with Pussy the cat" he said.

Millicent indicated that was the least that she could do. As Joseph walked her to the door they exchanged pleasantries about pet owners needing to stick together. After he bid her good night and closed the door Pussy emerged from the bedroom.

"*What a lovely woman Millicent is. Pussy shall make her a secondary servant. Millicent will like that for sure*"!

Joseph was stunned.

"You remembered her name!?"

"*Of course, there's nothing wrong with Pussy's memory*".

Joseph sighed in exasperation for so long and so deeply that he was in danger of feinting.

Chapter 19

The Ring and the Diamond

Joseph had just closed the door after seeing Millicent Williams out, when he heard an electronic warble. It certainly was not the sound that his mobile phone made. What on earth could it be? He followed the source of the sound to the kitchen when he noticed that there was a handset on the wall there. He lifted it.

"Dad"

It was clearly the voice of his son Austin.

"Son, where are you?" Joseph inquired.

"I'm at the security door, you need to buzz us in. Karalee is with me". Austin explained. Joseph was delighted. Both of his children had come to visit him. He briefly pondered if this was the kind of joy that his father felt whenever he received a visitor at the retirement home.

Joseph looked at the cradle for the handset. It did not take a genius to figure out that the way to allow entry to visitors was to press the button with the icon of a key on it. He did so and could hear the confirmation from Austin.

"We're in. See you in a second".

Joseph was relishing this moment. He resisted rushing to the door to open it and wait for his children to appear. Eventually there was a knock on the door. He took a breath and went and answered it. Standing there with incredulous looks upon their faces were Austin and Karalee.

"Hi kids. Thanks for dropping by". He said by way of greeting.

Joseph motioned for then to enter. They did so whilst looking high and low at the same time.

"I can't believe that you moved into Palazzo Versace without telling any of us. What does this place cost to rent? It must be an absolute fortune!?"

Austin was clearly flabbergasted at the new home his father was living in. Karalee then took up the mantle of questioning her father about the living and the career situations.

"Mum tells us that you've been made redundant from your job? So, have you spent the entire retrenchment package on renting this? Good heavens Dad. Why? Although, it is very beautiful, I must say".

He led them through the dining room and down the couple of steps into the sunken living room.

"You both may need to take a seat to hear this" Joseph said with a wry smile.

They did as they were instructed, both still looking around.

"Cool patio Dad. And your own private plunge pool too! Wow. But you'd never get me out of the lagoon pool from the main hotel section." Austin said.

"Karalee, Austin, this heavenly three-bedroom, fully furnished condominium is not costing me a cent to rent". He left the statement hanging in mid-air and waited for the obvious reaction. He didn't have to wait for very long. In unison both of his children asked.

"What? How?!"

With a growing smile he revealed the news to the two of them that he had kept secret for such a long time.

"You are looking at the WINNER of the RSL FIRST prize in their latest lottery; ME!"

Joseph even accentuated the news with a flourish of his arms. Austin and Karalee were clearly stunned.

"You?!" asked Karalee, unsure if her father was having a joke at their expense.

"Me!" he confirmed.

"You; seriously Dad, you?!" asked Austin in disbelief.

"Yes. Really and truly me. WINNER! OWNER! And now permanent resident of the Palazzo Versace. Isn't that fantastic?" he said.

Both of the twenty-one-year-old offspring were amazed. Although both a little dubious as well. Austin was the first to express his misgivings about the incredible news.

"I heard that the winner was a Social Housing tenant. A guy that had fathered five children, all to different mothers, by the time he was twenty. And was moving in here with all of them. And coming with some bombed-out car that he is stripping down for parts and selling bit by bit online to eek out a living. Imagine that parked in the security car space here!"

Joseph was horrified. How do these rumours get started he wondered?

"Well, obviously that isn't true" he said with a small amount of exasperation.

"Also, it is a dreadful stereotyping of social housing tenants. For shame Austin". He added.

Karalee pounced on the same grapevine of misinformation.

"I heard that it was a drug-lord that had won the prize here and was planning to set up a drug-lab in the bathroom and try to sell his narcotics to the rich residents!"

"WHAT?" Joseph was nothing short of horrified by this fanciful rumour.

"Who starts these gossip Chinese-whispers anyway?" he asked, not seriously expecting an answer.

"I did try to tell each of you the day that I received the call about my win. But you were both pretty wrapped up in your own little worlds. Your mother too. No time for the old-man!"

He said with a mock accusatory tone. Austin and Karalee were repentant.

"I am so sorry Dad". Karalee said.

"My fault entirely Dad; I apologise". Austin followed his sister's apology with his own.

Pussy chose this moment to appear from where she had been napping in the master bedroom. She recognised the former secondary servants and moved to ensure that they lavished affection upon her, as she wished.

"Hello Molly X!" said Austin when he saw the kitty.

Joseph felt it important to stay on Pussy's good side, so he corrected Austin immediately.

“Also, the cat’s name is now Pussy. Not Molly X. This is a classy establishment, and I can’t have the residents thinking that I’m a drug lord manufacturing ecstasy pills, or MDMA capsules in the bathroom, can I?”

Karalee and Austin looked immediately sheepish.

“Oh, you figured that one out, did you?” Karalee smiled an apology at her father.

“I’m not entirely twentieth-century you know. I know how things work. Which reminds me. Stop watching so much internet porn Austin. It is not a true representation of sex; and is ultimately demeaning to women”.

Austin was horrified at the accusation. He was about to object in the strongest possible terms when he realised that he was heating up. His face felt like it was on fire. He must be blushing a deep shade of red. It was a visual admission of guilt that he was powerless to control. If only he had known that it was Pussy the cat that had made the misdemeanour known to Joseph, he would have been even more embarrassed than he was.

“Busted!” Karalee laughed at her brother loudly.

Austin determined to claw back some credibility, or at least, wanting to change the subject as quickly as possible, queried his father about the suitability of the cat’s new name.

“How is Pussy a better name than Molly, exactly?”

“It’s more regal”!

Joseph’s reply had a mildly curt tone.

“Anyway, how about a full tour of my new home? And I’ll include the car spaces to prove that there is no old bomb parked there that I’m stripping for parts. You should see the actual cars that the people here own, kids. It’s just fantastic. And I think that we’ll finish the tour over at the marina, where my Yacht is moored”!

Austin and Karalee both jumped to their feet in anticipation.

“Yes please” she said.

“Let’s go!” Austin confirmed.

Karallee leant down and gave the cat a quick pat on the head.

“*You call that a proper way to greet Pussy”* said the cat in annoyance.

Joseph motioned with a single finger in the air.

“Did you hear that kids?” he asked hoping that they too would be able to hear Pussy speaking.

“Hear what?” asked Karalee.

Austin simply shook his head. Joseph was unsurprised, but a little annoyed. He had figured that he would somehow be the only one that could hear Pussy communicate.

“Ah, nothing; let’s start with the patio and work our way around the condo” he said.

***

By the time that they returned to the condominium and once more took seats in the living room, it was about an hour later. The Yacht had taken up quite a bit of time to go through. Thankfully, connected to power, it could light up like a Christmas tree and be seen in the night. Added to that, the marina was well lit as well.

“This place is breathtakingly beautiful Dad”! Karalee was trying to describe the Condominium, the fit out, the setting and the lifestyle that it afforded. But somehow superlatives did not seem to come close to the actuality of her father’s new living situation. In fact, his entirely new life.

“I am, believe-me, very happy”.

Joseph’s assurance was unquestionably honest. It was then that Karalee started to put together the sequence of events. Something needed more investigation in her mind.

“Let me get this right. You were retrenched from Big Lips Advertising. Then asked to work one more week to hand over. It was during then that you got the good news about winning the prize.”

Karalee’s retelling of the story was correct.

“That’s right”. Joseph confirmed.

“Who did you tell at Big Lips Advertising about the win. And how did they react? Did the news shoot through the office grapevine like lightening?” Karalee asked.

“Well, I decided after receiving the call about the win, to only tell those people in the company that I actually liked”. Said Joseph.

“So, who did you tell?” She asked.

“Nobody”

They all laughed aloud at the absurdity of the situation.

“Clearly you needed this to push you into a whole new mindset, Dad.” Austin remarked.

Then as if his comment had reminded him of why he was visiting he reached into his pocket for the small package he had picked up from the Jewellers earlier in the evening.

“Oh, and here is the diamond, returned as promised by Mum”.

He fumbled with the packet, opening it to reveal the diamond and the ring now separated.

Karalee picked that moment to question the instructions that Austin had received from their mother.

“Austin, are you sure that Mum said to give Dad the diamond and her the ring?”

“Yes, I’m sure that’s exactly what she said”. Austin confirmed.

Karalee shook her head and could not help but think that something was wrong.

“It doesn’t sound like something that she would do. Maybe keeping the diamond and giving back the ring, though. That would be more likely”.

“Nonsense” said Joseph.

“Your mother wants me to take-back the family heirloom. This diamond has been handed down in my family for three generations. Clearly your Mum wants to make a clean break and put the diamond back into the hands of the Whynees. She’s an absolute star”. He concluded.

Austin handed over the diamond. It was a beautiful cushion-cut absolutely-perfectly clear diamond of two and a half carats. Joseph lifted it up and admired it by looking through it at the central light in the living room. The diamond gleamed and glittered with amazing light flashes.

“Beautiful”

Joseph was always beguiled with this Whynee piece of history.

"One day, this could very well be yours".

"Whose?" Both twins asked in unison.

"Whichever of you gets married first".

They gave each other a sheepish look. Neither of them had been remarkably successful in the field of romance. But equally, they knew that there was still plenty of time to conquer that particular aspect of life.

Pussy made her presence known once more with a loud meow. Joseph looked down to admonish his pretentious cat.

"Keep it down Pussy, you know we have to keep you a secret here".

This alerted Austin and Karalee to the one thing that may be a blight on the magnificent life that their father had at Palazzo Versace.

"What? There are no pets allowed?"

Austin sought to verify the understanding that he had drawn from the statement.

"Unfortunately, no. It's the only downer about living here. My lovely old lady neighbour, Millicent Williams, was hiding a small dog for a while. But one of the other residents ratted on her! The neurosurgeon Charles Carver. Can you believe it?"

"Oh, Dad, you insurgent! This is the first time I think that I've seen you break the rules for anything, anytime, ever!"

Karalee was amazed at the expressed rebellious nature of her father. She had never seen it before. This was quite a new side to her conservative Dad.

"Well, let's keep Pussy a secret, shall we? I don't want to lose her. She means a lot to me".

The twins were amazed, but agreeable to the arrangement. Austin had a further point to clear up though that needed addressing.

"One last question Dad. Why is there a broken coffee table in the laundry?"

Joseph sighed and rolled his eyes so far upwards that they were in danger of never reappearing.

"It's a long story. I'll see about getting a replacement from the Manager tomorrow".

This statement from his father tweaked a further memory from Austin that he had to impart.

"Also, your front doorbell isn't working. We had to knock".

"I have a doorbell?" Joseph looked vexed.

"The white button beside the door". Austin confirmed.

"I'll look into it". He promised.

Joseph decided to open the bottle of champagne that he had received in the welcome basket. He would only allow Austin one flute after finding out that he was the designated driver for the evening. But between Joseph and Karalee, they made a good dent in its luscious contents.

It must have been close to ten o'clock when they finally said their goodbyes and left. With his head swimming nicely from the French bubbles, Joseph took another walk out to the patio to enjoy the lights of the building. The sound of the water in the water garden. And the stars in the sky.

He once more produced the diamond and looked through it at the stars above. Life really was just perfect.

Chapter 20

Designer Furniture is Expensive!

The following day, Joseph sprang out of bed, interrupting Pussy's slumbers as he did so. He figured that the first thing that he had to do was to stock the pantry and the refrigerator. Not having had dinner the previous night was beginning to make itself known. His stomach was churning loudly.

He decided to use one of the gift cards. The one for the Il Barocco would be perfect he decided, after first checking in the resident's folder that they served breakfast. They did. And the menu looked very appetising.

After showering and shaving and attempting to look as casual, but also formal, as his current wardrobe of clothes would allow, he headed off for breakfast.

When he arrived at Il Barocco he was greeted by the front-of-house person. A lovely young lady who arranged for a table. Joseph was seated and once more contemplated the menu. Everything looked good. It was going to be a hard decision. Eventually he settled on the Eggs Benedict and placed his order.

Whilst he was waiting and looking around at the opulence surrounding him, a familiar voice came from behind.

"Good morning, Mister Whynee".

Joseph turned around. It was the very person that he wanted to speak with.

"Ismail. I was going to come and see you after breakfast". Joseph said.

Ismail alerted to a resident's need wanted to know more.

"Is there something that I can help you with?" he asked.

"I had an unfortunate accident in my condo last night, whilst showing around my children. A framed print has been broken and the coffee table too; I'm sorry to say."

Joseph thought that the less he said about the entire incident, the better. Ismail was far too cultured to make a request for any further detail. He simply acceded to the unusual request and responded with an affirmation.

"I am sure that it is something that I can help you with. We have spares for all of the signature furniture. There will be a cost involved. I cannot quite remember off the top of my head what the print in the frame will cost. But I do recall that the coffee table, with resident's discount included of course, will be about fifteen thousand dollars".

Ismail delivered the shockingly high price tag for the replacement table in a matter-of-fact tone. Joseph, however, was horrified. His eyes bulged so much that he could feel that they were in danger of popping out.

"Is there something the matter mister Whynee?" Inquired Ismail.

Joseph took a moment to compose himself. He was beginning to get the picture that his beautiful furniture was also very pricey.

"Good heavens, what's it made out of? Gold?"

Realising that he sounded like a complete tight fisted scrooge, Joseph quickly changed tack.

“But, of course, I’ll happily pay for it. Thank you for being so understanding about my little accident”.

Joseph had to try with all of his might to look nonchalant and smile contentedly at Ismail.

“Alright then. I’ll get one out of storage and come by. What time suits?” Ismail inquired.

“Oh, and another thing, while I think of it, apparently my doorbell doesn’t work” Joseph interjected.

Ismail smiled and pointed to the ceiling with one finger.

“Good news, that won’t cost you anything. I’ll bring the electrician by later this afternoon. It’s probably just a loose wire.”

“Phew”. Joseph was visibly relieved.

The waiter chose that moment to deliver Joseph his breakfast. Joseph wanted to wrap-up the conversation as quickly as possible because he was so famished.

“I’ll be out shopping this morning, so please just come by whenever. I’ll leave the broken coffee table near the front door for you. And call me Joseph. I always think that my father must be lurking somewhere nearby when you call me Mister Whynee”.

Ismail accepted the authorisation without question. And appropriately modified his mode of address.

“Thank you, Joseph. By the time you get back everything will look as good as new”.

With farewells exchanged; Ismail parted leaving Joseph to get stuck into his breakfast. He was already planning the sequence of events. He would have to impose upon Millicent to shelter Pussy for the morning. The coffee table and print could be replaced whilst he was out grocery shopping.

One more thing popped into his mind though. The broken light fitting. He set himself a reminder to superglue the broken shard back into it before dropping Pussy off next door.

***

Austin had dropped Karalee off at her flat and elected to go home rather than drop in on his mother so late the previous night. Now, with a lovely Saturday morning ahead of him, he swung by her house to deliver the ring.

He found his Mum saying goodbye to a gentleman caller at the front door as he approached. Austin nodded and smiled politely at the stranger as they passed each other.

“Austin. I expected you last night” Isabella said.

Austin held up both hands in a surrender motion.

“I was unavoidably delayed getting the guided tour of Dad’s rather grand new home”. Austin said by way of explaining his circumstances from last night.

Isabella thought that it was an unusual excuse. How good could this rental be? And it was on Seaworld drive too. A tad too busy for her liking. She motioned for him to come inside and led the way to the kitchen.

“Can I get you anything?” She asked.

“Nothing for me Mum. And before I forget. Here is the ring”. He produced a small velvet pouch and handed it to Isabella.

She took it with some trepidation. Why did he call the diamond a ring? She thought to herself. Opening the pouch, she peered inside. Her fear was confirmed immediately.

"Austin! You were meant to give your father the ring, and me the diamond!"

Austin was confused. He was sure that he had carried out his mother's instructions properly. Wasn't he?

"Why would you keep the diamond? It's a Whynee family heirloom".

Austin appeared to have inadvertently trapped his mother in a moral dilemma. She was furious with her son for mixing up her original instructions. But pursuing the diamond in place of the ring would somehow now seem improper. There was nothing more to do, except go and get it from Joseph herself.

Not wanting to involve Austin for any more of her scheme, Isabella decided to change the subject.

"What's your Dad's new rental like? Nice?" She feigned interest, hoping that he would not see through her little ruse.

"Well. A couple of very important facts have not been entirely disclosed by Dad in this instance".

Austin allowed the question to hang in the air hoping to bait his mother into asking for further clarification.

"Such as?" She asked. Confused by the statement.

"Firstly; he is not renting his new home. He owns it outright". Austin produced the first of a few revelations that he needed to impart to his mother.

Isabella thought that it must have taken his entire redundancy package from his job to purchase something up at Main Beach. It was a rather salubrious neighbourhood. Surely, she thought to herself, he must have purchased the worst property in the best suburb. She requested confirmation of her assumption.

“Is it a small studio. Or a one-bedroom place? Something run down and cheap?”

Austin shook his head whilst he revealed the second extraordinary piece of news.

“Three bedrooms. His own private plunge-pool. Marble bathrooms. A real classy place all round”.

What Austin was saying did not make any sense to Isabella. Joseph was simply financially incapable of affording something that sounded incredibly expensive. She gave Austin a look as if to say, ‘are you having me on?’ It was then that Austin chose to reveal another morsel of information that was hereto unknown.

“Did I mention that the condominium is in Palazzo Versace?”

Isabella was now in a state of complete shock. Austin simply had to be pulling her leg.

“No!?”

The last piece of the puzzle was all that his mother would need to put it all together. Austin delivered it with wide eyes, leaving Isabella in no doubt as to his veracity.

“Dad was the most recent winner of the RSL lottery!”

It all made perfect sense now. Isabella was amazed but confused and a little bewildered at how the man that she had known for three decades, had managed to keep such a secret from her. After a suitable time to absorb the news, she spoke.

“I think that I’d better go and wish your father all the best for his win”.

***

By the time Joseph had done his grocery shopping and hauled it on public transport back to his fabulous home, it was noon. The doorman opened the doors for him. Joseph would have been incapable of doing so himself under the heavily laden circumstances. Having a doorman was one of the plethora of things about his new abode that he already absolutely loved.

He guessed that not many of the residents either did their own grocery shopping or were ever seen carting groceries through the lobby of the hotel. But none of the staff gave any indication that he was doing anything outlandish, which made him feel better about doing it.

He got to his front door eventually and fumbled with the key. Realising that he would need at least one hand free he put down the bags that he was holding in his right hand. Then, spying the doorbell for the first time he gave it a test push. Nothing happened. Joseph guessed that Ismail had not come over with the electrician to fix it yet.

As he opened the door, the next-door neighbour poked her head out of her doorway.

“Joseph is that you?” She asked.

“Hello Millicent”. Joseph smiled in return.

“Excellent. I’ve just had a call from the girls. We have a game of gin on this afternoon. I must make my way down to Paradise Waters to meet up with them. I’ll just grab Pussy for you”.

Joseph manhandled the groceries into the small foyer of his condominium. By the time he had finished Millicent was there holding Pussy in her arms. She let Joseph in on her observations whilst he was absent.

"I saw Ismail and one of the maintenance men deliver the new coffee table and framed print and take away the broken ones. So, the coast should be clear for the rest of the day."

Joseph knew that it was not. And that there was an electrician to appear at some time through the afternoon. But he did not want to impose on Millicent's good will for any longer.

"Thank you so much for watching Pussy for me. I've never played gin-rummy before. You'll have to teach it to me sometime".

Millicent corrected Joseph's misunderstanding of her planned afternoon with the 'girls'.

"Cards have nothing to do with it, Joseph. Providing there is Gin; we're happy!"

Joseph adjusted understanding of the idea that he had formed in his head. And reconstructed it in his imagination to picture a gaggle of old ladies drinking shots of gin and getting rather messy. He grimaced at the thought.

"Have fun!" he said with as must honesty as he could muster.

Pussy, now safely on the patterned marble floor, sauntered into the dining room and jumped up on the dining table. Joseph closed the door and lifted all of the bags onto the open-plan kitchen counter. He would have to decide if he wanted to keep a neat pantry, or one where everything is shoved in with wild abandon. He decided on the former, as it seemed to be more in keeping with his new surroundings.

"Millicent is a lovely secondary servant, Jacob. You could take a lesson or two from her on how to best look after Pussy".

Other than being somewhat insulted at the idea that he was less than a fantastic primary servant, Joseph was also miffed at being miscalled yet again.

"My name is Joseph, Pussy".

"Well, Pussy knew it was something beginning with a 'J' at least!" She retorted.

Joseph walked into the living room and looked at the sparkling new coffee table that had replaced the broken one. On the wall too, hung a perfect replacement for the print that had been smashed during the battle of the blowfly.

"What great service". He commented.

Joseph then busied himself packing his groceries neatly in either the refrigerator or the pantry. This was a great way to save money. He could only imagine what the other residents ongoing costs were if they ate in the onsite or other local restaurants constantly. Oh, to be rich, he thought. Well, at least he could fool himself that he was rich living here.

It was then that he noticed there was a piece of paper on the dining room table. He picked it up. It was the invoice for the rather expensive coffee table and the print.

"The combined cost is seventeen thousand dollars! Can you believe it?" He exclaimed.

Pussy had absolutely no interest in what Joseph was babbling about and removed herself from the situation so that she could lie in the sun streaming through the living room glass doors.

Suddenly, Joseph's daydream of living the high life began to evaporate. The stark reality revealing itself to him was that he needed to get an income so that he could afford continuing to live here.

Chapter 21

Everybody Loves Pussy

Joseph sank into a tub chair in the living room, incredibly depressed. What could he do about his current monetary situation? He could always get a job as an accountant again. But somehow that just did not feel right. He wanted something more, now that he had had a taste of the good life.

Deciding that he needed to find out more about his business idea of chartering 'Beat the Odds' he got his laptop from his room and brought it back into the living room. He would figure out what it would cost to get his Captain's licence. And what he could reasonably charge passengers for a day out on the boat, with him at the helm. Minus the running costs would be the total profit per journey; easy.

Pussy had been wonderfully quiet for the time that Joseph spent crunching the numbers. He looked up advertising costs. Website costs. Insurance and licence costs. It was going to be tough with the money that he had left. But he could almost do it.

The problem was that it would take time to build up the business. For his day-to-day expenses in the meantime, he was going to need an income to cover living costs. It was quite a dilemma. He would have to give it some more thought.

Pussy interrupted his musings with some of her own.

"Your problem is that you don't love Pussy enough!"

Joseph was shocked at the allegation. It was simply untrue. He had always liked cats, ever since he was a youngster. And when he found Pussy in the pet store a few all those years ago his heart absolutely melted. He had to correct this unfounded accusation immediately. He put aside his laptop, stood up and towered over the cat.

"I love you Pussy. You mean the world to me. I couldn't imagine my life without you".

Joseph hoped that his explanation would quell any misgivings that Pussy had of his affection for her. However, Pussy would not be swayed so easily.

"Pussy is not feeling the love. Tell Pussy with feeling, how much you love Pussy!"

Joseph had no option but to be much more dramatic with his show of affection.

"I love my Pussy!" he said with feeling.

Pussy simply shook her head and moved to hide herself beneath the newly installed coffee table. This shocked Joseph. He somehow felt that his cat was punishing him for not being loving enough. He renewed his vow of allegiance to his cat.

"I love my Pussy. I love my Pussy. I LOVE MY PUSSY!" Joseph shouted.

From behind him came a voice that startled Joseph so much he actually became airborne as he jumped with fright.

"Are you planning on a sex change operation?"

Joseph spun around mid-air to find Ismail Islington standing here along with a man in overalls, presumably the expected electrician.

"I'm ahhhhhh, errrrr, eeeee, what?" Joseph had no words to explain why he was standing in the middle of the living room shouting about loving his pussy to the visitors.

"Oh, my mistake. That was very insensitive of me. Of course, I meant to call it gender reassignment surgery".

Ismail seemed pleased with his politically correct nomenclature of the assumed proposed alteration to Joseph's gender. The electrician however was looking at Joseph like he was something that escaped from an asylum.

Joseph continued to look like a wild animal caught in a car's headlights. He glanced back at the coffee table. Pussy was well hidden from sight. At least he could be thankful of that. But in a fit of improvisation that should really have been thought through more carefully, he offered an absurd explanation.

"That's the name of the coffee table. I've given the furniture nicknames!"

Even has he said the words, Joseph could feel his stomach sinking. Ismail, for his part narrowed his eyes.

"And the coffee table is called Pussy?" Ismail asked.

"Yes". Joseph confirmed.

"May I inquire as to the name of the three-seat sofa?" Ismail was completely serious.

Joseph did not have time to come up with anything else, other than the first thing that popped into his head. After all, he was now committed to the charade. He had to make it seem real.

"Marshmallow".

He said in as deadpan a tone as he could manage. Ismail almost frowned this time. Ismail had to question further to re-verify previously obtained knowledge of Joseph's quirky nature.

"And you make makes kitty noises when you're pleased, and your phone also makes cat noises".

Again, Joseph had to content himself with the first thing that came to mind. Pity it was so incredibly lame.

"I have a thing with cats. I think that I was one in a previous life".

Ismail had to do his best to not look shocked at the bizarre statement.

"I see. I'm very happy that you love the new coffee table, er, I mean, Pussy so much Joseph".

Then changing the subject as quickly as he could, Ismail introduced the electrician.

"This is Ed, our electrician. He will be fixing your doorbell today".

The electrician was clearly not part of the staff, as his overalls had a logo and a name of some electrical company that Joseph could not quite make out. Mollycoddling the residents was clearly not part of his purview. With a less than genuine tone he asked Joseph.

"What's the name of the doorbell that I'm repairing for you?"

Trapped in his own lie Joseph decided that enough was enough. He had to get back to some semblance of normality in the eyes of these two men.

"I haven't got around to naming it yet".

Which was of course the truth. The electrician nodded and indicated that he would begin work immediately. But as he walked away, he could not help but throw Joseph another jibe.

"When you do give it a name, let me know".

Ed's tone was thinly disguised sarcasm. Joseph did his best to wrap up the scene, feeling that he had humiliated himself enough for one day. He thanked Ismail profusely and let him know that the money would be paid as per the invoice details as soon as possible for the coffee table and print.

He practically man-handled Ismail out of the condominium. As he was doing so there came a ding-dong sound from the door.

"Fixed. Just a loose screw. Although I bet it's not the only screw that's loose around here".

Ed's dig made Joseph feel like he was a schoolboy being denigrated by a school bully.

"Thanks for taking care of that so quickly. Have a great day both of you. Bye".

Joseph shut the door in the faces of both men. As he did so he breathed a sigh of relief. Returning to the living room he found Pussy exiting from her hiding place.

"Alright James, you may continue to be Pussy's primary servant".

"My name is Joseph!...........and thank you Pussy. I'd like that".

Chapter 22

Two Pussies Are Better Than One

It was later in the afternoon when Joseph heard the intercom buzz. Answering it he was surprised to find Isabella at the other end. He allowed her entry. This, he though, would be interesting. How would she react to his news? The kids would have most certainly told her everything by now. He was contemplating whether or not he should open the door and wait for her or let her ring the doorbell when the ding-dong of the doorbell removed that decision from him.

He opened the door.

"Why didn't you tell me Joe?"

Joseph had always liked Isabella's direct approach to finding out information that she wanted. His only answer was a huge smile and a single word.

"Surprise!"

Joseph opened wide his arms as if indicating his luxurious surroundings. Isabella was less than impressed at being kept in the dark from a piece of news so important. However, she could not help but be a little impressed at her former husband's ability to keep such a big secret. She smiled at him wryly and walked into the condominium looking around at the incredible detail.

"You know, we could always start the tour with my yacht and then work backwards from there?"

Joseph's offer was too tempting to refuse. Isabella had no intention of turning it down.

"Mister Whynee, you've got yourself a deal".

Joseph was quite skilled at showing off his new surroundings by now. He knew that by starting at the marina and working his way back to the condo, via the spa, gym, lagoon pool and restaurants, that the tour had the most impact. Well, it certainly did on him. So, he guessed that it would on others too.

***

By the time that they made it back to the living room of his condo, Isabella was a complete convert to the privileged lifestyle that she glimpsed. Settling into one of the tub chairs she waited for Joseph to come back from the kitchen with a sparkling water. As he handed her the glimmering glass, she summarised her admiration for his new living arrangements.

"Joe, this is heavenly. I could be not happier for you. It's just what you need to kick start the next phase of your life".

Joseph was happy that Isabella approved. And even more so that she saw it as a way to begin a new chapter in his life's story.

"Thank you so much Isabella. That is exactly how I feel about it too. Like a new chapter of the book of Joseph Whynee has been opened and is about to be written. This is something that I'll be able to tell the grandchildren."

Isabella was at this stage only half listening. She was planning to bring up the diamond and explain how she wanted to keep it as a souvenir of their married time together. But she was beaten to the goal posts by Joseph. Talking about the potential of one day having grandchildren reminded him of the inheritance that he would be handing down the line.

“Oh, and one more thing. I cannot thank you enough Isabella. You really knew what you were doing there. And I must confess, I did not think twice about it at the time. Not really at all until I held it in my hand. Giving me back the family diamond was a masterful stroke of genius on your part. It was very big of you indeed. And now it will go down the Whynee family line again to Karalee or Austin. I’ve promised it to whichever of them gets hitched first”.

Thwarted! Isabella listened with growing horror at each successive sentence from her oblivious ex-husband. She fixed her facial expression to not give away that she was completely flummoxed.

“Oh, that’s nice.”

Was all that she could respond with.

“Cheers to you my love”

Joseph lifted his glass of sparkling water and gave her a wink. Isabella breathed a huge sigh of defeat. There was now no way of getting her hands back on the diamond without coming across as a callous materialistic woman.

“Well, you know me Joe, always thinking of others”.

***

Karalee and Austin were out shopping together. They felt that they should get their father a house-warming present. But what? Austin put their conundrum into words.

“What on earth do we get the man who, suddenly, has everything?”

They were in the Pacific Fair shopping centre. It had been extended and modernised a number of times since it was built back in 1977. But now it was suitably glamorised to suit the more discerning customer that shopped in the approximately four hundred stores. Looking around Karalee was as unsure about what to buy as a joint gift for their father as Austin was.

"You know the one thing that Dad doesn't have, that we can't buy him, is permission to keep Molly X, I mean, Pussy there".

This seemed to light a spark in Austin's eyes.

"You have put your finger on it exactly".

Austin was clearly pleased at Karalee's unwitting revelation. Karalee did not know exactly how that point helped their situation.

"How so?"

"Come with me!"

Was all that Austin would say. He led Karalee through the crowds to a gift store of some description. They had passed it earlier but not seen anything that seemed to fit the bill. Inside Austin guided them to the back of the shop to a lower shelf. There sitting, or rather, curled up, were a number of hyper-realistic cat's all in various sleeping poses. One of them was an absolute dead-ringer for Pussy. Austin picked it up so that they could both have a closer inspection.

"It's uncanny. This is indistinguishable from Mol……I mean Pussy".

Karalee was amazed at the detail. But unsure of how this would help their Dad.

"But how……"

"Don't you see. This is exactly what Dad needs. If there are any accidental sightings of Pussy, we just ensure that this Pussy duplicate is used to explain the sighting. It will give Dad plausible deniability that there is actually a cat in his apartment. Or, rather not an actual cat in residence. If you know what I mean?"

Karalee was surprised at her brother's clarity of thinking in this matter. It left her utterly convinced that this was the right thing to do.

"That is perfect Austin. Well done. Let's take it over to him right now".

Austin hurried to the cash register of the store and plonked down the fake cat. He said to the old lady behind the register.

"I'll take it".

***

Joseph received the gift from Austin and Karalee with some trepidation. Removing it from the paper shopping bag he held the fake cat in his hands. He was astounded at it. Even the size was a perfect match to Pussy. He listened as they explained the rationale behind their purchase for him. This was truly the most amazing gift he had ever received from his children.

"This is perfect and exactly what I need kids. Thank you both very much".

Then looking down at the actual Pussy, who had come over to see what was going on. Joseph introduced the newcomer.

"Hey Pussy, meet your new twin. Pussy Two!"

Chapter 23

Briefs are Better for the Older Man, Not Boxers

It had been a hot day. Summer was really in full swing. Although he had access to air-conditioning, Joseph felt that he had better limit how much he ran it for fear of the cost of his electricity bill spiralling out of control.

It was now night-time on Sunday. Joseph was lazing about in his underwear. He was only wearing a singlet and boxers. It was not as if he had to dress to impress anyone whilst in his home. And as the living room glass doors that overlooked the plunge pool and only had the water garden beyond that, his privacy was assured.

Joseph was once more getting together information about attaining his Captain's license. He was sitting on the three-seat sofa fixated on the glowing screen of his laptop. Something that he was reading needed to be taken note of. He rose from his position and went into the bedroom to retrieve his note pad so that he could write it down. Upon returning he was rather surprised and somewhat annoyed to find that Pussy had taken his seat.

"I was sitting there, Pussy. You have the entire living room to choose from. In fact, the entire condominium to choose from. Why on earth do you want to sit right there?"

In her own inimitable unconcerned way, Pussy responded with a dismissive retort.

"Pussy sits where Pussy wants. No explanation is required".

This got right up Joseph's nose. In that instant he decided to take a stand and show Pussy that he was the Alpha in this household and not her.

"Well, that is my seat Pussy, so prepared to be crushed by my weight when I reclaim my rightful position!"

Joseph dropped the notepad on the coffee table unceremoniously, and then moved to be in position to sit-down right-on top of Pussy. She showed no sign of being concerned at the unexpectedly aggressive move. Unperturbed, Joseph made a big show of slowly but surely descending his buttocks toward the cat. By this time, she had sat up and was taking a bit of notice. Nevertheless, she remained determined to retain her spot at all costs.

Unfortunately, Joseph's precariously balanced scrotum chose that moment to dislodge itself from where it had been inside his boxers. The wrinkly, hairy, and rather oddly coloured sack of skin flopped out, and down.

Spooked at the sudden appearance of something that seemed like the ugliest mouse she had ever seen; Pussy lunged forward and sank her fangs into it.

The ensuing scream of unbridled pain echoed through the entire condominium. Joseph jumped so high that he almost hit the newly (but cheaply) repaired central light fitting. When gravity finally got around to pulling him back to earth, he landed slap-bang on the coffee table. And just as happened to its predecessor, the legs of the fifteen-thousand-dollar piece of designer furniture went flying off in four directions.

It was not something that Joseph noticed immediately as he was busy pulling down his boxers as quickly as he could to inspect the painful damage to his manhood. He had broken out in a sweat far greater that temperature could take responsibility for. He clutched his ball-sack tenderly in his hands as if it was priceless set of jewels.

Taking his time, he carefully felt around the testicles to ensure that they were not damaged. After satisfying himself that they were, indeed, intact, he turned his attention to the scrotum itself. Apart from some small blood spots where the top and bottom fangs had entered, it too was relatively undamaged.

Only then did he realise that he was standing upon the wreck of another Versace signature piece of furniture.

"Oh my. Oh No! Ohoooohhhhhh..........nooooooooo!"

Pulling up his boxers he surveyed the damage. He contemplated using the same tube of superglue that he had used to fix the light fitting, to reassemble the coffee table. But upon attempting to put the broken pieces together again, he realised that it would be beyond his abilities completely.

Facing another bill for fifteen-grand Joseph had to come up with a viable alternative that would not break-the-bank. He momentarily distracted himself from this seemingly insurmountable task by turning to admonish Pussy for causing the entire incident in the first place. She had long since left the commotion and had retreated to the main bedroom to get some peace and quiet. She really had no understanding of why her primary servant was carrying on in this manner. But it was of little concern to her.

Groaning with both relief for his not-so-damaged scrotum, and magnitude of the task before him, Joseph finally reclaimed his seat on the sofa. He opened a search engine and typed in the words 'furniture repair'.

As the results collated themselves onscreen, Joseph decided that from now on, it would be best if he wore briefs as his underwear of choice. Boxers presented too many hereto before unseen dangers.

***

The following day Joseph was walking through the main lobby on his way out to meet with a furniture repairer when Ismail intercepted him.

"Joseph, I'm glad I found you. May I please have a word?"

Joseph spun around and greeted Ismail and gave him the affirmation to proceed.

"It's about that rather painful scream that was heard coming from your condominium last night. Is there something wrong? Anything that we can help with?"

Without properly thinking about the answer, Joseph nearly gave away that it was the fault of his cat. But he managed to stop himself half-way through the admission and then found himself in need of completing the sentence in a way that would somehow make sense.

"Oh it was just my cat…cat….catt…..ummmm, errrrrr, my cataracts. Sorry Ismail sometimes I get a stammer. It was just my cataracts acting up. Acute pain. But all gone now".

Joseph smiled innocently at Ismail. Ismail looked horrified.

"Cataracts that are that painful? You poor man. I had no idea".

Trapped by the pathetic lie, Joseph had no option but to elaborate in order to imbue it with some semblance of credibility.

"Oh, it comes and goes. Quite rare, actually. But something I'm prepared to live with until I really need to get them taken care of. Nothing life-threatening you know".

Joseph's ad-hoc excuse was flimsy to say the least. Nevertheless, Ismail pressed him for further details.

"And you have a stutter too? I really didn't notice before; you must be very accomplished at covering it up?"

Joseph had to get this conversation drawn to a close as quickly as possible. This of course meant that he did not have time to properly think through what he said next.

"Yes, well it's really only the word c…c….cat, that seems to trip me up. And not always. Just most times………Pretty unique stammer eh?"

Ismail was flabbergasted. He put into words the entire list of things that he had managed to gather about the newest resident of Palazzo Versace.

"So, you make kitty noises when you are pleased. You have your phone programmed to emanate cat sounds. When you break wind, it bizarrely sounds like a cat meowing. You have pet kitty-like names for your furniture pieces. You think that you may have been a cat in your previous life. And, when you attempt to say the word cat, it may, or may not, invoke a stammer. Have I got all of that right?"

Ismail's absolute authenticity was palpable. And, in no way deriding or mocking of Joseph. It gave Joseph nowhere else to go except to accept the convoluted list of lies that he had up to this point managed to spew forth.

"That sounds about right". Joseph said with as much genuineness as he could muster.

Ismail nodded in complete agreement. Then, in order that the situation not evolve any further, Joseph made his excuses to leave and said a quick goodbye to Ismail. It was time to get to the furniture restorer to see if he could get his second coffee table repaired within a reasonable cost rather than admit to destroying another one and incur the horrendous expense of replacing it.

***

For once Joseph felt like he was outsmarting the situation that he found himself in. The furniture restorer had listened patiently to the description of how the coffee table had become disconnected to its legs. He looked at the pictures that Joseph had taken of the wreck. And he had come up with a price of around eight-hundred dollars in order to repair it. Joseph was relieved that he did not have to go to Ismail and acquire another overly expensive replacement. He was feeling quite pleased with himself as he returned to his glamorous home. Walking through the lobby he was claimed by Ismail who wanted to have a 'word' with him. Joseph stopped and waited for Ismail to catch up with him. After exchanging the usual pleasantries, Ismail told Joseph what should have been excellent news. But owing to the fact that it was predicated with a fanciful lie, Joseph listened with growing horror.

"Joseph I've let one of the other residents know of your acute pain and thankfully, he has agreed to see you tomorrow morning. The eminent neurosurgeon Charles Carver. Have you heard of him?"

Joseph was both stunned and confused at the same time.

"Well, yes, but I fail to see how a neurosurgeon would want to inspect my cat..cataracts?"

Joseph ensured that he stammered slightly on the word cat so as to keep up the pretence of his ludicrously specific stuttering problem.

"Charles Carver used to be an eye surgeon before altering his speciality into neurosurgery. Isn't that wonderful that he is one of our residents. And that he has made this opportunity available to you. Normally the waiting queue to see him can be up to a year. Here are all of the details. I hope that the time suits?"

Ismail handed Joseph a superbly written piece of paper, noting the time and date of the appointment. And the address of the surgeon's consultation rooms. It was quite nearby. Joseph felt a cold shudder come over him. How was he going to get this idiotic lie past such an accomplished professional?

"You shouldn't have".

Joseph said the platitude with much more heartfelt meaning than the phrase is usually delivered with. Pleased with the reaction from Joseph, Ismail smiled broadly.

"We cannot have our residents in pain now, can we? That simply would not do".

Ismail may have stayed to chat longer, but his mobile phone distracted him. He made his excuses and answered it whilst walking away and waving back at Joseph. Joseph did his best to force a grin that did not look like a grimace. It was not entirely successful.

"How much is this going to cost me?"

Joseph posed the question to nobody but himself. There was a sinking feeling in his stomach again.

Chapter 24

Charles Carver

All that Joseph knew about Charles Carver was what he had read in the papers. An incredibly talented surgeon credited for being able to perform surgeries that other surgeons, even other neurosurgeons would not attempt. Of course, now that he was a resident of Palazzo Versace, he had the insights of his neighbour too. Millicent did not seem to have anything nice to say about the fellow. And as he liked Millicent so much, he had assumed that her critique of the man would probably be the same as his.

Joseph arrived at the rather imposing looking rooms just prior to his ten-thirty appointment. They were in an old Queensland style of house, on the small and very exclusive Chevron Island. Thankfully Joseph was able to catch the tram down to the Cypress Avenue stop in Surfer`s Paradise and then walk across Thomas Drive to the home.

As he looked around at the hotel-sized mansions of Chevron Island, Joseph wondered why the man did not live here, close to his consulting rooms? Perhaps he liked to keep work and home very separate from each other?

Opening the door, he was directed by a brass sign to the waiting room. He expected to see throngs of people, given that the wait list for seeing Charles Carver was so long. Instead, there was a simple desk with a woman sitting behind it and some lovely furniture. The entire scene could have come directly out of a designer home-maker magazine. There was nobody else in sight. She looked up as he approached the desk.

"Joseph Whynee. I have an appointment".

Joseph cringed as he spoke the words. He certainly would not have been here otherwise. But under the circumstances he could not think of anything else to say.

"Go right in please Mister Whynee; you are expected".

The receptionist smiled and indicated the door that he should use. Without a further word, but with some trepidation, Joseph walked up to and then opened the door. Charles Carver could be seen in the room beyond. He was sitting behind a large mahogany desk which was situated in front of a large window.

Joseph entered and with a rather nervous inflection in his voice greeted the medical specialist.

"Hello, I believe that we are neighbours".

Charles looked up and indicated that Joseph should take a seat in front of his desk. He replied to the statement with a single word.

"Indeed".

This had the effect of making Joseph more worried than he was already. The tone too, sounded utterly devoid of any warmth. Joseph took a seat and waited for Charles to speak.

"I'm told that you have acute pain emanating from your cataracts. Is my understanding correct?"

The bald-faced lie that Joseph had told Ismail about his scream of pain, now put before him, filled Joseph with a growing sense of dread. He had to find some way to ameliorate the situation that he had created.

“Well, to be fair, it’s only ever an occasional thing. Nothing that I think needs the attention of such a busy man as yourself”.

But Charles would not hear of any trivialisation of the matter.

“Nonsense mister Whynee. This sounds serious. And to be quite frank, something that I may have to author a paper about for ‘Nature’ medical journal. Your highly unusual condition could be a vehicle for me to make a scientific discovery. One that is, as yet, unseen in our time. It is all very exciting”.

Charles clearly had further self-aggrandisement on his mind rather than any genuine concern for Joseph’s pretend condition. This really got up Joseph’s nose. But equally it scared him to think that a fib could be taken so seriously by such an accomplished medical professional. His mind began to race. How could he diffuse this situation as quickly as possible and with the minimum amount of embarrassment?

In an instant, Joseph decided to come clean with Charles. Perhaps if he threw himself on the mercy of the man, then he, like Millicent, could be a partner-in-crime? The crime of sheltering his cat within the luxury surrounds of their collective home. In the angst of the moment Joseph had completely forgotten that it was Charles Carver that had forced Millicent Williams to give up her pet dog.

“Let me see these cataracts of yours. I believe from your online health record that you are under the care of Doctor Monteverde?”

Joseph nodded. Charles stood up from his seat and reaching for the usual apparatus that an eye doctor would use to inspect eyes, he approached Joseph.

“Now, just sit still. This will be a little bright”.

Charles’ comforting words did nothing to alleviate Joseph’s tension. He had to bring up the subject of pet ownership as carefully as he could, without actually admitting to anything just yet.

"Lived at PV for very long?"

Joseph started with some small talk. Charles continued his inspection and answered in due course.

"About four years".

There was a short amount of silence before Joseph managed to blurt out exactly what he had hoped to slip into the conversation without raising suspicion.

"Any pets?"

He cringed as he spoke the words. What a stupid question, he thought to himself.

"No pets allowed at…..PV as you call it".

"Oh yes of course. I forgot. But no pets before you came to PV that needed to be rehoused? I hear that Millicent Williams had a dog that she put up for adoption. Or, something like that".

Joseph really wasn't thinking things through before speaking. Nevertheless, this unusual line of questioning resulting in dividends for him.

"It wasn't by her choice. She knew the rules but tried to shelter a dog. Annoying little noisy thing it was too. I was the one that let management know. It was then that she was forced to give it up".

Charles changed eyes and began his inspection of Joseph's other one. The realisation of this exercise in futility dawned on Joseph. He would never be able to get Charles Carver onside with hiding a cat in the complex.

"No sense in complaining about being betrayed by your own blood, I told her. Rules are there to be adhered too. It was unacceptable that she would not follow them. The rest of us manage to live there quite well without a dog, or a cat, or some other fur-shedding thing".

Joseph picked up on the rather unusual reference to blood. He had to seek clarification.

"I'm sorry; betrayed by your own blood? What does that mean?"

Joseph was genuinely confused. Charles finished his inspection and looked Joseph in the eyes.

"Millicent Williams is my mother. Didn't you know?"

Joseph gasped in horror. His eyes widened.

"You dobbed-in your own mother?"

Charles shrugged nonchalantly.

"Rules are there to be obeyed; not flaunted. The dog was put up for adoption. Never saw the yapping little thing again; thank goodness. I must say that your cataracts look perfectly normal for a man in his fifties. Certainly not worth removing just yet. I'd give them another few years before you would even need to consider it. They are not impairing your vision at all?"

Joseph shook his head. Charles continued. He had a look of concentration on his face.

"Your pain must be referred from somewhere deeper in your head. Perhaps along the optic nerve? Or where it connects to the brain itself? A good thing that Ismail referred you to me Mister Whynee. I believe that we need to investigate deeper. A brain scan is next up for you. I'll make the arrangements and let you know where and when that will be. I'll get to the bottom of this, you can count on it".

Joseph was horrified. Both at the man before him that could betray his own mother, and at the surgeon suggesting that he have what sounded like a very expensive investigative medical procedure. But there was something else that bothered Joseph. He put it into words.

"Why does Millicent have a different surname to you?"

"She was so upset at losing her dog that she reverted to her maiden-name to spite me. Father probably turned in his grave when she did that".

Charles got a faraway look in his eyes as he finished the explanation. Most probably recollecting the event as he told Joseph about it. It was one small mystery solved. The next would be finding a way to get out of this proposed brain-scan. A plan that did not involve coming clean about harbouring Pussy in his condominium. Charles Carver was a clear and present danger for his furry companion.

With the small talk all done Joseph thanked Charles for the consultation and retreated out of the door into the waiting room. It was still empty but for the receptionist. She smiled at him as he approached.

"Your bill comes to four hundred- and forty-five-dollars Mister Whynee". She said as he arrived at the desk.

Joseph audibly inhaled. He could feel the blood drain out of his face. This was by far the most expensive doctor's consultation that he had ever faced. Maybe Medicare would cover most of it? Almost willing his vain hope to be true, he pulled out his wallet and presented his Medicare card. The receptionist shook her head and confirmed his suspicion.

"Doctor Carver's fees have no Medicare rebate. He *is* a specialist surgeon. I am sorry".

Her tone indicated that she was anything but sorry. Joseph felt his stomach sink. There was no choice but to pay the exorbitantly high fee, for the disproportionately short visit. He begrudgingly did so and left the surgery feeling considerably poorer for the entire experience. Both figuratively and literally.

Chapter 25

Be Careful What You Attract at a Single's Bar

The only two things that had gone well during the following days was Joseph's registration for sitting his Marine License test and the smuggling of the coffee table parts out of the hotel to the restorer. The table parts just fitted into his largest suitcase. When asked by the doorman if Joseph was going on a trip, he spun a yarn about getting one of the suitcase wheels fixed because it jammed occasionally.

By the time Thursday came, Joseph was exhausted. There had been no word about the pending brain-scan. That was good news. He still had not yet come up with a viable plan to get himself out of that self-created mess. Besides there were more pressing things to occupy his time.

He had taken to the literature of the Marine licence studies and immersed himself for extended times over Tuesday, Wednesday, and Thursday. As the evening fell, he closed his books and decided that he would give himself a night out. A trip to Swipe Rite to visit his barman friend Gavin Grosvenor would be just the ticket.

Just as Joseph made that decision he heard his front doorbell ring. Rising from his desk in the main bedroom he checked that Pussy was safely ensconced on his bed (actually, her bed) sleeping soundly. As he left the master bedroom, he closed the door carefully so that she would not be disturbed.

Answering the door Joseph was surprised to find Ismail there looking somewhat troubled.

“Hi Ismail, what’s cooking?”

Joseph was in a cheery mood, anticipating his night out on the town.

“A rather delicate matter Joseph. I don’t really know how to say this, so I’ll just come right out and say it. One of the residents that lives above you says that they saw a cat sleeping in your courtyard this afternoon. I assured her that it could not possibly be the case. But here I am, just in case you know something about the situation?”

Joseph was more than prepared for this very contingency and indicated that Ismail come right in.

“I do indeed Ismail, come this way and I’ll show you what they saw”.

Joseph led Ismail to the living room and to the television cabinet and pointed downwards at the floor. Ismail looked puzzled until he came close enough to see around the cabinet at what Joseph was indicating. It was a sleeping cat. Ismail was horrified.

“Joseph! You know that pets are strictly forbidden here. I’m afraid that I’ll have to ask you to remove it immediately!’

Ismail was clearly very annoyed. But Joseph’s reaction was not what Ismail expected at all.

“Sure thing”.

Joseph reached down and lifted the cat up from the floor. It was as stiff as a board. He handed it to Ismail who took it in his hands rather nervously. Inspecting it, Ismail could see that it was just a stuffed toy. Incredibly realistic, but a fake cat, nevertheless.

“Meet Pussy Two Shoes. My pet kitty”.

Ismail was flabbergasted.

"What was it doing out on the patio this afternoon?"

He asked with some trepidation.

Joseph was unperturbed by the question and answered it without hesitation.

"I like Pussy Two Shoes to get some afternoon sun, so I put her out there. I move her around the house quite a bit. It helps me believe that I actually have a pet kitty in residence. Pretty neat huh?"

Ismail was almost at a loss for words. However, this was not the oddest thing that Joseph had managed to reveal about himself, so perhaps he should be grateful he thought.

"I suppose that we can simply add this to the growing list of cat idiosyncrasies that make you such a unique person".

Ismail had to dig deep to find a diplomatic way of phrasing what he was really thinking about Joseph's abnormal behaviour surrounding felines. Ismail then did his best to exit as quickly as he could, profusely apologising for disturbing Joseph and assuring him that the misunderstanding would be cleared up with the anonymous resident.

As he shut the door, Joseph breathed a satisfied sigh of relief. The plan had worked. It was surely a sign that the tide had turned, and things were now going his way. This was going to be great night out, with luck most definitely, on his side.

***

Joseph arrived at Swipe Rite around ten at night. He would have normally been worried about being out so late during the week. But he was now a man of leisure. He had only some more study for his boating licence to do tomorrow. There was no need to worry about getting up early to go to a job that he despised anymore. All of that was in the past now.

He waved to Gavin behind the bar, who reciprocated his greeting. The music was definitely louder at this time of night. And with a distinctly dance party rhythm too. It seemed to be crowded with quite a large number of people. They for the most part seemed contented to either stand around the makeshift dance floor in the middle of the bar or line-up for drinks. Joseph elected to take a booth as there was still one that looked vacant.

Taking his seat, he was surprised to find a waitress come up and ask for his order.

"I didn't know that you had table service here?"

He asked with genuine curiosity. The waitress was nonchalant with her reply.

"Only once a month sweetie. What'll it be?"

"A Cosmopolitan please".

With his drink order now in the works, Joseph was left pondering why Swipe Rite would bother with table service only once a month. Was it a way to check if the takings for the bar would be better against a normal night when there was no table service? If so, they would then need to deduct the cost of the waitress from the overall potential rise in profit. That way a true measure of the effectiveness could be gleaned. It was a question that had his accountancy brain intrigued.

He was still pondering the unusual situation when he was surprised by a visit from Gavin.

"Hey mister; what brings you here tonight?"

Joseph was amazed. The bar was still crowded with guests wanting to purchase something. It must have showed in Joseph's face, because Gavin answered the unasked question.

"I have more help with this particular night of the month than most. They can look after things whilst we have a chat".

Aware of the situation, or so he thought, Joseph started off with an observation about the club's name that he wanted to get off his chest.

"I've been thinking; why did you say the club was called Swipe Rite?"

Gavin was not at all bothered by the question. It was a clever turn of phrase after all. He indicated to the patrons.

"These people have the right to swipe right, when using a dating app, or to swipe left. They either want to look further into a hopeful candidate or dismiss them straight away. Sooner or later, swiping right will eventuate in a great romance. And that swipe right becomes a rite that they follow. Hence the name, Swipe Rite".

Without realising he was adding a pun Joseph continued with his question.

"Right. But how is using r.i.t.e instead of r.i.g.h.t wittier?"

Gavin answered with a somewhat laconic tone.

"We really need to work on your sense of humour Joseph. Anyway, what brings you here on this particular night?"

Again, Joseph managed to blunder through an explanation that unintentionally gave Gavin an entirely wrong impression.

"Gavin, I'm a free man now. Time for me to explore all of the things that I would never have done when I was married and in a dead-end job. This is my chance to really cut loose and have a good time".

Gavin nodded but had an expression of more amazement on his face than Joseph would have thought from such a minor revelation. So, he added to the explanation.

"I've ordered a Cosmopolitan".

With his misunderstanding of exactly why Joseph was at the bar this evening now garnished with a cocktail, Gavin was sanguine in his reply.

"Good for you Joseph. No need to do the same old things and get the same outcomes, eh? I'm sure that a guy like you will have a good time here tonight of all nights."

As he was finishing the waitress arrived with Joseph's drink and put it down. She was about to ask for payment when Gavin held up his hand.

"This one is on the house, Joseph. Drink a toast to the new you".

"I shall, thanks mate!"

Indicating that the waitress should attend the booth next to theirs Gavin then excused himself so that he could assist the two youngsters serving behind the bar. Joseph triumphantly lifted the cocktail to his mouth and had barely had a sip when a young man sat in the booth with him and said something rather peculiar.

"Hey Daddy. Sonny-boy would love a sweet drink of sugar".

It was perhaps the most perplexing thing that anybody had ever said to Joseph in a bar. Mind you, visiting bars was not really high on his 'to do' list during the years of raising a family. He regarded the boy sitting with him in the booth. He could barely be eighteen years of age. But he must have been because his age would have been checked at the entrance to the establishment.

Feeling that too much time had passed without an answer of any kind Joseph managed to string together a sentence that did nothing to clarify the situation.

“Sounds like someone has a sweet tooth”.

Although Joseph’s retort was completely innocent, it was misconstrued by the young man as a tease. He then responded with something that made Joseph feel rather uncomfortable.

“There are so many sweet parts of me Daddy. Which one would you like to taste first?”

It was now very clear that the fellow was gay and hitting upon Joseph. He had to find a way to extricate himself from this rather bizarre situation as quickly as possible.

“Um, I’m a diabetic. Sugar would probably kill me”.

The young man looked like he had just been slapped in the face. With a growl and a harrumph, he exited the booth mumbling something beneath his breath. No doubt it was nothing complimentary.

Relieved to be alone again in a bar full of people, Joseph took a large swig of his Cosmopolitan to settle himself. He had barely swallowed a second mouthful when another young man moved into the booth. Like the first one, he seemed rather well groomed and overly young to be bothered chatting with a man in his mid-fifties.

“Daddy, you got rid of that leach like a seasoned professional. Great spotting. He is practically a rent boy! Clearly what you need is the company of someone that isn’t going to suck on your wallet for the evening”.

Joseph wasn’t sure if that was a question that needed a reply or a statement that should have provoked one. But either way, he felt that he should say something. If only he had though it through more thoroughly, he may not have progressed the situation from bad to worse.

"Company that doesn't suck would be a good start, I suppose?"

Unfortunately, this gave the new interloper an opportunity to take the conversation to a dark place rather quickly. He smiled broadly at Joseph and relaxed further into the curved seat, spreading his arms widely across the top of the backrest.

"Oh, I never said that I don't suck. I just like to suck the right things. And I suck so well, so incredibly well you cannot even imagine it!"

Once more Joseph was plunged into territory that he was completely unfamiliar with. He broke out in a cold sweat. What on earth was he going to do? He was still racing through scenarios that may extract him from the situation when the youngster added to his growing list of sexual innuendo.

"Maybe I should start off sucking something really slowly, and then push it up a gear and suck hard and fast?! What do you think?"

The young man moved further around the semicircular booth to be closer to Joseph. This alarmed Joseph much more than he would have thought possible.

"You know; sucking so much will give you broken capillaries in your cheeks. That would be a pity eh?"

It was perhaps the lamest of all retorts that Joseph had ever come up with in a hurry, but it did manage to diffuse the rampant sex cravings of the fellow. He shot Joseph a look of incredulity. Then he followed it up with a single worded question.

"What?"

Joseph was scrambling to find something to say that would get rid of the intruder.

"I'll stick to sucking on my cosmopolitan, thanks. Less chance of swallowing something unknown. If you know what I mean?"

Actually, Joseph himself, did not know what he meant from that blubbered excuse. Nevertheless, it had the desired effect. With an indignant look and tone the young man exited the booth and fired a verbal retort to Joseph.

"You're too much hard work".

He walked off and disappeared into the growing crowd in the bar. Joseph breathed a huge sigh of relief. Was it a full moon tonight or something like that? The crazies were certainly out in force. He downed another large swig of the cocktail to help calm his now frazzled nerves. Before he had even had the chance to swallow it, two young men joined him in the booth. Joseph managed to gulp down the mouthful of drink and gave them a look of inquisition.

They were both perhaps in their mid-twenties. Both well-groomed and well dressed. Fearing another thinly disguised sexual advance, Joseph was relieved when one of the men spoke.

"Hello, my name is Barry, and this is my partner Tymon. We've been watching you and felt that you needed rescuing from the daddy hunters".

Joseph was visibly relieved. This was a normal way to introduce yourself to a complete stranger. He responded appropriately.

"Hello. It's nice to make your acquaintance. My name is Joseph. What on earth is a Daddy hunter?"

This garnered a smile from both young men. It was Tymon that answered. He clearly had an accent of some description, but not one that Joseph could readily identify.

"We could tell that you were out of place. I said to Barry, we've gotta do something about that straight guy. He is going to get eaten alive by the daddy hunters".

Barry then took up the remainder of the explanation.

"Swipe Rite has a gay-themed night once per month, called The Closet. It's tonight! And you have been attracting the young gay guys that want to be looked after by a sugar-daddy. The grey hair is a magnet for those types".

Sudden realisation dawned upon Joseph's face. Then shock at the context that Gavin would have thought Joseph had meant by coming here tonight to 'explore things he'd never done before whilst married', or words to that effect. Gavin must have thought that he was coming out of the closet after years of marriage!

"Oh no! My friend Gavin is the head barman. He must think that I've deliberately come here tonight to pick up a guy! What have I done?"

Tymon nodded sympathetically. Barry offered a condolence.

"I'm sure you can explain it to him later. Remember to tell him that a couple of boring accountants saved you from the piranhas".

The irony of the situation was incredible. If this was a typical Swipe Rite straight night, then Joseph was what could only be considered as dating poison. Middle aged and paunchy. But here in The Closet he was pulling in the goods. Albeit not the goods that he would have liked. Anyway, Barry had just said something that got his attention. It struck a chord with Joseph immediately. They were fellow accountants. He felt an immediate affinity with them.

"Accountants, eh? What a good solid job that is. I used to be one myself. Where about are you working?"

Tymon answered.

“We’ve only arrived today. We met when studying in Queensland University. And we’ve been together ever since. It’s too hard to make a living and pay rent in Brisbane, so we though that we’d pack in our jobs, and start up again here”.

Barry finished the explanation.

“We’re staying in a cheap hotel until we can get jobs and find somewhere nice to rent”.

That was the starting point to the three of them conversing solidly, over cosmopolitans for the next hour and a half.

As it turns out, twenty-five year old Barry, was originally from Wagga Wagga, and was so gifted at figures and successful in his school, that he was awarded a partial scholarship to study for a degree in economics at Queensland University. Although he never mentioned it when talking about his family, Joseph got the impression that they were not as aspirational as Barry.

Tymon, also twenty-five years of age, came from Poland. He immigrated with his parents only seven years ago to Brisbane. The small town they left behind was Zakopane. Tymon was correct, Joseph had never heard of it. Zakopane is a resort town in southern Poland, at the base of the Tatra mountains. It is a popular departure point for winter sports and summertime mountain climbing and hiking. Nearby ski resorts like Kasprowy Wierch and Gubalowka can be reached by cable car and funicular. The township is noted architecturally for its wooden chalets, which have become synonymous with Zakopane.

Barry seemed the more level-headed of the two. Whilst Tymon appeared to be full of rather outlandish advice. Which always managed to begin with the phrase ‘what you gotta do is this!’” By the time the fourth cosmopolitan was served, Joseph had forgotten about his embarrassment. So what if Gavin thought he was coming out of the closet, by attending The Closet!? Who cares?!

Besides, a small plan was forming in Joseph’s mind. These were two very employable young men. Both qualified. Both would clearly be able to pull in a good wage. Barry especially seemed to want to wash away his upbringing and make a good life for himself and his partner. Joseph took a gamble and made them both an offer that he hoped that they would not refuse.

"Guys, you know what you need? A stable roof over your heads. A place from which you can go out and get those high paying jobs that you a looking for. You simply cannot do that whilst doing your washing in a common laundry. And think about this. What home address will you be putting on your job applications. It won't look good, if it is a cheap hotel. What you need is a home base with credibility. And I think that I can provide that for you. If you want? And if you can keep it on the low down?"

The offer was too intriguing to refuse. What on earth could Joseph mean by that?

"Sure" said Tymon.

"What have you got in mind?" asked Barry.

"I have a three-bedroom condominium. I could rent one of the bedrooms to you. You could have a lovely place to come home to, from your job interviews. Your own bathroom. Great kitchen. Private patio. Plunge pool, and other amenities in the block that you just won't believe. But there is just one thing. Nobody can know that you are paying me rent. You'll know why when I tell you the address. What do you think?"

As it turns out, Joseph did not have much convincing to do in order to get acquiescence from the two young men.

"Joseph, our hotel is so old that the cockroaches have never heard of the internet".

Barry's quip brought a howl of laughter from Tymon and Joseph. Tymon was the first to accept the proposal.

"That would be great for us Joseph. I agree. How about you Barry?"

Barry nodded and then asked the obvious question.

"What's the address?"

Joseph paused for effect and then spoke slowly and deliberately.

"Palazzo Versace".

The eyes of both men widened considerably. Both of their mouths dropped open in unison.

"You are joking with us" demanded Barry.

"No. Come live with me in P.V. as we residents call it. If anyone asks, I'll just tell them that my nephew and his partner are staying with me for an indeterminate period".

Joseph indicated as he spoke, pointing to Barry as the nephew and Tymon as the partner. Joseph then added a small caveat that he thought he had best let the guys know about.

"Neither of you are allergic to cats, are you? Because I have one".

Barry was so completely enamoured at the thought of living somewhere so prestigious that his reply was loud and ebullient.

"You could have a panther living with you and we would still love to be there. Wouldn't we Tymon?"

Barry elbowed his partner, hoping for an equally positive response. He was successful.

"I love kitty cats. I love this idea!"

And with that Joseph now had two housemates other than Pussy the cat to share his home.

It was arranged that they would give notice to their hotel the next day and move in immediately. Barry, whose surname turned out to be Bougainvillea would let anyone know that Joseph's (imaginary) sister, was his mother. Hence the different surname.

Tymon whose surname was actually a little funny given that he was from a ski village in Poland and living on the Gold Coast of Australia, was Surfski. It unwittingly paid homage to both the surf of the Australian beaches, and the skiing in the Tatra Mountains. The accountancy side of all three came into play before the negotiations were complete and a suitable price was agreed. Paid monthly, directly into Joseph's bank account.

Joseph's big night out had achieved something that he desperately needed. A way to stop haemorrhaging money. Even as they left the club, Joseph was on such a high that he did not bother to correct Gavin's misunderstanding of why he was there that evening. Instead, he gave him a friendly wave of farewell as the three of them left The Closet together.

Chapter 26

Kransky Does Not Equal, Skanky

Barry and Tymon moving in with Joseph barely raised an eyebrow from Ismail Islington. He accepted the explanation that Barry was Joseph's nephew, and that the two newcomers would be around for the foreseeable future. Even Pussy turned out to not have a problem with the guys. Annoyingly she managed to learn their names immediately and let Joseph know that she would turn them into supplementary servants in no time at all.

Joseph managed to sit the written part of the Marine Vessel Licence test and passed first go with flying colours. Now all he needed was more experience on the water. It was the following week when Tymon announced that he had secured a job. Not to be outdone, Barry had a job offer the next day. Both young men started in their new roles the following week. So, in a way, it felt like this would be the end of their settling-in period.

To celebrate Tymon insisted on shouting everybody breakfast at a small place on Tedder Avenue that he had 'discovered'. On a grey morning, they set out to walk down the lengthy street to find out why Tymon had rated this short-order diner so highly.

"Here it is!"

Tymon was clearly enthusiastic about the forthcoming breakfast experience that he was about to share with Barry and

Joseph. They approached the nondescript diner and entered. It was ordinary in every way possible. Given that most of the restaurants and cafes along Tedder Avenue were rather stylish, this seemed to fall short by a significant margin. The disappointment must have shown on both Barry and Joseph's faces. Tymon spoke up offering them an explanation for his choice of breakfast menu.

"It's nothing to look at. But what you gotta do is try the food! The Kransky sausage with bacon and egg on a roll is fantastic!"

Tymon's enthusiasm was obvious. Barry and Joseph gave each other a look as if to say 'why not? They walked up to the counter to order, as there was a sign instructing them to order first before taking a seat.

The breakfast menu was extensive. Omelettes, full Irish, English, and Scottish breakfasts. And then there was the before mentioned egg and bacon rolls, including the various iterations of them. High on the third column of text in the overhead menu was the one with Kransky sausage.

"I know exactly what I am having".

Tymon indicated to the woman behind the counter that he was ready to order. The woman was Asian as was the man hovering at the grill barely an arm's length from her. It was then that Joseph assumed that it must have been a husband and wife run business. Just the two of them pumping out short order food on an otherwise prestigious foodie street. It could work, he thought.

"I'll have the bacon and egg roll with Kransky please".

Tymon had barely finished his order when the wife turned to her husband and shouted the order to him as if he were in another room.

"ONE BACON AND EGG ROLL WITH SKANKY!"

She turned back to Tymon and in a much more convivial tone queried if there was to be a sauce with the order. He elected for

Tomato. This too was shouted at the husband in a volume that could have woken the dead.

"TOM-TOE SAUCE ON THE SKANKY!"

Joseph watched the entire amusing scene in mild surprise. Maybe the hubby was mostly deaf? He pulled Tymon back from the counter to have a quiet word to him.

"I'm sure that it is not pronounced that way; is it?" He inquired.

"No, but it the real joke comes later. I'll let you know at the table". Tymon smiled in his reply.

Barry and Joseph gave each other a look in inquiry. What were they each going to order? It was Barry who took the next step.

"One bacon and egg roll with kransky and barbeque sauce please".

Right on queue the wife turned to the husband and shouted a second order at the top of her voice.

"ONE BACON AND EGG ROLL WITH SKANKY AND BARBY SAUCE!"

This was too much for Joseph and Barry who began to giggle beneath their breaths. Although Joseph would have preferred an omelette, he could not resist getting the wife to scream a skanky order at the husband just one more time. He dutifully took his place at the front of the counter and ordered, but this time asking for dark mustard as the accompaniment.

"ONE BACON AND EGG ROLL WITH SKANKY AND MUTTARD!"

Joseph laughed aloud but managed to cover it up as a hacking cough. He did not want to offend the woman.

Tymon dutifully paid for the orders, and they took a seat in a booth to await their breakfast. Tymon was the first to speak.

"You know what is really funny about the kransky sausage they serve here?"

Barry offered the obvious explanation.

"That it is called skanky instead of kransky?"

Joseph and Barry looked to Tymon expecting him to verify that they were correct. Instead, they were both mildly shocked to find him shaking his head.

"Nope. The sausage served is actually Polish kielbasa sausage, cooked pork and beef and then smoked. It's not German kransky at all. Isn't that hilarious!?"

The fact that Tymon seemed to be completely unaware of the comedic aspect of the husband-and-wife team miscalling kransky and mustard and so on, did not even rate a mention with Tymon. After shooting a knowing look to Joseph, Barry just shook his head in mind bemusement. Joseph, however, had to probe a little deeper.

"Is the cook, who I assume is the husband of this duo, a bit deaf?"

Once more Tymon indicated in the negative.

"Nope. When he delivers the order, he will want a brief chat about the weather or something. I'm certain that he can hear just fine".

This time it was Joseph's turn to shake his head in befuddlement at the situation. Clearly Tymon had completely missed the real hilarity of the situation happening around him.

***

Ismail Islington was born to a Lebanese mother and an English father. His parents had both met whilst living (separately) in Australia. It was a whirlwind romance, and the wedding took place appropriately on a white sandy beach. Ismail was born a year later and raised up to the age of five before he was uprooted and moved to London owing to work commitments of his father.

As he was clearly not particularly English looking, but boarding in a very English school, he never felt like he was one of the crowd that was accepted or fitted--in with everyone else. That feeling stayed with him all the way through his teenage years and then during his first years in his hospitality roles at the Goring Hotel in Westminster, and later at the Savoy Hotel in Charring Cross. By the time Ismail was thirty he had had enough of English pretentiousness and moved back to Australia.

Thankfully, he fell into the welcoming arms of Palazzo Versace and had happily taken on the role of Residential Relationship Manager with great gusto. This was a place that celebrated diversity and one in which he felt very comfortable indeed.

Ismail was busy dispatching his normal duties when something odd came into his field of vision. He was in attendance of Condominium number three. Technically this was one of the penthouses, although it was on ground level. It was larger than the usual condominiums and to ensure that extra level of privacy, there was a ground floor wall that separated the patio from the plunge pool of condominium number four, next door.

A creeping vine had managed to grow a little out of control and was threatening to begin spreading upon the ceiling of the outdoor room. Rather than wait for the gardeners to take care of it, Ismail had climbed up on the plant bed and pulled down the offending creeper himself. From this rather precarious vantage point he could see across the plunge pool of number four and into the living room.

To his absolute amazement, on top of the television cabinet he could see a cat grooming itself. Ismail was shocked. He had to take a second long lingering look to be certain that he wasn't imagining it. Yes, he was sure now. There was a cat sitting on the television cabinet doing the normal things that cats do to preen themselves.

There was nothing for it. Ismail had to investigate. He excused himself from the owner's residence and made his way into the corridor.

Meanwhile, inside number four, Pussy had finished grooming herself. She liked the strategic position at the top of the television cabinet. From here she could see any danger approaching. She gave a rather distasteful look to the stuffed toy that looked to her like a grotesque parody of a feline. It was directly beside her. If only primary servant hadn't put that ugly thing up there with her, she may have stayed longer to observe the goings on outside. Judging the distance below, Pussy jumped deftly down to the sofa and then onto the marble floor.

Deciding that she needed a nap, she moved into the main bedroom to have a snooze beneath the bed. It felt safe and secure there, hidden away from any prying eyes. As she made her way down the hallway she pondered about Tymon and Barry. Where had the supplementary servants gone? In fact, where had primary servant gone? She supposed that it didn't matter. All in good time they would be back to see to her every whim. Within a minute she had settled beneath the bed and was fast asleep.

Ismail had stopped at the door to number four. Now that he was here, he was suddenly unsure about what he had seen. He rang the doorbell. Nothing. He rang it again. Still nothing. He knocked loudly upon the door. No response. Although it went against all of his training in the role, to never enter a resident's condominium without permission, Ismail felt that this was an extenuating circumstance. He would simply have to find out what was going on. It was then he opened the door with his master key. Gingerly walking in he called out.

"Anyone at home. Ismail calling".

As there was no response, Ismail entered and made his way to the living room. He walked up to the television cabinet and faced the toy cat. To him, especially given what he had just witnessed, it was real. It must be. He poked it with a finger. There was no reaction. He lifted up the toy. Amazingly it was just as he had first found it. This was a hyper realistic inanimate cat. It was most definitely not real at all.

But that did not make any sense to him. He knew exactly what he saw. This thing was moving. It was doing cat-like things. Now it was simply a stuffed toy again. Were his eyes playing tricks on him? Was his comprehension of reality somehow flawed?

"I'm sure that this thing was alive!"

Ismail realised that he had spoken the words that he only meant to think. The sound of his own voice suddenly made him very insecure about being inside the condominium. He decided that it would be best to exit. But on the way out, he couldn't help a quick peek in all three bedrooms. There was nothing out of place at all.

And where on earth was the coffee table that should have been in the centre of the living room? He would have put more thought into conducting a thorough search except for his feelings of discomfort. They dissuaded him entirely.

Admonishing himself for his suspicious mind and now overwhelmed with feelings of guilt, Ismail exited the residence quickly and quietly. Perhaps he had been working too hard? Maybe he was tired? There had to be some rational explanation that would account for his imagination running rampant like it had.

One saving grace was that nobody had seen the intrusion, so he had nothing to explain to anyone. Ismail breathed an audible sigh of relief as he scurried away, without looking like he was in a particular hurry.

Chapter 27

Never Try to Fake it!

Joseph had spent the day sailing aboard 'Beat the Odds' with his instructor. He was tired when he returned home. Although it was the weekend it felt like any other day to him now that he was living his newfound dream to not work a normal nine to five job. Tymon and Barry were in the living room when he arrived home. After exchanging the usual pleasantries about how each other's days went, Joseph slumped into a tub chair and began to ruminate on the forthcoming party that he had to host.

Aware that something was weighing on Joseph's mind Barry inquired as to the nature of his sombre expression.

"Why the long face Joseph?"

Joseph had to collect his thoughts and organise them into a priority of misgivings that he was currently harbouring.

"I'm worried about how much this party is going to cost. The one where we get to meet the other residents. But actually, above that, I have been very aware that the other residents that I have met in passing all seem to wear the most extraordinarily good-looking clothes. Whenever I'm having a chat with one of them, I always feel under-dressed. Or at least a little impoverished by comparison".

Even as he said the words, Joseph was cognisant that it sounded somewhat childish. But it was nevertheless a concern that had cultivated itself within his innermost insecurities. Barry was sanguine about the perceived problem and shrugged as if to say that it shouldn't really matter. Tymon, however had a ready-made solution to Joseph's feeling of inferiority. He piped-up in his typically enthusiastic manner.

"What you gotta do is this! Don't pay full price for these designer clothes. Nobody does! I'll give you a website that can deliver any of the latest designs to you, at eighty to ninety percent discount on the full price. You can dress like a king on the budget of a pauper. It's genius!"

Joseph was equal amounts of intrigued and suspicious.

"Is it a legit site? I mean, Are they real designer clothes or cheap knockoffs?"

Barry was already rolling his eyes at Tymon's hair-brained scheme. Tymon offered a different kind of assurance to the one that Joseph was expecting.

"All of these designer clothes are made in the same place. What happens is that the factory managers put these clothes on this website to make a little extra cash on the side. Everybody knows that they do it. But as long as the factory delivers the orders that the designer label wants, nobody loses".

Although still somewhat doubtful as to the veracity of this explanation, Joseph agreed to at least look at the website in question. He got his laptop and logged in before handing it over to Tymon to put in the web address. This, Tymon did with great speed and handed the PC back to Joseph. The three of the gathered around the screen to look at the men's clothing offerings.

True to Tymon's word, the site contained the very sorts of clothes that one would expect the residents of P.V. to attire themselves in. Joseph homed-in on the one and only label that he wanted to attire himself in. He flicked through the shirts, trousers., shoes and jackets. With expert opinions from both Tymon and a still dubious Barry, they settled upon an outfit for Joseph. The sizes that he needed were available and all he had to do was create an account and pay for the purchases.

Within minutes he had completed the purchase. Joseph felt pleased with himself for cheaply solving what would otherwise have been an expensive shopping expedition. Now he could at least look the part during the forthcoming celebration. But that was only half of the battle there was still the overall cost of throwing a swanky party for people with expensive tastes. He posed the question to his flatmates and received the solution from them both. Barry began the explanation. Tymon followed up.

“Discount grocery chains are your friend in this case Joseph”.

“But they offer a world of dangers for a single straight male”.

Joseph was again so enthralled he had to ask for further details.

“You’re going to have to elaborate on both points for me guys”. Joseph said.

Tymon and Barry both became quite animated. This was clearly a subject that they both enjoyed discussing. Barry began with his expanded explanation of why Joseph was best to use a discount grocery chain for the party supplies.

“You will be able to get all of the snooty supplies for the residents meet-and-greet party at a third of the cost of the regular supermarkets. So, it won’t be an arduous financial burden. They stock the same stuff that that the exclusive food emporiums do, but at reasonable prices. Well, at least at prices that won’t give you heart palpitations”.

Then following on from the logical part of the dialogue, Tymon chipped in with his cautionary tale. It sounded very much like a gypsy fortune teller warning of impending doom.

“But be warned. It is not only groceries that you can accidentally pick up at these places. What you gotta do is this. Watch out for the suburban singles, wanting to improve their situation. If you know what I mean?"

Tymon's explanation left Joseph none the wiser at all. He scratched his eyebrow and confessed that he did not understand the warning at all. Tymon offered further information to illuminate the danger that Joseph would be facing.

"Suburban women don't hang out at Swipe Rite, you know, or places like that. They don't have the time. Too much to do at home with the kids. So, they improvise. Discount grocery chains are the new pick-up joints nowadays".

Tymon's revelation piqued Joseph's curiosity all the more. He indicated with a rolling gesture of his hand that further detail be added. Tymon was only too happy to oblige.

"Aldi. Full of single mothers, usually with one child, on the hunt for a new husband. Costco is entirely different. It attracts the widowed women from former polygamous marriages. Hubby usually died from sexual exhaustion. Now a replacement is needed. What you gotta do is stick with a place like the discount grocery outlet in Southport. That will have the age demographic that you are part of. Older women, not that fussy about paunchy middle-aged guys. But still hot-to-trot, if you know what I mean?"

Tymon finished is description with a nod and a wink. Joseph was stunned on a couple of levels. Firstly, that an entire world of hook-up places surrounded him without his knowledge whatsoever. But moreover, that Tymon saw him as a paunchy middle aged old guy.

Joseph made a promise to avoid Costo and Aldi and shop for the supplies from the discount store in Southport. But all the while he was concentrating on his mid-section. How did he let himself become so out-of-shape over all these years?

Then a lightning bolt struck him. He still had vouchers for the spa. He could have some sort of fat reduction procedure. The thought certainly held more appeal than dieting and endless cardio exercise in the gymnasium. Besides his chosen exercise nowadays was sailing. That would be his keep-fit regime from now on. And by getting his fat dealt with by some other means meant that he would get a head start.

Satisfied that he had come up with the perfect plan of attack for his physique. Joseph felt a smug glow envelope him. Living here offered him more benefits that he would have thought possible.

***

It was Tuesday of the following week when Joseph had just arrived back from yet another sailing lesson that he was startled by the telephone ringing. It was quite a novelty having a landline when he had come to rely upon his mobile phone so completely.

The condominium seemed a little empty without the guys now that they were at work. Pussy was ‘busy’ sleeping in the sunlight that was streaming through the living room glass sliding doors. Joseph picked up the phone. It was one of the internal staff.

“Mister Whynee. You have a delivery in the mail room. Would you please come and collect it?”

Joseph knew that the mail room was situated behind the resident’s mailboxes. They were all clustered in a very stylish way, neatly hidden away from the prying eyes of the hotel guests. Joseph made his way there. He assumed that his online shopping had come. Now he was congratulating himself for paying for expedited shipping. It hardly took any time at all to show up.

When he arrived at the mail room it had a few of the other residents already there. No doubt they were picking up their own packages. The staff member saw Joseph enter and motioned to two men that Joseph did not recognise. They had suits on and what looked like badges on their pockets. Not quite police, but something very similar. Who could they be he wondered?

They approached Joseph and one of them sought verification of his identity.

"Mister Joseph Whynee?"

Joseph blinked innocently back at them.

"That's right. May I help you with something?"

By this time the attention of the other five people in the mail room was drawn towards Joseph.

"Did you purchase some clothing online recently?"

With that one of the rather tall and imposing men indicated the box that was resting on the counter. Even from this distance Joseph could see that it contained his name and address on it.

"Yes, I did. I assume that is it there on the counter".

Joseph replied and indicated to the box. The other man took up the dialogue.

"Could you please open it and confirm that the contents are what you purchased please Mister Whynee?"

It sounded more like a threat than a request. And it was quite a bizarre one at that.

"What's this all about?" Joseph was perplexed.

"If you could please just open the box and verify the contents first. Then we will provide an explanation Mister Whynee".

You could have heard a pin drop as Joseph approached the counter and found the tear to open tab on the long flat box that had his name on it. Rustling through the packing tissue paper he produced a Jacket, shirt, pants, and pair of shoes. They were all in dark colours, understated and bearing the name Versace on the labels strung to them. In with the clothes was an A4 printed sheet of paper stating the items individually and the amount that Joseph had paid for each of them.

The two men could be seen visibly shaking their heads. One of them reached in and took hold of the invoice.

“Fakes!” Said one.

“And bad fakes too!” Said the other.

There was a collective and rather loud sharp in-drawing of breath from the residents in the room. All of them looking accusingly at Joseph in admonishment and astonishment. The first of the men to talk with Joseph then identified himself and his colleague.

“We’re from the customs department. We noticed this package arrive from……well you tell me mister Whynee? Where did you expect this delivery of garments to come from, given the maker’s label?”

Joseph felt like he was about half of his usual height. His throat was dry. He could feel his stomach turning into mess of knots. The world seemed to recede around him. All he could sense were the stares of his fellow residents and their appalled expressions. Somehow, he managed to squeak an answer in a pitch that was far above his normal conversational voice.

“Italy?”

Both men shook their heads simultaneously. Each had an expression that could easily have been read as thinking of Joseph as absolutely pathetic. Joseph’s mind raced. He hadn’t felt this kind of pressure since his final educational exams. He had to find a way to answer these fellows correctly. Maybe that would help this unbelievably embarrassing situation? But instead of answering with the most likely country to rip-off a major designer, he clung to the desperate hope that his garments were somehow still genuine.

"The U.S.A?"

This only managed to elicit an impatient and frustrated look from both men.

"Wrong hemisphere!" Said one of the customs agents.

Joseph was immediately on the back foot. Was the fellow referring to the eastern and western hemispheres or northern and southern hemispheres. There was no time to ask for clarification as the second customs officer took over the conversation.

"Mister Whynee! We would normally confiscate such obviously pirated merchandise at the border and send you a letter informing you of the Customs Department decision to destroy it. And then provide you a warning about purchasing such things in the future. However, given that this was addressed to Palazzo Versace we felt that a visitation in person was in order. Were you aware that this was fake merchandise?"

If Joseph had felt small before, he was now positively minuscule in size. There was a heat emanating from his face which could only mean that he was blushing like a pubescent schoolboy. He stammered a reply, that although honest, felt like he was refuting a guilty verdict in a court of law.

"Umm, well, errr……I thought they were a bargain price..So, um, no".

Far from getting Joseph out of trouble, this only seemed to inflame the two customs officers.

"When have you ever before seen Versace clothes offered at such unbelievably low prices?"

The customs officer was displaying the invoice to Joseph to reaffirm the unrealistically small amount of money that he had paid for the clothes.

"Saks off fifth avenue?"

Joseph sounded like he was trying to make amends with his answer. Unfortunately, it was construed as being trite by both men. The other blasted back at him in an overly loud voice.

"Not even Saks discount Versace up to ninety-five percent buddy! What were you thinking?"

Joseph had nowhere to go but utter capitulation. Embarrassingly he lowered his head and gave in to the admonishment.

"I guess I wasn't thinking"

"No, you weren't!" Replied the first.

Not even a little bit". Added the second.

As if the discomfiture wasn't bad enough, the next words out of the first customs officer was a nail in the coffin of his humiliation.

"I am afraid that in this instance we are going to have to issue you with an infringement notice and fine of one-thousand dollars. Your obviously fake merchandise will be destroyed. And you will receive a note on your immigration file that you have attempted to bring illegal merchandise into the country. That won't bode too well for you the next time that you pass through border security in any of the member nations of the Organisation for Economic Cooperation and Development countries. That is to say all of the O.E.C.D participating nations".

Joseph could feel his often-fantasised Italian holiday evaporating faster than his sense of self-worth. They would never let him into the country now, knowing that he was a fake-merchandise customer.

With their threat hanging in the air, both customs officers said a rather grim farewell to Joseph. One picked up the box of fake clothing and they left the mail room. Joseph watched them depart. He then became acutely aware that everyone in the room was looking at him. Even if he couldn't see them, he could surely feel their eyes burning into the back of his head. He skulked out of the mail room without a shred of dignity left in his body.

Chapter 28

If it's not from Champagne; then it's Sparkling Wine

Joseph was sitting in his condominium feeling like a complete failure. He also had feelings of betraying the community of which he was now a part. He had bemoaned the entire situation to Pussy upon his return from the mail room. But she was completely disinterested and let him know in the most direct way possible. The worst part for Joseph was that some other residents had witnessed the entire sorry incident. It would have certainly by now, been spread throughout the entire residential enclave.

There simply had to be some way to make amends. But how? And this wasn't the only worry weighting heavily on Joseph's mind. The forthcoming party too was filling him with financial dread. There was nothing to it, he had to take steps to solve at least one of these. So, he picked the party as the first problem to be solved. The solution was to put on the 'suggested' menu at a huge discount.

Ismail had kindly provided the usual catered menu for such parties that the kitchens would provide. However, Joseph was convinced that by shopping in a discount grocery store he would be able to come up with the same or similar products at a greatly reduced price. Now, all he needed was transportation.

He phoned Isabella who was willing to help by lending him the car for the afternoon to do his penny-pinching shopping. However, when he explained the overall plan to her, he could feel her eyes rolling on the other end of the phone.

“Joseph are you sure that you want to cheap-out on this party? I thought that the idea was to impress the other residents with your worldly sophistication?”

Joseph was sanguine in his response.

“Providing I don’t pronounce sophistication as sof-iss-ti-mah-cay-shun, or epitome as epee-toe-hmm, then I think that I’ll be fine”.

Arrangements were made for Joseph to come over to Broadbeach Waters to pick up the car.

***

After a further brief exchange with Isabella, who once more tried to dissuade him from this ‘mean’ course of action, Joseph pointed the car toward the discount grocery outlet in Southport. He was lucky enough to get a great parking spot not too far from the main entrance to the store.

Inside the store he found a trolley and began a methodical march through the isles to find the foods that he was looking for. First up was the foie gras. Sure-enough, thanks to the individual pricing that the kitchens had provided on their menu, Joseph was able to make a direct comparison between what they would have charge him, and what he was able to obtain here in the store.

It was nothing short of extortion. The price was around one third of what the kitchens were going to charge him. If everything else on the list worked out as relatively cheap as this, then he was going to get away with spending two-thirds less on the food than was originally thought. Joseph was feeling a sense of smugness as he continued his shopping expedition.

One by one he managed to tick off the overtly pretentious foodstuffs as he added them to his shopping cart. Even the caviar, which was listed on his menu as running past one thousand dollars, he managed to get for a price, that although still horribly expensive, way less than he would have paid.

By the time he had reached the end of the grocery isles he was grinning in victory. A quick addition of the items in his head revealed that he was indeed correct. It was going to be cheaper than planned. He had to temper this fact with the realisation that this was going to be the most he had ever spent on throwing a party in his life. But Joseph felt that it came some small way toward making amends for his failure with the pirated clothes incident.

"I'd love to come to *that* party!"

A woman's voice interrupted Joseph's meanderings. He looked up to see who was talking to him. A lady, well dressed, rather pretty and seemingly upon first glance, in a similar age bracket stood there. She smiled and indicated the opulent foods within Joseph's trolley. It took him a few moments to readjust his thoughts to one of conversation.

"Oh, this? It's just a small gathering of the residents in my apartment building. A way to say *hello* to as many of them as I can in one go".

The woman was having none of Joseph's projected modesty.

"Well, with a new resident as generous with the goodies as you are, I'm sure that you'll be a bit hit".

It was a simple compliment. But it sounded so deeply genuine, and Joseph was in such dire need of approval in any form, that it resonated strongly with him.

"Thank you very much. I certainly hope so. My name is Joseph".

He smiled as he stretched out a hand to formally introduce himself to the lady. She responded in kind.

“Joseph, what a lovely name. I’m very pleased to make your acquaintance. My name is Josephine”.

With the introductions complete, the duo could now turn their conversation to other similarities they perhaps shared. Joseph took the lead.

“We share a similar name I wonder what else we have in common?”

It was the perfect open-ended question. Without fully realising it, Joseph had provided Josephine with the opportunity to find out more about him, whilst extolling the virtues of her interests.

“Well, I’m a retired financial adviser, early retirement that is. I prefer public transport to driving a private vehicle. Except for doing my grocery shopping of course. I live in the Q1 apartments in Surfer’s Paradise, top half of the building. And when not catching up with the ladies for lunch, tennis, or mah-jong, I can be found visiting my mother in her opulent retirement home in Coolangatta”.

It was a perfect summation of a rather perfect looking lady as far as Joseph was concerned. He felt a little giddy with fascination for his shopping isle friend. He responded with a similar vein of descriptions about his own life.

“Newly retired Accountant, and newly divorced too. I’m learning to sail my Elan Impression forty-foot yacht. It’s moored in Main Beach, where I live with my precocious cat and two housemates”.

He was going to make his explanation longer but thought that the briefer he kept it the more likely it would be to sound interesting. He was correct.

“I love cats, especially precocious ones. I mean, is there any other kind?”

She laughed, and Joseph was immediately drawn further into his fascination with Josephine. What a lovely laugh she had. And a cat lover too; perfect.

"I should introduce you to her sometime. I'm sure that she'd like you. In fact, she likes anyone that will lavish affection upon her".

Josephine was quick to take up the offer.

"Sounds like my kind of girl. When is good for you? I'm free tomorrow afternoon. The ladies have cancelled tennis for this week".

Joseph was mildly stunned. He had never recalled in his youth being able to get on the good side of the opposite sex so quickly and easily before. But it made sense. They both had time on their hands. They both had a similar working background in finance. Why not? What did he have to lose?

"That sounds perfect. Let me give you my phone number and my address. Shall we say two p.m?"

With the arrangements all but set, the two of them continued to chat all the way through the checkout and even whilst loading groceries into their cars. And without even trying, Joseph had secured a mature-aged date with a lovely lady.

As he drove back toward Main Beach, there was something niggling in the back of his mind. What was it? Something that he had to do tomorrow. And then like a flash he recalled it. He had made an appointment in the Versace Spa to get his paunch taken care of. That was it!

He briefly panicked before realising that the time difference was easy enough to manage. His spa appointment was at eleven o'clock in the morning. There would be plenty of time to get ready for his 'date' for two o'clock that same afternoon. All was well. Joseph basked in the glow of his accomplishment. Things were finally starting to go his way.

***

After dropping off the groceries at his home, Joseph returned the car to Isabella in Broadbeach Waters. He was walking toward the tram stop to return to Main Beach when he decided that whilst he was in the area he would pay a visit to Gavin at 'Swipe Rite'. He guessed that Gavin would have started his shift by now. But it was always quiet until the evening crowd brought the place to life.

He was correct. Upon entering Swipe Rite there was nobody inside except for Gavin. He walked up to the bar and greeted his friend, taking a stool so that they could chat over the bar.

Joseph was quick to impart the news of his forthcoming 'date' to Gavin. Gavin was congratulatory and enthusiastic, but cautious too.

"That's great news. Remember to use condoms! You don't want to take any chances that she is experiencing a late menopause".

Joseph was horrified. He had not even considered the possibility of sex at this stage of the game.

"I hadn't planned to get to third-base so quickly Gav". Said Joseph.

"You have to plan for every contingency Joe. You don't want the financial liability of a child at this stage of your life. You'll end up like that leader of the whatchamacallit party that had it off with his staff member and now he has two young boys. At *his* age! No thank you!"

Joseph was unsure of the reference that Gavin was making. He shook his head in a signal that he did not know the politician in question. Gavin tried to elucidate.

"You know, the old bugger. The adulterer! Looks permanently drunk. A red face only a mother could love. And even then, she'd need a stiff gin beforehand".

Unfortunately, Gavin's further clarifications could be applied to so many local, state, and federal politicians that it was utterly meaningless. He decided instead to change the subject completely.

"I'll take all necessary precautions against any unplanned pregnancy. Mostly by planning to have a celibate date with this lovely lady."

Gavin was curious and wanted to know more about Joseph's last visit to Swipe Rite.

"When I saw you leaving with those two young guys, I assumed that you were going to have a three way with them. What happened to put you back to liking women? Was it bad?"

Once more Joseph was caught in a situation predicated by misunderstanding.

"I had no idea that it was a gay themed night. But all was not lost. I now have two boarders that have good jobs and can help me out with the exorbitant homeowners association fees, when I finally have to start paying them. "

Joseph's explanation received a sigh of relief from Gavin.

"You're a bit too past it, to start experimenting with the same sex anyway", Gavin said.

Joseph was not going to be baited. He had come here looking for inspiration for one of his problems. Having earlier let Gavin know about the Palazzo Versace situation, he brought up the latest problem that was giving him angst.

"Anyhow, I have another more pressing problem that needs a solution", said Joseph.

"What's the problem?" Gavin asked.

"The resident's party next Wednesday. I have to come up with a crate load of champagne. That is something that I can't find in abundance at the discount grocery store. It's going to cost me a fortune".

Gavin held up a finger triumphantly to let Joseph know that he had a solution. He turned around and lifted down a magnum of champagne from the top shelf of the rows of bottles behind him. Resting it on the counter he indicated with a flourish that his was the answer. Joseph was a little confused.

"It's an empty display bottle of Champagne Tsarine. A magnum by the look of it. How can this help me?"

Gavin indicated the top shelf of the bar. There were about ten of the bottles on display. Joseph hadn't paid them any attention before. The bottles were green and had a lustrous green swirling pattern to the surface of them. They certainly looked expensive, even if they were display bottles only and not filled with anything. Joseph indicated with a shake of his head and a shrug of his shoulders that he was not interpreting how this was of assistance to him. Gavin detailed his plan to help Joseph out of his champagne quandary.

"I'll carefully open all of these up, fill them with cheap sparkling wine that I have on tap and then replace the cork and caplet, I have a hand press machine out back that can do it. Whenever you open one it will give the expected pop. And who can really tell the difference between champagne and sparkling wine anyway? This will only set you back one tenth of the price of genuine champagne. What do you think?"

Gavin's plan sounded hair-brained enough to actually work. Joseph liked it a lot. But as if he needed any more convincing Gavin sealed the deal with the final icing on the cake.

"And I'll drop them off to you in our 'Swipe Rite Bottle Sales' delivery van. We do lots of business up at main beach… P.V. have had their fair share of deliveries from us in the past. Nobody will suspect a thing!"

It sounded like the perfect crime. Nothing could possibly go wrong. Joseph loved this super cost cutting plan. Gavin added a simple caveat that Joseph was only too pleased to accept.

"Just remember to keep the corks, caplets, and bottles for me, so I can put them back on display here, ok?"

"No problem!"

Joseph was elated. A huge expense for the party had just been expertly circumvented. Things were once again all going in the right direction. But of course, that is usually when somebody pulls the rug out from beneath you. Just be sure that it isn't you doing it to yourself, without realising.

Chapter 29

Fat Freezing Should be Confined to Hollywood Celebrities

The day had come for Joseph's spa treatment and his 'date' with Josephine. He was very excited. Barry and Tymon had wished him 'luck' with the potentially blossoming romance as they departed for work. Even Pussy was more generous with her well wishes than normal.

"*I do not know why you would need anyone in your life other than Pussy? But if it's human companionship you require, then Pussy can always do with another servant*".

This, Joseph decided, was as much praise as he was ever going to receive from his cat. So, he accepted it with a gracious thank you to her.

"*What is the potential new servant's name*?"

"Josephine".

"*Josephine? Sounds vaguely familiar for some reason*".

Joseph thought better of entering into a lengthy explanation of how her name was a feminine version of his. Up to this point, Pussy had still not managed to accurately remember his name. Besides, he didn't want anything to dampen his enthusiasm for the day.

“I have an appointment at the spa that I have to attend to directly after my sailing lesson today. I won’t be back till the afternoon”.

With a spring in his step Joseph picked up his backpack and left to meet up with his sailing instructor.

***

It had been a gruelling day of sailing. Mostly because it had been so hot. And his instructor had really run Joseph ragged. But it was constructive, and it all helped Joseph get closer to the time when he could begin to take paying passengers aboard ‘Beat the Odds’.

He arrived back at dock and raced through the usual mooring tasks before hurrying back to his condominium. He was running too late to have a shower before he was required in the spa. He hoped that he didn’t stink too much. Dropping his backpack in the bedroom, he could see Pussy sunning herself out on the patio.

This was one of the great things that he loved about his new home. He could leave the doors open to the pool and patio without concern. The water garden acted as a barrier to any potential intruders. And security here was exemplary.

With a feeling of smugness, he made his way to the spa. By the time he arrived he was running a couple of minutes late. He presented himself to the lady at reception.

“Mister Whynee, we were wondering if you’d stood us up?”

“No chance of that, I’ve been looking forward to this. I’m a bit intimidated though. Can you tell me more about the whole process please?”

Joseph, now that he was in the spa, and ready to go with his treatment, was suddenly quite apprehensive about it. The young woman nodded sympathetically and sought to allay his fears.

"Our beauty therapist will go through all of the process with you mister Whynee. Please come through this way".

She indicated that he should proceed through a doorway to small white but rather ornate corridor that had three subsequent doors in it. The one at the far end opened and a thickly set lady emerged. She spoke with a heavy Russian accent. The short black hair with obvious grey streaks helped give her an air of authority. The overly loud voice helped too.

"Hah! Mister Whynee! This way please!"

Joseph walked down the short corridor and through the door that the woman was indicating. Inside where was a massage table and three machines to one side of it.

"Please sit on the table! Mine name is Zlata! You want to get rid of pot belly. Yes?!"

The request and subsequent question had all of the finesse of a bull in a fine-china shop. Joseph sat on the raised table. He nodded his reply to her. As if either sensing his misgivings about the procedure or maybe performing the usual sales pitch Zlata gave Joseph the rundown of his options. Pointing to each machine, she summarised the purpose, effectiveness, and overall expense of the treatments.

"This; melts fat with high temperature, inexpensive, but not very effective. This; freezes fat, expensive and effective. This; blasts fat with ultrasound, most effective, and most expensive!"

It was easy. All he had to do was choose the one that would be the most effective, but not the most expensive. He was about to point to the middle machine, when he thought the better of it and pulled out the voucher that he was going to use for payment.

Zlata took the voucher from him and studied its relative value. She made the decision for him.

“This voucher will get you this machine!”

Zlata indicated the middle one. The one that Joseph would have chosen anyway. Perfect! With a nod and s smile Joseph awaited the next instruction.

“Remove shirt and lay down on table. I put oil membranes on stomach to protect from frostbite. This gets cold as Moscow winter day. Then add two suction cups to trap fat and freeze it. Yes?!”

To be fair Joseph did not entirely understand what he was getting himself in for. And the explanation only managed to confuse him all the more. But the result, fat quite literally frozen away somehow, was the quick-fix and head-start he needed for his new physique. He removed his shirt. Zlata took if from him and hung it on a hook on the wall. Then she busied herself readying the appropriate fat freezing machine.

Joseph lay there pondering the fabulous new body that he would get after the procedure. His musings were rudely interrupted by Zlata laying an oily cloth on the top part of his stomach. It was really cold! Joseph drew in his breath in shock.

“Cold; yes?” Zlata said.

“Yes!” Joseph replied.

There was a second one put on the lower part of his stomach. Then one by one Zlata positioned two large rectangular suction cups with hoses on the upper and lower stomach. When activated they sucked in the skin and presumably the fat too within their capacious innards.

With both upper and lower abdomen now securely held within the machine’s suctions Zlata announced the start of the actual freezing process.

"You go numb soon. Then, not so uncomfortable. Watch this display. It count down to zero and I return to finish process!"

Zlata indicated a timer that could be clearly seen from where Joseph was lying. It was set at forty minutes and had started counting backwards when Zlata began the freezing procedure. Nothing for him to do now but wait for his fat to freeze-away.

***

Joseph had managed to have a little snooze during the process. Zlata was correct. He no longer felt any sensation of coldness as his stomach had gone completely numb. When the alarm sounded that indicated that the freezing part of the procedure had finished, Zlata reappeared.

"Good! Next, I roll frozen fat to destroy cell membrane. Then body absorb it over next month and expel. Drink lots of water!"

It sounded so forceful that Joseph felt intimidated enough to acquiesce immediately. Zlata produced what looked like a paint roller brush, but smaller and somehow more clinical looking. After detaching the machines and disposing of the membranes that had protected his skin, she began to roll the frozen fat with quite a force. He could hear it crunching as it was smashed beneath her relentless rolling.

It went on for quite longer than he had anticipated. Eventually Zlata announced that he could wipe himself down with a small hand towel that she had provided and put his shirt back on.

"Done! One month from now you will not have such ugly pot belly mister Whynee!"

Joseph couldn't help but think that Zlata's overly-direct manner could do with some rounding-off at the edges. He was also a little perturbed that there was such a lag between the process and the result. He hadn't fully understood that aspect of it. Nevertheless, it was done.

Just as he was about to leave Zlata offered one final point of useful information.

"Bruising may occur. Natural part of process. Nothing to worry about. Yes?!"

It was as if he was being offered a warning when it was already too late to heed it. With a raised eyebrow and a quizzical look, he responded.

"Thank you Zlata. That was quite an experience".

Satisfied that he had spent his voucher wisely, Joseph contemplated a quick workout in the gym, but his stomach felt like someone had punched it. Now that feeling was beginning to return to his abdomen, Joseph was aware that there may be more payback for undergoing the process than he had originally anticipated. Which was none. That is to say, he had not anticipated any downtime or unintended outcomes at all.

Joseph decided to lie in the sun on his patio to warm up for a while. He returned to his condominium and found Pussy occupying one of the sun lounges near his plunge pool. Pussy roused as Joseph settled into the adjoining sun lounge.

She gave him a slow blink of acknowledgement, which Joseph returned. Then they both closed their eyes and drifted off to sleep beneath the hot summer sun.

***

Both Joseph and Pussy were rudely awakened by the intercom buzzer. Joseph sprang up from his lounge and went to answer it. Pussy yawned and stretched and began to groom herself. Joseph was trying to shake the sleepiness from his head as he inquired as to who was calling him.

"Joseph! This is Josephine. You didn't make our rendezvous in the lobby. The concierge pointed me in this direction".

Joseph was quite taken aback. He looked at his watch and realised that he had been asleep for far too long.

"Josephine; I'm so sorry. I fell asleep on the patio. Here, let me buzz you in. Straight down the corridor to the right".

Joseph was cursing himself for not making the arranged meeting with Josephine in the lobby. Also, he was acutely aware that he had still not managed to have a shower since returning from sailing in the morning. All of that time lying in the baking sun had not helped matters any.

He fussed in front of the mirror near his front door. Satisfied that this was as good as he was going to look under the circumstances, he opened the door. Josephine glided into the doorway.

"There you are!" She smiled; Joseph swooned.

"I cannot apologise enough………"

Joseph's planned lengthy apology was waved away by Josephine. Her tone and demeanour clearly illustrating that she did not harbour any ill feeling over the matter.

"Joseph, pay no mind to it. We've all been there. Now where is this adorable kitty that I've come to meet?"

As if on cue, Pussy arrived to see the newcomer.

"*This must be Josephine. Pussy will mark her as property*".

With that, Pussy sidled up to Josephine and began to push her rear hind leg flanks against Josephine's calves. Josephine, being typically human, misunderstood this marking of ownership for affection.

"Oh, she's absolutely beautiful. And so friendly"

Joseph shut the door for fear of any other resident walking past.

"Come through to the living room". Said Joseph.

They moved as a trio to the sunken lounge room, all the while Josephine looking around in admiration of the condominium.

"Lovely condo Joseph. It must have cost a fortune?"

"Five dollars" He replied.

"Very funny. There's no need to tell me of course. After all we only just met. But if I wanted one of these, how much would it set me back, ballpark figure?"

Josephine was clearly not going to take no for an answer. Strangely, Joseph liked that. It showed he that she was a determined woman. It was a very attractive trait.

"No, seriously. This cost me five dollars. I was the winner in the R.S.L lottery, this was the prize".

Josephine spun around and looked at him open mouthed. A look of incredulity on her features.

"That was you? I heard that it was a convicted murderer that somehow got off his charge on a technicality and now the other residents were all living in fear of their lives".

Joseph was appalled, and he let it show.

“How do these rumours get started. You wouldn’t believe the list of them that I’ve heard so far”.

Shooing the words away from the air, Joseph tried to reset the conversation.

“Please take a seat”

They both sat adjacent to each other. Pussy once more affirming her ownership of Josephine.

“*Thank you, Jeremiah! Josephine will make an excellent supplementary servant*”.

Joseph could hardly answer Pussy under the circumstances. He felt a twinge of annoyance at being called Jeremiah. And why exactly had Pussy managed to remember Josephine’s name after hearing only once before? It was an argument that he would have with Pussy later. Right now, there was a more pressing need. One to impress his newfound lady friend.

“What is her name?”

Josephine’s question was a simple one. Without realising the ramifications of blurting out the name of Pussy he began to answer. After just the ‘P’ had left his lips, he caught himself and thought the better of it. He attempted to name her Molly as she was known previously. There were no female anatomy connotations linked to that name. But in the end, it came out as a hybrid of the two.

“Polly”.

“Hello Polly!”

Josephine, only after greeting the cat, realised that it was a name more often associated with a parrot. She took this to mean that Joseph had a sense of humour.

"Very droll, Joseph. I like it"

Pussy on the other hand, was less than impressed at being misnamed.

"POLLY! HAS YOUR I.Q. SUDDENLY DROPPED JEROME? DOES IT LOOK TO YOU LIKE PUSSY IS SITTING ON THE SHOULDER OF A PIRATE?!"

Joseph had never had Pussy get so angry with him before. So, he was unsure of how to diffuse the situation.

"LOOK AT PUSSY'S BODY MISTER! This is black silky fur, not blue and yellow feathers!"

Joseph knew that he had to end this rant from Pussy as quickly as possible if he was to have a meaningful conversation with Josephine.

"How about a kitty treat for beings so lovely?" Joseph said to Pussy.

She ceased her tirade and her ears moved forward. Pleased that he had circumvented any further input from the cat he made his way to the kitchen to make good on his promise. All the time chatting with Josephine.

"Speaking of treats. I haven't had lunch yet. Are you hungry?"

"I'm hungry for many things Joseph. Lunch is but one of them".

The sexual subtext to the reply brought a smile from Joseph. He enjoyed a bit of banter in this way. It made him think however that perhaps the youth of today did not partake of such flirting.

"I like the way you think Josephine. You know, if we were young, we would have met using an online app, not in person in a grocery store". Said Joseph

Josephine's reply was supportive of his viewpoint.

"If we were young, we would have already swapped pictures of our genitals by now".

They both laughed raucously. Pussy did not concern herself with the goings on as she was now tucking into a healthy dental treat for cats.

Joseph thought that it would be best to get showered and then continue the conversation over a nice lunch. He suggested 'Ladybird' restaurant. It was on the boardwalk between Palazzo Versace and Marina Mirage shopping centre which was directly adjacent to Versace. With lovely water views overlooking the marina and an excellent reputation for food, it was appropriately 'romantic' for a first date.

Joseph fixed Josephine a quick gin and tonic before making his excuses to go and shower before they headed out to lunch together.

"Please enjoy the patio, it is wonderfully serene out there. I won't be long".

With his promise of a quick turn-around, he left Josephine to her own devices. She carried the drink to the patio and looked over the plunge pool to the water garden beyond. It really was lovely. But then her mind turned towards more amorous thoughts.

She pondered the question of effectiveness. Which approach to getting hooked-up was the better one? The young, who rely on applications and picture swapping before jumping into bed with each other. Or the more traditional approach that she and Joseph were taking. Chance meeting, leading to discussing common interests. A first non-threatening meeting. Then an actual 'date' of some description, that may or may not result in getting to the 'business!'

Josephine decided that there was a lot to admire about the immediacy of the youthful approach. Thinking that she really had nothing to lose, she downed the gin and tonic in a few gulps and decided to make her move.

Meanwhile, Joseph had made it to his luxurious bathroom and disrobed. He was about to get into the shower without a second (or even first) look in the mirror. But something made him take a look. Maybe it was to check that he still had some meagre skerrick of sex-appeal that would help him in the forthcoming lunch date.

His pupils dilated almost to their maximum extent in shock when he witnessed the "bruising" that Zlata had warned him about. It was unbelievably grotesque. His entire stomach was literally black and purple and brown blotches of bruising. The surface of his belly was uneven and severe dimpling had appeared here and there.

"What on earth?" Joseph said to himself aloud.

Another thing too. His testicles seemed to have reacted unusually to the numbing cold that his stomach had endured. They had retreated so far back up from his scrotum that it was like he had no balls at all. Joseph regarded his genitals. They looked awful and unbalanced. He hoped like crazy that this was only a temporary situation. Also, his penis had shrunk to a point that made it look shrivelled and very unappealing.

There was nothing to do but continue with his shower. Zlata had not exactly been overly forthcoming with the amount of bruising that he would develop after the fat freezing procedure. And certainly, no mention had been made as to any effect on the surrounding organs! Shaking his head in disbelief he started the shower and waited for it to be the perfect temperature before entering.

He had lathered up his body when surreptitiously, Josephine entered. She had considered disrobing herself and joining Joseph in the shower. But her naturally cautious nature prevented her from taking that course of action. In the moments to come she would thank her lucky stars for that decision.

The clear frameless glass door of the shower was already steamed up and obscuring Joseph's figure within. Josephine's approach was further obscured as Joseph had turned to face the shower spout to help rinse the lather from his body. She reached out for the door flung it open and with a loud voice frightened Joseph's relative serenity.

"SURPRISE!"

Joseph nearly jumped out of his blotchy and unattractive skin. He spun around revealing to Josephine in all of his glory, or lack thereof, his battered and meagre body. Josephine gasped loudly as she saw the hideous shape and colours of his stomach. Then without even realising that she had moved her gaze southward to judge his genitals, she managed a small scream upon viewing them.

"AAarrrgghhh !"

Josephine was horrified beyond belief. The incongruous abdomen and laughable penis and apparently non-existent testicles all served to repulse her in a way that she wouldn't have thought possible.

"Wait!"

Joseph shouted in horror. Although he was unsure of exactly what he was asking to happen under the circumstances. Wait for him to finish the shower? Wait for his testicles to drop again? Wait for his penis to unfurl and return to its normal size? Or wait for the weird bruising on his pot belly to fade? Perhaps it was a subconscious call for Josephine to wait for all of the above to happen?

But, waiting around to make sense of all of this was not what Josephine had in mind. Thanking her good sense, that she had kept her clothes on, she was able to make a mad dash for the front door. The patterned walls were a blur as she ran faster than her schoolgirl athletics days to exit the apartment with as much speed as humanly possible.

From his embarrassed position in the bathroom, Joseph could hear the front door close automatically with a thud. Joseph felt that the sound of the closing door had a double meaning. It was not just the exit of his lunch date, but the closing of the door on his potential new love life.

Looking down at the outlandish body that he possessed, he breathed a huge sigh of regret. Part of that sigh included his customary question to the universe in such situations; why me? Pussy appeared in the bathroom and sat at the door of the shower watching Joseph.

"*What happened to primary servant's stomach*?" She inquired.

"I'd rather not talk about it". Joseph answered.

"*That's good, because Pussy isn't really all that interested*".

Joseph couldn't help the obvious double entendre retort under the circumstances.

"No pussy is interested in me, Pussy".

Completely ignoring the comment, Pussy exited the bathroom and set herself up in the window of the bedroom ready to observe the seagulls coming and going. That was without doubt far more interesting than why her primary servant's stomach was black and blue.

Chapter 30

Genuine Designer Clothes are Expensive!

Joseph had really hit rock bottom. He had explained the debacle of his 'date' to Tymon and Barry upon their return home from work. It was great to have them there so that they could sympathise with him. Both were horrified at the state of Joseph's stomach after the fat freezing. But they hastened to remind him that a month from now, the bruising would be gone. It was a small comfort under the circumstances.

Hoping to make Joseph feel a little better Barry and Tymon took him out to dinner. They suggested 'Ladybird' restaurant but settled on a Greek restaurant on Tedder Avenue. It was a lovely dinner and upon their return to Palazzo Versace, the boys made their way toward the Versace boutique within the main lobby. It was closed at this time of night. But they wanted to window shop.

The three of them stood their looking at the expensive merchandise. The outfit that was in the main window on the male mannequin was particularly fetching. And the younger men commented to that effect. This began the spark of an idea in Joseph's mind. Which is the usual point when things start to go terribly wrong for him.

***

With the day of the resident's welcome party fast approaching Joseph had hatched a plan to get some credibility back that he had lost recently. He would fork-out for a genuine Versace outfit, the one that he saw in the window, in its entirety. But he would wait for the busiest time in the lobby so that as many residents as possible could witness the purchase. Hopefully, they would relay back to the others that he was making amends for his online fake merchandise debacle.

As it turned out, he had observed that it was a Monday around lunch time that the residents were most active. They appeared to be meeting in the lobby before departing for various regular commitments. That was when Joseph made his move.

Marching purposefully up to the Versace boutique he stood and looked admiringly once more at the complete outfit that was displayed on the male shop dummy. Then feigning some contemplative thinking he brazenly entered the store.

There were three customers already either browsing around or in conversations with one of the sales assistants. This left one of the sales assistants free who approached him and with a friendly smile introduced himself.

"Hello mister Whynee, my name is Frederique, may I help you find something today?"

Joseph was taken off guard.

"You know who I am?" Joseph asked.

"Your reputation has preceded you mister Whynee".

Joseph was not very happy to hear that titbit. It was sure to bad news that had circulated throughout the establishment. Trying his best to look as if he was pleased to hear it, he carried on.

"That's wonderful. I was hoping that you could help me find that exact outfit in the window, in my size of course".

Joseph indicated the desired look that was on display. He glanced back through to the lobby hoping to find some residents looking back at him. If they were, then they were being very discrete.

Frederique was a well presented handsome young fellow. He certainly presented a friendly face to buying such premium priced clothing. He smiled as he acknowledged the items that Joseph sought.

"Certainly. If you'll please take a seat, I can get some sizes ready for you to try on in the change rooms".

The whole process was going very smoothly. Joseph felt his initial apprehension of entering the pricey store begin to evaporate. He sat on one of the available chairs and awaited the return of Frederique. Looking around the shimmering store, Joseph actually deluded himself that he could get used to this kind of shopping. It was so completely different to K-Mart.

Frederique, true to his word, returned but was strangely empty handed. Joseph gave him a puzzled look. Frederique responded with the answer to the unspoken query.

"I've set up a couple of sizes for the entire outfit in changing room number one for you mister Whynee. Right this way please".

He was led to the appropriate door and Joseph entered. Even the change rooms were glamorous here. There was a leather chair, multiple mirrors so that he could see his reflection from multiple angels and various clothes hooks. There were two examples of the entire outfit available for him to try on.

“I’ll be back soon. May I suggest this size first. I’ve put the entire look together from a separate top, jacket, pants and shoes collection. I’m very glad that you like it”.

With that he discretely exited allowing Joseph to disrobe and attire himself in the outfit. Everything felt very smooth and silky to the touch. When he had put on the entire look, he regarded himself in the mirror. He looked like a million dollars.

Frederique returned and knocked politely on the door before asking permission to enter. When he saw Joseph in the clothes, he was very complementary. Joseph had to thank his good eye for size, because the first outfit was a perfect fit in every way. There was no need to try on the second.

“This is absolutely perfect. I’ll take it!” Joseph declared.

“Wonderful, would you like to wear the outfit now or take it home with you packaged up?”

“Packed please” Joseph said.

The next few minutes were a blur of endorphins as Joseph prepared himself for what would no doubt be a price tag that he had never before faced for clothing. By the time that he joined Frederique at the counter he had mentally prepared himself for the transaction.

“It feels wonderful, doesn’t it? The Jacket, pants and top are a viscose and silk blend”.

Frederique was making light conversation whilst preparing the clothing.

“Isn’t that just a fancy way of saying polyester?” Joseph joked.

Unfortunately, the ‘joke’ went down like a lead balloon with Frederique. His face turned from jovial to judgemental in the blink of an eye.

“No. It isn’t” Frederique replied with more than a note of curtness.

Thinking that he had better get out of here as quickly as possible, before putting his foot in his mouth again, Joseph produced his credit card and the voucher he received in his welcome pack. Frederique took the voucher and to Joseph’s surprise found out that it would only cover the cost of the shoes, rather than, as he would have hoped, at least a third of the cost of the entire outfit.

Joseph steeled himself for the final cost. Frederique seemed to be taking ages to get the entire thing packed into a couple of boxes and then into an oversized carry bag, thankfully with the brand emblazoned across it for all to see.

“That will be eight thousand dollars please mister Whynee”.

The reality of purchasing these clothes hit Joseph in the face like a slap.

“Are you sure?”

Joseph had a vague hope that somehow the price had been miscalculated. And that maybe an extra zero had been added by mistake. Frederique, to his credit, did not miss a beat and rang up the cost of the items again, then subtracting the value of Joseph’s voucher. He presented the number to Joseph without flinching.

“Confirmed. Eight thousand dollars exactly”.

Joseph handed over his credit card, but his hand was visibly trembling. Frederique took it and put it through the usual process to extract the amount required. Joseph’s mind was racing. There was nothing on the card at the moment was there? His limit should cover the exorbitant cost, but somehow, he was now usure. He began to break out in a cold sweat.

“Oh, I wasn’t expecting that!” Declared Frederique.

“What! What?” Joseph flinched as he asked.

"It went through". The salesman confirmed.

Either unaware of the implied insult, or perhaps just happy to make the sale and oblivious to all else, Frederique handed over the bag to Joseph. Taking his card and the bag, Joseph thanked Frederique for his help and exited the store proudly displaying to all the bounty he had purchased.

He walked slowly, nonchalantly, across the length of the lobby to the residential access hallway and disappeared from view. Safely away from prying eyes, Joseph let out a huge sigh of relief.

When he entered his condominium, he was already having major buyer's regret. He had never before paid such a mammoth price for clothing. But he consoled himself, it would help in win back some kind of credibility or respect from the other residents. He planned to show it off to everyone at the party.

Entering his bedroom he unboxed the Jacket, pants, and top. They were all on a branded coat hanger. Regarding the outfit with a mixture of pleasure and disbelief that anything could cost so much, he hung it on the hook on the back of the door.

Then looking around suspiciously, as if expecting a burglar to be present somewhere, he closed the door with a resounding thump. Unfortunately, that action caused the outfit to sway heavily enough to fall from the hook and lie in a mess on the floor.

Disturbed by the noise, Pussy emerged from where she had been sleeping beneath Joseph's bed. After a yawn and a downward stretch, she regarded the clutch of clothes lying on the floor. They really were the ugliest that she had ever seen. Guessing that they must have been put there by primary servant, you know, what's-his-name, Pussy moved forward to get a closer look. Yes, indeed, they were hideous. But the material that they were made from looked perfect for sharpening her claws. And Pussy's claws could always do with more sharpening.

Approaching them with her usual boldness, Pussy extended her claws and began to sink them deeply into the jacket, pants, top combination. The tearing of the material made the most pleasing sound for Pussy. She purred loudly as she continued to eviscerate the clothes.

But then something unsettling happened. Somehow, simultaneously, a thread from each of the garments became caught in various front claws. As pussy pulled her claws out they were clearly captured in some way by this intruder to her bedroom. Further clawing did not release the clothes grip on her. Taking fright Pussy leapt directly upwards in the hope of freeing herself from the assailant. No luck!

She dashed back under the bed pulling three perfectly continuous threads from each of the garments with her. Noting that the threads were somehow following her to one of her most secure hiding places, she reacted accordingly.

Pussy ran in circles around the base of the bed posts. Each lap pulling more and more viscose and silk combination thread from the garments. After about eight complete laps, one of the threads broke free. Only two more to go!

It took a further three laps around the base of the bed in order to completely free herself from the aggressive clothing. Hissing each time seemed to help break the bonds that bound her. The clothes were ruined. Various threads in contrasting colours now looped from the clothing and around the base of the bed.

Satisfied that she had won the battle against the intruder, Pussy jumped up to be on top of the bed and glare down at the offending clothes. That would teach them to intrude upon her territory and attempt to capture some of her front claws. Still suspicious of the garments, however, Pussy elected to sit there for quite some time staring at them in unmasked disdain.

***

It was about an hour later that Joseph returned to once more bask in the munificence that was his first designer outfit. It had been on his mind the entire time that he was away from it. The thought of hosting the welcome party in the splendid clothes went some way toward ameliorating the excessive cost of the garments.

The horror of the scene that greeted him upon entering his bedroom however was so much of a shock that he screamed like a radio actress being terrorised by a zombie.

"What happened?!" Joseph demanded of Pussy.

"Primary servant's ugly clothes attacked Pussy! However, Pussy was victorious!"

As that was all that Pussy was prepared to say on the subject, Pussy trotted past Joseph and made her way to her water dish. All that running around was thirsty work. Joseph still unable to grasp the horror of eight thousand dollars of ruined Versace clothes, began to simper.

"Oh…nooooo; whyyyyyy meeeeee?".

It was in that instant that Joseph understood why his former work colleagues had nicknamed him the way that they had. Why me Whynee. Upon reflection, he did tend to say that whenever he felt that the world was conspiring to prevent him from achieving something that he desired.

He looked at the rags once more. They were dismembered to the point of being useless, even as dust cloths. Joseph fell to his knees and picked up the remnants of the clothes as if they were a close friend dying slowly in his arms. He had a vague flash of incredulity. Maybe, he could return them, and say that they fell apart in the bag!?

Thankfully that insane thought lasted only a brief part of a second before he dismissed it with a healthy dose of common sense. The reality of his folly was clear. Real designer clothes are expensive. And not something that he should not have attempted to indulge himself with.

Chapter 31

Diamonds and Cubic Zirconia Should Never Mix

True to his word, Gavin Grosvenor had delivered the 'champagne' to Palazzo Versace. It had been received with admiring glances from the staff as it was transferred to the main kitchen refrigerators to chill them nicely before the welcome party on the evening of the following day. There simply wasn't enough room in Joseph's refrigerator for so many magnums of Tsarine Champagne.

As luck would have it, the coffee table was delivered from the furniture restorer at the same time as the champagne. Thankfully, it was wrapped in layers of felt, nicely disguising it from prying eyes. With 'champagne' and coffee table now on site, Joseph breathed a sigh of relief. Things were going his way, finally!

It was a good feeling and helped Joseph get over the tragic loss of his clothes the other day. Another great positive was the written exam for his Marine License. He passed it with flying colours. Now all that he needed was to pass the practical examination, conducted on his boat with an examiner putting him through his paces. It was scheduled for the end of the week. Just enough time to get over this dreaded welcome party on Wednesday evening.

He had all of the necessary components to put the party on as required by the other residents. All he needed now was to go through the motions and get to the other side of it. The intercom alerted him to a visitor. He was surprised to find it was Isabella. He let her in and greeted her at the door, showing her through to the kitchen where he was taking stock of everything, just to ensure that there was nothing missing.

"Now you are clear on the specifics of my newly extended family, right?"

Joseph was referring to his convoluted explanation of having adopted Barry as his nephew, even though Joseph was an only child.

"Yes, Joseph, and Austin and Karalee are all briefed as well. Have you let your father know that he has a long-lost daughter that lives down south somewhere?"

Isabella was more than a little sceptical that such a deception was either necessary or wise.

"Yes, he is completely on-board with it". Joseph affirmed.

"The old devil is actually bringing a date with him. Someone from Golden Years. Isn't that great?"

Joseph upon hearing his own words of praise for his father, realised that he was completely dateless and without prospects. It was a sobering thought. His self-pity was interrupted by Isabella.

"How are you going to display all of this? With some aplomb and flair, I hope?"

Isabella's question caught Joseph off guard. He had not contemplated how he would be arranging the various expensive foods.

"Maybe".

Was all Joseph could think of in reply.

Resisting the urge to roll her eyes, Isabella committed to helping him design the layout for the spread. As the air conditioning was already turned up, they had the opportunity to put the various foods out on the table from the refrigerator without fearing spoilage.

Isabella, true to her word, was masterful at making the entire thing look both appetising and somehow very classy. This was perfect thought Joseph. And completely in keeping with the attendees and the general surroundings. By the time she was finished, the dining room table looked a million dollars.

The caviar was the raised centrepiece of the display. Both Joseph and Isabella stood back to admire their handywork.

"Beautiful. Thank you very much Isabella". Said Joseph.

"You're welcome. You know, you could thank me by giving me another look at that lovely diamond that used to grace my finger. I'm thinking of buying something similar and wanted to get some inspiration from it".

Isabella smiled innocently at Joseph as she made the request. Little did Joseph know that this was just the prelude to a devious scheme that Isabella had dreamt up to secure the diamond once more. It was the real reason that she had unexpectedly dropped by to see him today.

Without realising that there were serious machinations happening around him, Joseph agreed and went to the bedroom to recover the family diamond from the safe. In the meantime, Pussy had arrived in the kitchen and addressed Isabella. It was a pity that Isabella couldn't hear Pussy's words.

"Well, if it isn't Griz-a-bella? What are you doing in my new home?"

If Isabella had heard Pussy and then cared to answer honestly, the answer would have been shocking. Isabella had dreamt up a little scheme to once more get her hands on the beautiful diamond that she had counted as hers ever since the engagement. In her purse was a very cleverly commissioned imitation of the cushion cut diamond but made from cubic zirconia. It had still cost a lot of money to get made, for a forgery, but it would be worth it when surreptitiously swapped for the real thing. Now all Isabella needed was the opportunity to palm-off the fake to Joseph and get away with the real thing.

"Still deaf as a door post?"

Pussy's insult went unheard and un-returned. Whilst she waited Isabella took in the spectacle of the table that she had designed with the delicacies. Joseph returned with the diamond in hand and noticed her admiring her handy work.

"Do you know that looking at black caviar through a diamond is meant to be good luck? Tymon told me that. It must be an old Polish superstition"

Joseph's unusual comment had indeed, not been heard by Isabella before. And she let him know.

"Well, let's put that to the test, shall we?"

Isabella took the top of the large tin of black caviar. Joseph handed her the diamond and Isabella held it up to her eye and regarded the glistening contents.

"Not feeling any luckier than I already am Joe". Isabella commented.

"Try getting closer, see it that helps any?" Joseph suggested.

Isabella leaned forward over the table and could see the caviar refracted multiple times through the intricately cut diamond. At that moment, tired of being ignored by somebody that she didn't even like, Pussy decided to raise herself upon her hind legs and push her front paws into Isabella's right leg, just above the knee. Her claws were deliberately extended. Firstly, to ensure good grip, and secondly to spite the woman for invading her territory.

At the precise moment that Pussy's claws entered Isabella's skin, the unsuspecting woman let out a small shriek and flicked the diamond into the air. It all happened so quickly, yet both Joseph and Isabella managed to see the entire thing in slow motion.

In a movement worthy of an Olympic diver, the diamond did a quadruple somersault and plopped into the very centre of the caviar. It was immediately obscured in the shallow depths of the can by the black viscous contents.

"Oh NO!" Exclaimed Joseph.

"Molly! I mean, Pussy; bad Girl!" Bellowed Isabella.

Isabella actually made to reach into the can with her fingers to recover the diamond, but Joseph stopped her.

"No; don't! I have a mother of pearl spoon here somewhere for that. We don't want to ruin the stuff."

They both moved into the kitchen to find the spoon that they could use to reclaim the diamond from the caviar tin. Unseen by both of them, Pussy jumped neatly up onto the table and sniffed at the little black pearls of fishiness. As far as food goes, these little morsels were quite the most beguiling thing that she had ever encountered.

Joseph had failed to find the spoon in the draw with the rest of the cutlery. He looked at Isabella with a worried expression.

"What have you done with it?" She inquired.

After thinking briefly the answer came to him. He raised a finger in the air in triumph.

"I put it in the refrigerator to cool down". He said.

They both went to the refrigerator and opened it up. Between the two of them they managed to locate the spoon and with it in Joseph's hand they returned to the table.

The site of Pussy tucking into the expensive tin of black gold filled both of them with horror. They both shouted in unison.

"PUSSY!"

Disturbed by the noise Pussy raised her head to see what all the commotion was about. It was at that precise moment that she swallowed the largest mouthful of the tasty treats. It was hard. But it went down a treat. Both Joseph and Isabella heard the louder than normal swallow emanating from Pussy's throat.

Hurrying, Isabella lifted Pussy down from the table and placed her on the floor.

"Quick! Check the tin!" She exclaimed.

Joseph needed no encouragement. He dug deeply through the remnants of the caviar and swirled it up and over the spoon over and over again. It was useless. The diamond was gone!

"She must have swallowed it. I'll take her to the nearest vet and have her cut open to retrieve it!"

Isabella's horrendous suggested course of action was met with an equal and opposite rebuff from Joseph.

"Nobody is opening up my Pussy!" Joseph shouted.

Frustrated that her secret plan had come so completely asunder, Isabella demanded an alternative course of action.

"What are we going to do then?"

After a moment scratching his head, Joseph came up with an alternative.

"Let's ring the Vet and find out what to do?"

Joseph, being a responsible cat owner, had the phone number of his veterinarian clinic stored in his phone. He produced it and dialled them. Isabella watched on helplessly as Joseph explained the problem to the vet. They appeared to be more interested in the size and shape of the diamond that she would have thought. Eventually after what appeared to be a lengthy and rather unusual conversation Joseph hung up the phone and looked at Isabella.

“Apparently this is more common that you might think”.

“What? Cats often swallow two and a half carat cushion cut diamonds that have fallen into caviar? Really!”

“No, no. But cats swallowing something that is inert. Not large enough to warrant an operation to remove it. And something that will in time, pass through and can be recovered in her kitty litter. Lucky it wasn’t a brilliant cut diamond, or it could have been a big problem. Too many sharp edges. But my diamond, none. It will come out the other end without a problem. Phew!”

Joseph wiped the perspiration from his brow as a way to underline the course of action.

“You’re kidding Joseph. You’re going to wait and get it out of her poop!” Said Isabella incredulously.

“That’s what the Doctor said”. Joseph confirmed.

Isabella rolled her eyes and simultaneously sucked in a deep breath to let out an extensive sigh of frustration. Her plan to swap the real diamond with her fake may have been temporarily thwarted by this unfortunate circumstance, but it could still proceed at a future date.

Isabella and Joseph packed away the foodstuffs into the refrigerator. Mostly to keep them fresh and ready for tomorrow evening’s party. But also, to prevent Pussy from gorging herself on anything else that was meant for the guests. Joseph made the obvious smarmy comment.

‘Pussy sure does have expensive tastes!”

He laughed expecting at least a smile from Isabella. He was disappointed. Instead, he got a glare of impatience. When the food was securely put away, Isabella moved to the patio to bask in the sunshine for a short time.

Joseph stayed int the kitchen to admonish Pussy for her theft.

"Naughty Pussy. That was very expensive stuff, and it was for the other residents. And swallowing a diamond could have been very dangerous".

Pussy was having none of it however. She replied in her usual dismissive way.

"*Everything here belongs to Pussy. Keep that in mind Jackson!*"

"Joseph!"

But in her usual inimitable way, Pussy had stopped paying attention and had started to make her way out to the patio to further admonish Isabella for invading her territory.

Isabella had in the meantime, taken out the fake diamond to ponder exactly when she would be able to swap it with the real thing. Again, just as before, Pussy crept up on her and deliberately sank her claws into Isabella's calves.

With a small scream, Isabella jumped. The cubic zirconia flying out of her fingers. It fell to the ground and bounced a couple of times before coming to rest on a small metal grate that was nestled neatly in the terracotta tiles.

With a look of alarm on her face she leapt forward to recover it. Sadly, the very act of attempting to get her hands on it with too much speed caused it to fall through the grate and make the sound of a very definite plop into the hidden depths below.

Frantically, Isabella attempted to remove the grate. It remained stubbornly in place, unyielding to her efforts. She stood up in frustration.

“Why me? I’m not a Whynee anymore!”

Joseph couldn’t quite make out what Isabella had said as he joined her on the patio.

“What was that?” He asked.

Indicating the grate, Isabella asked for some unusual information.

“Where does that grate lead?”

Joseph thought that it was a rather odd question. But as he knew the answer, he thought nothing of providing the information to his ex-wife.

“It’s one of the stormwater drains. I imagine that it runs through to the mangroves further up the broad water. Why? Is it important?”

With her devious plan now completely asunder, Josephine couldn’t think of any reasonable excuse for her curiosity.

“I need a drink” She said.

“Oh. OK. Nothing too heavy surely. You drove here, right?” He asked with some concern.

With a force of resolution that was not to be argued with Isabella let her wishes be known.

“One dry Martini for me, make it a double. Nothing for you, because you’re driving me home”.

Misinterpreting Isabella's tension as concern for Pussy's well being, Joseph went to make the drink without any further query or comment.

Chapter 32

One Pussy Too Many

Joseph and long since dropped Isabella home and made his way back to P.V. via public transport. By the time he arrived Tymon and Barry had returned from work that day. They were horrified to learn of Pussy's predicament. Both agreed to ensure that any "deposits" made in her kitty litter, would be set aside for proper inspection rather than thrown out.

Then surprisingly, Tymon insisted on making a traditional Polish dish for the party the following evening. So, they left to get the necessary ingredients. Joseph was at a loose end. He was wondering what to do next when the front doorbell rang. Answering it he found Ismail asking permission to come in for a chat. They moved to the living room.

"I just wanted to ensure that you are ready for the party tomorrow evening." Ismail asked.

"Ready and willing, Ismail. I have everything. How punctual will the guests be?"

"Everyone will arrive within the first hour, unless they are held back by work commitments, As I expect Doctor Carver to be".

Ismail was still responding to the question when he glanced down at Pussy Two Shoes near the patio door. There were two of them now. Also, the coffee table that had been missing the last time

Ismail was here, was suddenly back where it should be? He wondered where it had been? Ismail finished his reply and then pointed to the newcomer.

"I see that you have another 'pet' Joseph"

Joseph looked over to where Ismail had indicated. There lying in exactly the same pose as Pussy Two Shoes, was Pussy. The real cat was indistinguishable from the stuffed toy. And thankfully at this distance, Pussy could not be visibly seen to be breathing.

"Let me guess the name of the newcomer" Ismail Said and then paused to contemplate what it might be.

Joseph knew that any mention of the name Pussy would alert his cat which could wake her from her slumber. Panicked he spoke over the top of Ismail as he began to formulate his guessed name.

"Harrold!" He said a little too loudly.

Ismail was somewhat perplexed. The naming of this one didn't seem to follow the usual conventions for cat names that Joseph had imbued onto the furniture, and the first of his stuffed toy cats.

"Oh. That's…nice" Ismail responded.

Joseph could see that Ismail was more than a little confused at the name but thought the better of attempting some convoluted explanation to rationalise it.

"Actually, I was thinking of giving this one to my ex-wife. You know, to keep her company. Living in that big house all alone. I thought it would be a nice gesture".

Ismail failed to respond, so Joseph added to the explanation.

"After all, I wouldn't want people to think that I'm obsessed with felines or anything like that. Would I?"

It took all of Ismail's self-restraint to both keep his eyes from opening widely and replying in a manner that did not seem either condescending or incredulous.

"No. Of course not".

Thinking that it may be better to leave now before the conversation became any more ridiculous, Ismail pardoned himself, citing many things to take care of, and left Joseph and the two cats to their own devices.

"I'll see myself out. Till tomorrow evening; goodbye".

After Ismail had left, Joseph let out a sigh of relief.

"That was a close one Pussy" He said.

Pussy opened her eyes, lifted her head, and glared at Joseph for disturbing her nap.

***

Barry and Tymon had arrived home from shopping for ingredients, and set about immediately to make their contribution to the party. Tymon was directing Barry how to help him create the two Polish dishes. Boiled cabbage seemed to feature prominently, and it filled the apartment with its unpleasant smell.

After quite some amount of time, the dishes were done. Tymon proudly introduced them both by spelling them, and then pronouncing them. In both cases the spelling of the foods did not seem to have a close resemblance to the way they were spelled.

“The cabbage rolls are stuffed with turkey meat. Spelling is; G.O.L.A.B.K.I but pronounced gwompkee. And the mini sausages are a regional version of K.I.E.L.B.A.S.A, but pronounced killbassa. We make them smaller in Zakopane than in the rest of the country”.

Joseph couldn’t help but make reference to the most recent sausage that he had encountered.

“What, No skanky kransky?”

The three of them had a little chuckle about it.

Without fully thinking the sentence through, Tymon asked Joseph.

“Do you think Pussy would like a bit of sausage?”

And without pondering the reply completely enough Joseph answered.

“I’m sure she would”.

It was only Barry’s snickering that alerted them both to the obvious double entendre that they had stumbled into.

They had dinner together and arranged their day tomorrow. Barry and Tymon would leave work early so that they could help Joseph set up for the party in the early afternoon. Joseph had organised for Millicent to hide Pussy in her condominium for the duration of the party. It all seemed like it would come together nicely in the end. What could possibly go wrong?

The only thing that did not work out to everyone’s satisfaction was the fact that Tymon had brought up Zakopane. It was just the catalyst that he needed to regale Joseph and Barry with boring story after boring story about the small town of his birth. By the time they retired for the evening Joseph and Barry were worn out.

***

When Joseph finally arose the next day from his slumbers, it was quite late in the morning. By the time he showered and got himself ready it was even later. Somehow, he did not feel like the usual breakfast given that it was more like brunch time. Surveying the contents of the fridge his eyes settled on the cabbage rolls that Tymon had prepared.

If he heated up a couple of those, nobody would be the wiser. He did so and marvelled that he really enjoyed the traditional Polish dish. They went down quite a treat, along with a nice hot cup of tea. All he had to do now was relax until the afternoon when he and the boys would set up everything for the party and await their guests.

Chapter 33

Umbilical Cords Should Always Be Severed

Joseph was lying on his bed stroking his Pussy.

(Editor: That sentence should read 'Joseph was lying on his bed stroking Pussy, the cat').

[Author: I tells it like I sees it]

(Editor: Eye rolling emoji: I don't know why I even bother to try!?)

[Author: I don't know either; but I wish you'd stop!]

As I was saying before being so rudely interrupted. Joseph was gratuitously stroking his Pussy whilst lying on his bed. And we all know that stroking Pussy with gusto is always preferable to a soft tickle!

Pussy was lying on Joseph's chest. Which is not exactly where you want Pussy to be, but close enough is good enough. So pleased was she with the stroking that she sat up and began kneading Joseph's chest and purring a most agreeable manner.

Across the way, on the very top level of the building, Ismail was helping a resident unfurl one of the rooftop apartment's sun umbrellas. He was standing on a chair and doing his best to untangle the mess. It was an occupational health and safety nightmare. Ismail was standing on a chair and from that unusual vantage point he could see down four levels to the ground floor condominiums.

In fact, he could see straight into the bedroom of Joseph's condo. There appeared to be a cat upon Joseph's chest, doing that kneading thing that they do. He watched incredulously as the cat then walked a circle before settling down on Joseph's chest to rest.

Ismail rubbed his eyes. Had he seen that correctly? He was still contemplating and craning his neck to see if he could get a better viewing point, when a sudden gust of wind threatened to hurl him over the balustrades. Alarmed at the immediate threat to his safety, Ismail jumped down from the chair. Serendipitously, the umbrella managed to fix itself at that very moment, removing the need for him to put himself in any further danger.

There was nothing to it, Ismail had to do some further investigation on the scene he had witnessed. Or, at least, thought that he had witnessed. He excused himself from the resident that he had been helping and returned to his office. There he kept a pair of binoculars. These were to see any details of the building that he needed to inspect from afar. But today, he would most definitely be using them to spy on Joseph Whynee.

Ismail had made his way to the board walk that separated the building from the broad water. Between him and Joseph's bedroom windows was the water garden. And if he clambered upon one of the hefty timber poles that supported the board walk structure, he would have enough height to see properly into Joseph's bedroom.

He was too busy trying to keep his balance on the thick post, whilst attempting to see what was going on in Joseph's bedroom to notice that a couple of the residents were rapidly approaching him.

Mister Otieno Mwangi and his wife Missus Hamima Mwangi, originally of Kenya, observed Ismail in his precarious position. They looked at each other in vexed confusion. Neither made any attempt to conceal their approach to Ismail. But he was so preoccupied with his spying that he did not register them at all. So, it came as quite a shock when Otieno inquired as to the nature of Ismail's position.

"Ismail, what on earth are you doing up there?"

Startled by the question and feeling more than a little guilty about being caught spying on one of the other residents, Ismail jumped down to the boardwalk. He had to think quickly. Admitting to what he was actually doing would be career suicide. As well as a major breach in trust that the residents put in him as their relationship manager.

"I'm…….trying to scare off the seagulls from the water garden". He said rather unconvincingly.

The moment the words came out of his mouth he regretted them. What an incredibly flimsy and ridiculous excuse. He admonished himself mentally. Otieno and Hamima however, accepted his explanation without a second thought.

Do binoculars help? Otieno is asked.

Ismail could not for the like of him think how binoculars would aid him in his manufactured endeavour.

"No". He replied feebly.

Hamima took up the point and offered an alternative.

"Then maybe you should use something that will help. Like a fake owl to scare off the seagulls. What about that?"

She offered the sensible suggestion with a flourish of her hand. Otieno, thinking that he could improve upon the idea piped up.

"Only if it is gold coloured and has a medusa's head. So that it is in keeping with the design theme for the establishment".

Hamima briefly contemplated the thought of a golden owl with medusa head positioned to be a seagull deterrent.

“A golden owl, with the head of Medusa would scare the beegeebies out of me. I think that is a wonderful idea Otieno” she said.

Glad that his wife approved of the idea, Otieno offered the obvious counter point of view.

“But will it be effective in scaring away the seagulls do you think?”

Ever the logical one of the relationship, Hamima offered her viewpoint.

“Well, it couldn’t do a worse job than using binoculars to frighten them; could it?”

Both husband and wife nodded in agreement to each other and then turned their gaze once more to Ismail. Otieno offered these parting words before they continued with their mid-morning walk.

“Ismail, perhaps you should workshop the idea, before spending any good money on it”.

Satisfied that they had helped the situation they excused themselves and went about their day. Ismail scratched his head. He often felt that small exchanges like these with Mister and Missus Mwangi went nowhere. This was just the latest in a series of them that he managed to come away from, feeling worse-off for some reason.

***

Joseph had had a relaxing day. Far from being stressed about the forthcoming celebration, he was now rather looking forward to it.

Why did he leave it so long? He asked himself. But alas, all was not well in the Joseph's bowels. The cabbage rolls were beginning to make their passage through his intestines known to him.

It started with a very definite cramping he felt in his lower abdomen. At first Joseph worried that it may have been food poisoning. But an almighty rush of very unpleasant smelling wind from his rectum confirmed that it was just the aftereffects of the Golabki.

"The stack 'o pain from Zak-o-pane!"

His reference to the Polish dish causing him angst went unheard by everyone except Pussy, who didn't bother responding. She did however unwittingly acknowledge the effects of the rolls by trotting off at a quick pace the moment the offending smell was registered by her sensitive nostrils.

Any hope that Joseph may have had that the situation would ease throughout the day were dashed by repeated and more stinky eruptions. The only positive side was that for some inexplicable reason the noise quotient subsided. So, ultimately Joseph was releasing silent but very deadly (to one's sense of smell) farts.

By the time that Tymon and Barry came home Joseph was panicking about the situation. Both young men knew something was amiss when they entered the condo.

"What is that horrible stench!?" Said Barry. Nose shrivelled up in disgust.

Joseph appeared from the bedroom and told them the bad news.

"It was me! And that is with all of the doors and windows open too! It just lingers around and stays. I had a couple of gwompkee for brekkie. And now I can't stop farting!"

In unison, Barry and Tymon nodded and acknowledged their understanding with a combined 'uh-hhahhh'. Barry quipped.

"That's the only problem with those things. They come back to haunt you".

Joseph was a little incredulous at receiving a warning that was far too late to be of any use.

"Those gwompkee are going to come back and haunt everyone! Not just me!"

He was clearly exasperated. But without missing a beat Tymon had the perfect solution for him.

"Here's what you gotta do Joe. What you gotta do is, sever the fart umbilical cord".

His explanation raised more questions rather than solving the problem at hand. Or solving the noxious smell in the immediate atmosphere. Joseph frowned in perplexed pithy.

"The, what?" Joseph asked with more than a small note of incredulity.

Tymon was only too happy to explain in excruciating detail.

"The fart umbilical cord Joseph. Here is what happens. Let's say that you drop your guts here in the dining room, and then walk into the kitchen. The fart travels with you because it still has the fart umbilical cord attached from your behind to the stink lingering in the air. You pull it along with you. So, what you gotta do whenever you feel one coming on, is excuse yourself. Go to your bedroom. Let it rip, and then sever the fart umbilical cord with a swift waft of your hands behind your bum. Then the fart is released and cannot follow you. Leave it in the bedroom and close the door. Problem solved!"

Tymon was clearly overjoyed at the absurd solution he offered to Joseph. It was as if fart umbilical cords were a proven scientific fact that somehow Joseph had previously never known.

Seeing his disbelieving expression, Barry chipped in with further proof of the existence of the invisible thing.

“Air crew do this all the time in economy. And sometimes in business class. But I imagine, never in first class. If they take offence with the passengers for whatever reason, they slip out a silent but deadly one. And then walk the length of the cabin dragging it with them to spread it around”.

Barry sounded so completely convinced that what he was saying was true that it was somehow hard to disbelieve him. Tymon finished off the explanation.

“They call it crop dusting!”

Joseph was struggling to think of a way to tell the boys that it sounded totally irrational to him when his bowels alerted him to a forthcoming stench-explosion. He settled very quickly on a course of action.

“Let’s put it to the test, shall we? I can feel another one coming on now. I’ll drop it in the bedroom. Sever the fart umbilical cord. And come back here. If we don’t smell anything then I’ll believe you”.

“It’ll work, you’ll see”. Said Tymon encouragingly.

Joseph scurried away to this bedroom and waited for the inevitable out-gassing. Sure-enough it was a big one! He frantically waved his hand behind him to break the invisible cord attaching the fart to him. Then careful to close the door behind him he returned to the dining room.

The three of them stood there in silence. Joseph was the only one waiting for the inevitable stinky reprisal from his outpouring. But nothing happened. No acrid, foul-smelling odour assaulted anyone’s sense of smell. Joseph had a dawning of realisation upon his face. There really were more things in heaven and upon the earth than were dreamt of in his philosophy. And the existence of an umbilical cord between the fart and the originator was one of them.

Now absolutely convinced of the reality of them, Joseph thanked Tymon for his newfound knowledge on the subject.

"Perfect. Thank you very much Tymon. I had my doubts. But this is all of the proof that I need".

Chapter 34

It's the Fault of the Foie Gras!

Joseph, Barry and Tymon set about setting things up for the party, that would now, thankfully be free from offensive smelling odours. However, putrid odours were not going to be completely extinguished by the guys just yet. Un-witnessed by any of them Pussy had retreated to the laundry so that she could make use of the kitty litter.

"*That caviar went right through me*!" Pussy said to no one in particular.

After depositing the small cigar-butt shaped cylinders into the kitty litter, Pussy set about covering up her faeces with the small pellets. Pussy was a big fan of her kitty litter. If she was an outdoors cat, she would be forced to bury it in a planter box, or some other soft soil hiding hole. But this was so much easier and neater. And primary servant was always very good at cleaning up after her. Satisfied that the job was now done, Pussy trotted off and past the guys who were busy setting the dining room table up with all of the nibbles and other expensive treats.

The familiar smell of a kitty deposit soon registered with the three of them. The pellets would eventually suppress the smell, but there was the diamond to consider. It was probably a bit too early to hope that it was in this bowel movement. But better to be safe than sorry.

Joseph volunteered to recover it from the tray and set it aside for later. A thorough going through was required, but there simply wasn't time right now. He used one of the small Versace side plates to house the poop. Using some disposable latex gloves, he removed any errant pellets of kitty litter. He wasn't even sure why he did it. Soon enough the poop would have to be disassembled to see if it contained the family diamond. Certainly, upon first inspection, it did not appear to be present in this lot.

The intercom alerted them to an external visitor. Joseph answered it and to his surprise found that it was his father.

"I came early to help you set up". Said Harrington through the intercom.

Joseph let him in and introduced him to the guys.

"You must be my long-lost grandchild from Wollongong?" Harrington said with a wry smile.

"Wagga Wagga. That's were my family lives". Said Barry by way of correction.

"We have to get our stories straight for this to work Dad". Cautioned Joseph.

"I'm an old man Joseph. People will forgive a lack of specific knowledge at my age".

Joseph nodded in complete agreement. He too had come to expect that his father had let some pertinent facts slip through the cracks. Although he wasn't entirely sure if that was the result of old age, or that he had been a politician for his entire working life.

Many hands make light work, and soon enough all of the foods were displayed ready for the party. Joseph asked everyone if they would like to sample the champagne. Most of it would be delivered during the party, but he had secured one bottle earlier in the day and it was chilled nicely in his refrigerator. After giving his father the brief two-minute tour of the condo, Joseph pulled out the ornate bottle to show the guys what they would be celebrating with. They were all very impressed.

With a satisfying pop, the cork was pulled away from the bottle and Joseph poured each of them a flute. As per his deal with Gavin, the wire holder, caplet, and cork were secreted away into an urn in the living room for later recovery and return. They all retreated to the patio to cheers the success of the party.

The four of them looked like they did not have a care in the world. However, that is when you should probably be doing the most thinking about what could possibly go wrong. Pussy sidled her way up to the table. There was nobody around. With a lithe jump she was upon the table. It was full of the most wonderful smelling things.

Unfortunately, she could not see any of that 'caviar' anywhere. She reminded herself to let primary servant know to get some more. It was fabulous. But equally there was something else that caught the attention of her acute olfactory sense. Peering at the lid of the package that was displayed near to where the paste like thing was, Pussy couldn't quite make out what it was meant to spell? F.O.I.E. G.R.A.S?

Whatever kind of animal it was, one thing was certain, it smelled heavenly! So, naturally she tucked right into it. And she was correct. It was the most delectable thing that she had ever had in her life! Thankfully there was quite a lot of it too.

Pussy continued to devour the foie gras uninterrupted until Joseph decided to grab a taste of it himself. Maybe a bit on a cracker to see what all the fuss was about. When the site of the nearly completely demolished foie gras met his eyes, he shouted at pussy in a torrent of anger.

"PUSSY! WHAT THE HELL ARE YOU DOING!"

Disturbed and somewhat frightened by the tone of primary servant's voice, and volume, Pussy leapt down from the table. Tymon, Barry and Harrington hurried inside to find out what all of the commotion was about. When the scene greeted them, it was immediately evident what had happened. Joseph was furious. And he let Pussy know it.

"The foie gras isn't meant for you Pussy, it was for our party guests!"

Pussy was having none of it however and responded in a most condescending manner.

"*If those fwah grah didn't want Pussy to eat them, they wouldn't be so tasty!*"

Was that pure logic, or puerile logic? Joseph was unsure. Either way, this was something that he couldn't let Pussy get away with.

"What sort of idiotic excuse is that!" He said tersely to her.

Harrington was surprised to say the very least. Who was Joseph having this conversation with exactly? It's not as if the cat was talking back to him.

"Who are you talking to son?" He asked, with a worried look upon his features.

It was then that Joseph realised that he shouldn't be arguing with Pussy in front of anyone. Especially as nobody else seemed to be able to hear her. He had to backtrack quickly to prevent anyone from thinking that he was losing his grip on reality.

"Oh, umm. What… I meant to say was……She looked innocently at me. As if to say, I'm cute so I can eat anything I want".

Joseph hoped that the explanation was adequate. He must have succeeded as he saw his father roll his eyes in mild resignation and acceptance of the odd excuse.

"What am I going to do? The residents are ineffably snobbish when it comes to this stuff. I'm told that they won't eat pâté. And it's too late for me to go and get some more foie gras".

A knock at the door and a quick check that Pussy was safely out of site, revealed nothing to further alarm the situation. It was Millicent. There were quick introductions to Harrington.

"I'm here to get kitty settled in my place comfortably before arriving at the party a little later".

At least this was something that Joseph could solve. Harrington could see that Joseph was distressed and offered a course of action.

"I'll clean this up and see what else can be done. You help get Pussy and her paraphernalia out of here. OK?"

Joseph once more expressed his gratitude that Millicent was his partner in crime when it came to concealing Pussy from prying eyes. He bundled the cat up and helped Millicent transport the cat, her water bowl and food bowl and the kitty litter to Millicent's kitchen and laundry.

In the meantime, Tymon and Barry had removed the decimated foie gras leaving a rather obvious blank space on the otherwise lovely table setting. Harrington went to the refrigerator and scoured the contents. There was nothing that could be used as a centrepiece, replacing the foie gras. But then the words of Joseph echoed in his mind. If they weren't going to eat pâté, then why not put something there that simply looked like it.

Harrington searched through the cupboards until he found what he was looking for. Cat food done as a thick paste. In fact, it was even called Chicken and Quail pâté. It was perfect. Nobody would know the difference. And nobody would be eating it anyway. So, what did it matter?

Pleased that he had solved the immediate problem, Harrington opened the foil pack and pressed it out onto a small plate. It even looked like the stuff that you'd buy in the delicatessen. It was the perfect crime and absolutely nobody would get hurt. He gave it pride of place on the table.

Just in time too. The doorbell rang. When Barry answered it, it was some of the kitchen staff delivering the magnums of champagne. Thankfully they also supplied some rather large and very ornate ice buckets with ice to keep them chilled. One was set up on the patio and the other on the kitchen bench top.

Two of the staff would remain to serve the drinks. It was then that Joseph arrived back from Millicent's place. Ismail too had arrived by then and brought with him one of the residents. All of the commotion conspired to push the foie gras problem out of Joseph's mind. Ismail spoke.

"Joseph Whynee, I'd like you to meet Missus Yarrani Jagamara. Yarrani has been a resident with us for the past three years now".

Joseph was a little stunned. Yarrani Jagamarra was an Australian First Nations Aboriginal artist of quite some repute. He had no idea that she lived in the complex. His mind shifted into socialisation mode.

"I'm very pleased to meet you. I'm a fan of your work". He said taking her hand in greeting.

Yarrani looked him up and down and asked a question that immediately put Joseph on the back foot.

"I'm pleased to meet you. I was hoping to see the outfit that you purchased in the boutique the other day".

Joseph had to try his best not to sound exasperated. How was he going to explain that it had been trashed by the cat he was hiding in his home?

"It was a present for a friend. Who happens to be the same size as me. Which is why I tried it on. And…there you go".

Nothing that came out of Joseph's mouth managed to surprise Ismail by this stage. So, he didn't even flinch at the unusual explanation. Yarrani however, blinked in bemusement.

“What a lovely friend you are”. She said politely.

“Come in and let’s get this party started”. Said Joseph hoping (successfully) to end talk of the tragic outfit.

Chapter 35

If You Don't Know the Champagne Maisons; Someone Will

It did not take long for the remainder of the people to show up. About thirty other people showed up and soon the welcome party was in full swing. A late addition was Millicent Williams. And then a few minutes behind her was Charles Carver. Last to arrive was Isabella with Austin and Karalee in tow.

Ismail took it upon himself to introduce Joseph to the entire assembled crowd of residents in small batches. Starting out on the patio, Ismail introduced Joseph to Otieno and Hamima Mwangi. Their beautiful dark Kenyan skin hid the fact that both were over the age of fifty and in the same ballpark as Joseph. But they didn't look that old. Joseph was complimentary to their sense of dress as well.

"That reminds me. Didn't I see you in the lobby the other day with a new Versace outfit? Where is it? I'd love you to show it off"

Hamima Mwangi had unwittingly hit the sore nerve about the outfit. That was twice in as many minutes. Joseph groaned internally and made the same poor excuse that it was actually meant for somebody else. Otieno took the conversation in a different direction.

"We're both very glad to meet you, Joseph. Of course, Hamima and I heard that the winner of this condo was a former leader of an unspecified African country. Guilty of the most atrocious human rights abuses and a war criminal too. Somehow he had fled persecution and ended up here and with the winning ticket".

Joseph was stunned at the incorrect allegation. He shook his head in both disbelief and to reaffirm that he was definitely not the man at the centre of such an outlandish rumour.

"That's the first time I've heard that one. But I can assure you both, that I'm just a simple retired accountant. Newly divorced too. And looking for a quiet life here in at P.V. I'll bring my ex-wife and children over to say hello, shall I?"

The pair indicated that Joseph should do just that. As he left to fetch them, he heard the most unusual question from Hamima to Ismail.

"Have you given up using binoculars to try and scare away the seagulls from the water garden?"

Joseph almost turned around to see what Ismail's response was to the odd inquiry. But he elected to instead bring over Isabella, Austin, and Karalee to meet the Mwangis.

With the small chat out of the way, it was time once more for Ismail to move onto another couple of the residents. Next up were Mister Daan and Missus Saar Govender. Also, a similar age bracket to Joseph. If this was the average age for the residents, then he may have truly found his new tribe here amongst the rich and subdued. After the formal introductions and handshakes, Ismail added that the Govenders had moved from Mumbai to live permanently here.

Joseph couldn't help but think how exotic that was. He had never managed to visit India. He asked them for a bit of guidance for any future tourism that he may get around to one day.

"I've never visited India before. If I ever get around to it; where should I go first?"

Daan and Saar seemed to contemplate the question for a short time before Daan began the answer and Saar finished it off for him.

"I suppose it doesn't matter where you go. Just be sure that there is a five-, six- or seven-star hotel to stay in".

“That way you are assured to have a wonderful time”.

Completely oblivious to the fact that they had just discounted seeing any of the natural wonders that India is known for, Joseph was somewhat deflated. He noticed that neither had a drink in their hand and motioned for one of the staff to correct that oversight.

“What is it that we’re drinking?” Asked Daan.

“Tsarine Champagne”. Replied Joseph confidently.

“Oh, I know it well.” Began Saar.

“From Maison Chanoine founded in 1730. The Tsarine branded line began in 1741 when founder Pierre Chanoine met with the Tsarina Elisabeth Petrovna in Russia. He tailored his wines to suit her tastes and that of her royal court. Isn’t that interesting?”

The specificity of information from Saar Govender sent Joseph into a cold sweat. How could anybody possibly know a champagne so thoroughly? Even as the waiter poured Daan and Saar a flute of champagne Joseph was trying to come up with some clever reason why his cheap sparkling masquerading as champagne would not taste as they would expect.

In unison they both raised the glasses to their lips and had the smallest of sips. As if some comedic duo, their expressions changed from expectation to rude awakening as the flavour of the wine made itself known to their palettes.

“Oh, my goodness, I think that it is corked!” Exclaimed Daan.

“This is without doubt the most hideous champagne I have ever tasted!” Said Saar.

Ismail gave them both a worried look. He shot a glance to Joseph hoping for some refuge from the awkward situation. Finding no support whatsoever, he offered a defence of sorts.

"It came from a reputable supplier. The bottle shop associated with Swipe Rite down at Surfer's Paradise." Ismail's tone sounded anything but assured.

Thinking of Gavin Grosvenor as 'reputable' was not exactly how Joseph would have put it. But as he was complicit in this deception, he had to find a way to explain the disparity between real Tsarine Champagne and this cheap swill.

"I've heard that they sometimes bring in grey imports, you know, to cut costs".

Joseph hoped with all his might that the flimsy excuse would explain the dramatically different taste to the actual champagne.

"What on earth is a grey import?" Asked Daan.

Joseph was then forced to elaborate on his fib in order to give it more credence.

"When a champagne order is cancelled whilst still aboard a cargo ship. The freight forwarding company can then resell it while it is still en-route. The trouble is that the ship may be in the equatorial region for a lengthy period of time. That could have affected the champagne. I mean, I don't know for sure of course. But it would be one explanation".

Daan and Saar, thankfully nodded in acceptance of the situation. However, Ismail interjected with perhaps the worst possible alternative explanation for the unusual tasting champagne.

"Perhaps it is a consignment of fake champagne?"

It was like having a nail in the coffin of his credibility hammered home. Joseph cringed as he heard the hypothesis. It felt like he was on public trial. There was nothing further that he could think of to deflect suspicion from falling upon him.

"You'd know all about fake merchandise Joseph. Do you think that it is?" Daan asked innocently.

The question hit Joseph in the heart of his integrity, or lack thereof. He was struggling to come up with any answer that would dissipate the accusation. Saar however came to his inadvertent rescue with some obvious logic.

“But the champagne was delivered by one of our regular suppliers. Surely, they would be the ones that had succumbed to the fraudsters? Not Joseph.”

Saved by the sudden turn of events, Joseph breathed a soft sight of relief. But it was to be very short lived. Ismail offered a way out for all of them.

“Why don’t I send down to the kitchen for a regular bottle of Tsarine champagne. We can do a blind taste testing and see what the differences are. I’ll send you the bill later if that is alright Joseph?”

Trapped by his desire to make a good impression on the crowd, Joseph had no alternative but to accept the expensive offer. Even as he nodded his acquiescence, he could feel the dollars flying out of his wallet.

As it transpired, the real item arriving from the kitchen caused a sensation amongst the guests. Not some, but all of them had registered that something wasn’t quite right with the champagne that was being served. Joseph could hear comments like “swill”, “acid on my tongue”, “Possum pee”, and “vile fizz”.

Without exception each of them fell like dominoes, requesting replacement champagne from the kitchen. Ismail was only too happy to oblige. Each time looking at Joseph for a visual nod of agreement. Before he knew it, the condominium was filled with bottles of real Tsarine champagne.

Joseph broke out in a cold sweat as he tried to add up in his head, how much this was going to cost him. Luckily, or unluckily, depending upon your point of view, Ismail was busy distracting Joseph with further introductions.

Chapter 36

Some Pâté is More Palatable than Others

Harrington Whynee was chatting with a lovely couple that had moved from New Zealand to live in Palazzo Versace. Mister Ari and Missus Tia Nanaia, a native Māori couple had run a very successful string of hotels on the South Island of New Zealand. Now basically retired, they decided that a warmer climate overall was required and made Queensland their new home.

Luckily, they were not aware of the specifics of Harrington Whynee's long political career. Nor his status as an only child. So, they took it for granted that when Harrington introduced Barry to them, that he was indeed Harrington's grandson.

"You have to try one of the kielbasa sausages. My partner Tymon made them himself. He's from Poland".

Barry indicated the small sausages on the table. Both husband and wife availed themselves of the opportunity.

"Lovely" Said Tia

"Very good" Affirmed Ari.

It was then that Ari noticed that there was no foie gras being served. He commented to Barry and Harrington.

“I see that Joseph has decided not to serve the recommended foie gras. Is he an animal liberationist?”

Neither Barry nor Harrington knew of Joseph’s stance on animal rights. They gave each other a worried glance as if asking for any input on the subject that may shed light on the subject. Finding no help Harrington ventured with a generic (and consummate politician’s) answer.

“Of course, making foie gras in the traditional way is animal cruelty. So, Joseph decided to take a stand and only serve pâté. You understand?”

It was a very diplomatic answer. And it played into Harrington’s hands perfectly. It would be best if nobody touched the kitty food at all. To his horror however, Ari was more than willing to support a change of appetite.

“Living here has really spoilt Tia and I. Maybe you’re right Harrington. Perhaps it is time that we made more ethical and sustainable food choices. I’ll give it a go. What type is it do you know?”

Harrington had a growing sense of horror as Ari surrendered to the possibility of eating pâté instead of foie gras. He tried to intercept Ari’s sense of politeness.

“No need to go out of your way to accommodate Ari. Ismail warned Joseph that nobody would touch the stuff. No need to be a pioneer”.

But the dissuasion had no effect on Ari whatsoever. He reached for a small cracker and used the small serving knife to spread some onto its surface. He offered it to Tia first, who took it from him. Then Ari set about preparing another for his own consumption. Harrington tried to remember the flavour of the kitty food that he had substituted for real pâté. As Ari and Tia both put it into their mouths, Harrington was able to confirm the category of the food.

“I believe that it is chicken, with a hint of quail”. He said almost gagging as he finished the sentence.

Ari’s expression left everybody in absolutely no doubt that the substance was not to his liking at all. Nevertheless, he persevered and with final push, swallowed the morsel. Tia too could be seen to visibly wince at the tang of the flavour.

“It’s an acquired taste”. Tia commented.

“Not the sort of taste that I’d like to acquire anytime soon”. Responded Ari.

Much to Harrington’s relief, Ari and Tia washed the unusual flavour out of their mouth, each with a swig of champagne. Ari voiced his escape from any further assault upon his taste buds.

“I think that I’ll stick to the cheeses, and of course, to those lovely kielbasa sausages”.

The sound of the intercom interrupted them. Barry was closest and answered it. He looked at Harrington and then pushed the button to allow entry.

“Grandfather, you have a visitor. Someone by the name of Cool Allah?” Barry said.

Harrington corrected Barry and explained who the newcomer was.

“Cru-Ellah. My date for the party. We live in the same facility down at Coolangatta. You’ll love her. She is an absolute riot”.

Chapter 37

The Fastest Way to Destroy Dental Work

Isabella had somehow become stuck talking with Charles Carver. It did not take her long to realise that he was a complete snob and didn't mind everyone knowing it. She looked around the room hoping to find some excuse to get away from him. But there was no visible opportunity that afforded her an escape. Resigned to listen the bore prattle on and on about himself, Isabella sighed internally.

But then something intriguing happened. He made mention in passing about her ex-husband's case. It was something to do with a consultation that she was unaware of that Joseph had had with Charles Carver.

"Wait just a minute please Charles. Did you say that you'd been speaking about Joseph to your colleagues? May I ask about what exactly? Does he have some sort of neurological disorder that I was unaware of?"

Ethically of course, Dr Carver was unwilling to discuss such matters in any way except nonspecific detail.

"I couldn't say anything without contravening the doctor and patient confidentiality bond. You understand of course?".

Charles looked about the room as he spoke. He caught Joseph's eye and motioned for him to join them.

"But, if he were here with us, then I'm sure that the situation would be different".

Joseph managed to extract himself from the latest mini conversation that he was having with another couple that Ismail had just introduced him to. After promising to return to Ismail's side so that he could continue to do the rounds, he sidled up to Isabella.

"Interesting crowd, aren't they?" Joseph said.

Isabella had not really had the opportunity to find out, and let Joseph know it.

"I need to circulate more and find out. But in the meantime, Charles was telling me that he has had a consultation with you? What is that all about?"

Joseph suddenly and inexplicably put on the expression of a trapped animal. Isabella picked up on it immediately. But Charles seemed oblivious. Perhaps because he was so completely self-centred. He did interject with some further detail that was hinted at previously, but now became stated explicitly.

"I've been consulting with some of my colleagues about your case Joseph. All seem in agreement that such a thing simply could not be based within the realms of their experience. That is why I have not proceeded with the brain-scan. I'm perplexed with what the next step should be?"

'What on earth has he got himself into now?' Thought Isabella. As if able to read her mind, Joseph attempted to explain the 'problem' in a way that she would understand but Charles would not.

"I've been having trouble with my cataracts. It felt like a little set of sharp fangs had pierced them a couple of weeks ago. But nothing since. I'm sure that it was just a one off. No need for any further action I'm sure".

Lucky for Joseph the reference to 'fangs' had indeed alerted Isabella to the fact that somehow Pussy the cat was involved.

Nothing that he could talk about openly with these guests of course. So, she made a snap decision to support his point of view. And, if possible, sure it up.

“Yes, indeed Joseph. No need to hurry into anything. It could all just be your over-active imagination. Couldn’t it?”

Isabella’s inference to Joseph’s overly alarmed demeanour came as no surprise to Charles. He looked at Joseph for confirmation of the assertion. As luck would have it (bad luck that is), there was a natural lull in the conversation throughout the party. Therefore, when Joseph hurriedly spoke to support his ex-wife’s explanation, his voice could be heard clearly throughout the condominium.

“I’m a complete hypochondriac really, there’s nothing more to it!”

People’s heads turned to look at Joseph. Shocked by the sudden echoing of his own words around the crowded but silent apartment, Joseph visibly stiffened. He could feel the blood rushing to his face. Frantic for some way to divert attention from himself, his gaze settled upon the table. The plate of kielbasa sausages was the first thing that came into sharp focus.

“How about a Polish sausage. I think that you’ll really like them?”

Without waiting for a response from either Charles or Isabella, Joseph scurried over to the table and picked up the small plate. He did not register that there appeared to be more of them on the plate now, than when the party first started.

***

Whilst the conversation between Charles, Isabella and Joseph had been happening, Harrington had let Cru-Ellah in, and was busy showing her around the condominium. She was very impressed and commented that it was even more luxurious than their living arrangements in the Golden Years retirement village.

At some point he even poked his head into the laundry. Maybe it was worth showing Cru-Ellah this as it had lovely marble floors and a patterned ceiling.

"Check out this laundry Cru. Even the utility room is ornate".

Harrington had barely finished complimenting the room when he noticed a small Versace plate of what looked like the kielbasa sausages.

"Look at this Cru. Someone has been hoarding the sausages!"

Cru-Ellah offered her resolution to the unusual situation.

"Take them out to the dining room. Someone is sure to eat them". She said.

Harrington picked up the plate of small cigar-butt shaped objects and continued with the tour. When they finished, it was back in the dining room where it had begun. Harrington dumped the sausages onto the same serving plate as the other ones.

"Let's grab a drink at go outside to the patio". He suggested.

"I've got a better idea". Cru-Ella offered, with a mischievous grin.

***

Joseph made it to the table to retrieve the kielbasa sausages in record time. The general chat noise levels of the party had mercifully returned to a normal din. He fronted up to Isabella and Charles offering them the plate in one hand and a small clutch of napkins in the other.

Isabella took a sausage and a napkin and proceeded to eat it. She produced a yummy sound as she did so and gave Joseph and Charles a look of approval of the little morsel. Charles was next he lifted one suspiciously from the plate. It seemed to be a little malleable in his fingers. After contemplating for a second, he decided to just pop the entire little thing in his mouth and chew.

He did so and it produced an immediate and startling reaction. His face screwed up as if he was in agony. The bite into the sausage released the most putrid flavour he had ever encountered in his life! Almost as a reaction he bit down the second time but instead of finding compliant paste like sausage, his upper and lower molars met with an object of unbelievable hardness.

"AAAARRRRGHHHH OOOOHHHHMMMMPHHH !"

Charles instinctively expelled the entire contents of his mouth into the napkin, whilst coughing and objecting in sounds rather than words. Isabella and Joseph looked on with mounting concern.

"Oh my goodness Charles, are you alright?" Asked Joseph.

It took a few moments for Charles to compose himself enough to explain what had happened. He did so whilst uncrumpling the napkin to examine the contents. There were three distinct objects in it. Firstly, the mashed remains of the 'sausage'. Second, a piece of one of Charles molar teeth. Lastly, although covered in slimy residue, the Whynee family cushion cut diamond.

Joseph was stunned.

"My family diamond! How did it get into the sausages?"

Joseph handed the plate to Isabella to free up one of his hands. Then without asking for approval, Joseph reached forward and plucked the diamond from the mess Charles was holding. He gave it a wipe with one of his napkins and held it up triumphantly.

"Yes, that's it alright. I don't understand".

Even as he spoke the words the realisation of what must have happened dawned upon him. He shot Isabella a look, who had reached the very same conclusion. Somehow the diamond had made record time through Pussy's innards, and he had served up a cat turd to one of his neighbours. Joseph suspiciously gave the diamond a single sniff. The resultant stench confirmed his worst fears. Scrambling for an explanation that would somehow cover up what had really happened he spoke without really thinking it through.

"Do you think that one of the sausages went rancid from sitting out too long?"

Charles was far from concerned with the hideous taste of the Polish delicacy. Instead, he was clearly fuming over the state of his teeth.

"I've chipped a sizeable chunk off my porcelain crown. I can feel it with my tongue. It's sharp!"

Charles was focused upon the state of his dental work, which luckily distracted him from the foul aftertaste in his mouth from the sausage. Isabella did her best to help the situation.

"Best if I throw these sausages away in case there is more than one that has turned bad".

Joseph nodded frantically in agreement. Eyes wide as he regarded the plate full of objects in alarm. Grateful to get out of the situation, Isabella made a quick exit to find a bin in which to deposit the plate of sausages.

Ismail, alerted to the commotion came over to see if there was anything that he could do to help.

"Can I be of assistance Doctor Carver?"

Charles was angry and he didn't mind letting everyone know it.

"Yes, actually. You can tell me how a diamond can get cooked into a rancid sausage and served to me?"

The question of course, could not be answered by Ismail. Naturally he looked to Joseph searching for some kind of reason within the unbelievable event. In reply, Joseph could do little but look completely stunned. It was then that his bowels reminded him that he was still suffering from the effects of the cabbage rolls. He decided to excuse himself and retreat to the bedroom to dispose of the forthcoming flatulence.

Leaving behind Charles and Ismail, and a number of the other party attendees that had been watching from a polite distance, Joseph moved with haste down the short hallway to his bedroom door. It was closed. Nothing suspicious there, as he had earlier on, deposited a little unpleasant smelling invisible cloud in the master bedroom. And severed its umbilical, ensuring no escape.

Guessing that it would have dissipated by now and without any hesitation he swung the door open. The site that greeted him made him loose control of his sphincter and he let rip an abnormally loud fart. It would have surely been heard back in the dining room and beyond.

His embarrassment at breaking wind was completely obscured by the fact that he found Harrington and Cru-Ellah engaged in wrinkled senior citizen sex. The sight of his father penetrating

Cru-Ella doggy style was too much for Joseph. He shrieked at volume.

The scream brought Isabella, Tymon, Barry and Ismail running to find out what had alarmed Joseph so much. Harrington and Cru-Ellah to their credit, stopped grinding each other long enough to give Joseph a surprised look. Which rapidly turned to disapproval at being disturbed.

Suddenly aware that multiple people were approaching down the hallway, Joseph reached in for the door handle and slammed the bedroom door shut. The least that he could do in the situation was preserve the privacy of the amorous couple.

By now the small party had arrived to an acrid smelling hallway. Each of them reacted in their own ways. Isabella frantically fanning the air and accusing Joseph verbally of the misdemeanour.

"Joe, what on earth have you been eating!"

There was no hiding from it. They all heard it. And now they were all smelling the evidence firsthand. Even the usually unflappable Ismail Islington had to pause and cover his nose with his cupped hand.

"What seems to be the problem. Other than the obvious one of course?" he inquired.

Joseph was at a loss. What could he possibly say to cover up the fact that he had caught his dad and dad's partner in his bedroom having sex? He need not have bothered to even attempt to gloss over the situation. A muffled but still easily heard explanation came from Cru-Ellah herself.

"OHHHH HARRINGTON!"

Immediately, the entire small group understood what must have been happening in Joseph's master bedroom suite. There was a moment of pure collected embarrassment that passed between them all. Unwilling or unable to think of anything that would lessen the awkwardness of the situation one by one, each of them gave Joseph a knowing nod of understanding before moving back to the living room.

Tymon motioned to Joseph to sever the umbilical of this particularly noxious invisible cloud. Certainly, nobody wanted it to follow them back to the party.

There was still the matter of Charles Carver to contend with. He appeared from the guest water closet where he must have been rinsing out his mouth and inspecting the damage that the diamond had done to his dental work. Even though Joseph had no idea how he was going to explain how the situation came about, he couldn't help but feel relieved. At least he would not have to pay for an expensive brain scan. The situation had worked out for the best.

Charles was clearly annoyed and let Joseph know it.

"One molar chipped, and my lower crown mostly destroyed".

He looked accusingly at Joseph as if silently demanding an explanation of the events. Figuring that this time it would be better to not say anything, Joseph put on his best expression of concern.

As there was no further information forthcoming from Joseph, Charles decided to lay out his plan of action.

"Luckily, my dentist is one of the best in the country. I'm certain that he will see me as soon as possible to get the damage repaired. I will be sure to send you the bill. Good evening, mister Whynee!"

With that, Charles made a rather angry exit from the party. Joseph's former feeling of being freed from the cost of the brain scan, was jarringly replaced with expensive dental work. His eyes sank to the floor. He even went to say his usual 'why me' catch phrase but caught himself before it came out of his mouth.

Ismail decided that it was time once more to restart Joseph's introduction to the residents that he had not yet met. It was a merciful distraction for them both. As it turned out, there was quite an eclectic mix of people from around the country and around the world. The residents came from such diverse places as South Africa, Mexico, Colombia, Chile, and the United Kingdom.

Millicent Williams wanted to know what had upset her ostentatious son so much. When Ismail explained that he had damaged his teeth on a Polish sausage she laughed raucously.

"Serves him right!" She said.

Thankfully there were no follow up questions about exactly how a '*kielbasa sausage*' had managed to accomplish such a feat.

Chapter 38

Credibility is a Fragile Thing

The party was going rather well. Joseph had now met everybody and was busy circulating. He was puzzled by a few of the residents pointing out how good the pâté was that he had served. Whilst others were not so praising of it. He made a mental note to find out from his father how he had come up with a replacement for the foie gras.

At some point he noticed that Ismail was standing by himself beside the cabinet in the living room. He was holding something and looking at the floor. Joseph decided to investigate. He approached from behind to ascertain what was happening without being seen by the residential relationship manager.

To his surprise, Ismail was using a laser pointer on Pussy Two Shoes. He was flicking it around the floor in the impossible hope of getting the stuffed animal to chase it.

"You know that it's not real right!?"

Joseph's exclamation took Ismail by surprise. He jumped with fright. Then looking somewhat guilty at being discovered he offered his lame excuse to Joseph.

"It looks so completely real, that I couldn't help myself".

For the first time since moving into the exclusive residence, the shoe was on the other foot. This time it was Joseph looking incredulously at Ismail instead of the reverse. But Joseph's moment of superiority was short lived.

Harrington and Cru-Ella had finished their tryst in the bedroom and were re-joining the party. Harrington was carrying the coat hanger that contained the mangled jacket, top and trousers that Joseph had purchased from the Versace boutique in the hotel lobby.

As they appeared at the top step leading down into the sunken living room, Harrington held up the outfit for everyone to see and said loudly over the various conversations.

"I found this mangled Versace outfit on the back of your bedroom door son. What's the story?"

As people took in the sight of the expensive clothes that had been shredded there was an audible collective gasp from the crowd. Silence replaced the conversational party atmosphere. All eyes turned from the clothes toward Joseph. He could feel everyone staring disapprovingly at him.

How on earth was he going to explain this one? Chancing a brief look to confirm his worst fears, he found expressions of horror and criticism painted on the faces that he managed to take in. The room suddenly felt empty of air and Joseph was finding it difficult to breathe. He was unsure if he was blushing or not. But the prevailing feeling of doom prevented him from caring about his appearance.

Then as luck would have it, Joseph caught sight of Yarrani Jagamarra. In that instant he was struck with either the most inspirational flash of brilliance that he had ever had in his life, or the most idiotic. Only time would tell.

A long time had elapsed from Harrington asking Joseph about the clothing without resulting in an answer. Taking in a deep breath Joseph told the crowd exactly what the reason was for the unusual sight.

"It's… art!"

There was a confused 'huh?' from most of the people present. Frowns of judgement turned into expressions of confusion. There was nothing to it now; Joseph had already started down this road, there was no going back. He decided to throw himself into the lie boots and all.

"Yes. Art!. And the reaction that you all gave was exactly what I was hoping for. Thank you all very much. It is very gratifying to find that I can achieve what I set out to do with this piece".

Conversation began again but only as a soft murmur. Probably people discussing their understanding of Joseph's outrageous claim. Joseph acted quickly to underline his position with a few small embellishments.

"I spent hours and hours getting it just the way that I wanted it. That is no random destruction of clothes you know".

It was the local artist that offered some of alternative viewpoint to the bizarre piece of textile art. Yarrani asked from where she was standing talking with a few of the other residents.

"Joseph, is this some kind of response to the *incident* in the mail room with the custom's officers?"

There was a general consensus of approving noises from the residents. Perhaps Joseph had had some kind of mini nervous breakdown, or the like. Scrambling to keep credibility on his side Joseph did what he does best and improvised.

"You know, I think that must have been an influence on me yes Yarrani. I saw this outfit in the boutique window and knew immediately what I wanted to do and what I wanted to achieve with the outcome. All I need to do now is get it framed and then put on sale."

Without realising it, Yarrani had become an unwitting supporter of Joseph's fabricated fantasy. Her next words only served to play further into Joseph's ploy.

"Then you will probably want to sell it on consignment at the Dalozzo Art Gallery in the Marina Mirage centre. They can arrange for the framing for you as well. I have a couple of paintings on sale in the gallery at the moment".

Yarrani's support was exactly the voice of credibility that he needed to make his lie become the truth. Harrington gave the garments another look and offered his take on the validity of the destroyed garments as a piece of art. His tone was of obvious incredulousness.

"Somebody is expected to pay for this?"

Austin leapt to his father's defence though.

"I never knew you had an artistic bone in your body Dad. Good on you!"

With the immediate disaster averted, Joseph gave a very humble thanks to Austin and Yarrani and the crowd for supporting his newfound artistic endeavour. Harrington was resigned to accepting the prevailing opinion of the group. Shaking his head in disbelief he returned the hanger and its controversial contents to Joseph's bedroom.

***

The party continued along for a while quite nicely after the series of dramatic earlier events. It was getting close to the time when people would start to excuse themselves and make a polite exit. Joseph guessed that it was because the plethora of cheeses had all but run out and there was no more of the mysteriously appearing pâté that seemed to be a hit with half of the snobbish crowd. Harrington had insisted on refreshing that particular morsel himself each time. And then disappeared to the laundry to do it for some odd reason. Joseph made a mental note to ask him about it later.

As if reading his mind, Harrington appeared with Cru-Ellah in tow.

"Great party son. Who knew that rich people could be so lovely!"

Joseph was a little offended by the snide comment.

"Dad, I don't think that being rich and being obnoxious go hand in hand".

Harrington was quick to correct his son's viewpoint.

"Tell that to Doctor Charles Carver".

Indeed, with that particular person, ineffable snobbishness did manage to permeate his entire being. Joseph would have perhaps attempted to argue the point some more but Cru-Ellah interjected with her own line of inquiry.

"Joseph, darling. Does your artistic flair stem from a more deep seeded need to express yourself and perhaps make up for other.......shortcomings in your life?"

It was an odd question to say the very least. Joseph had no context and quite frankly did not understand what it was that Cru-Ellah was asking. He attempted to get to the heart of the matter to clarify his understanding.

"I suppose that could be. But I'm unsure of how trying something new such as textile art has a connection to any of my perceived deficiencies. Could you please be more specific?"

It was Harrington that interjected at this point. His demeanour was one more akin to shady businessman rather than a loving father.

"Come on son. We have no secrets here. No need to be bashful about your little.........problem".

His Dad's comment fell upon fallow ground. Joseph had absolutely no idea what he could be referring to.

"Dad whatever it is that you want me to admit to you had better let me know. Because we're not going to get there by pussyfooting around".

The direct request for specifics seemed to catch both Cru-Ellah and Harrington off guard. They blubbered a little. Mostly about not wanting to blurt it out or anything like that. But Joseph was insistent.

"What is it? Please tell me Dad".

Harrington gave Cru-Ellah a knowing look and then proceeded to open the veil of secrecy a bit at a time until the entire terrible scene was laid bare.

"Cru-Ellah is very close with her daughter. They share everything. No secrets you know. That kind of thing".

Joseph indicated that his father should continue to elaborate.

"It was Cru's daughter that told her of a recent misadventure and Cru told me. You understand we have the knowledge firsthand from a reliable witness".

Joseph indicated with a facial expression to his father that he still needed more information.

"Well, it was easy to figure out. How many people live here at Palazzo Versace and go shopping at the discount grocery store in Southport?"

Joseph shrugged indicating that Harrington needed to provide further illumination on the subject.

"And how many of those people are named Joseph and have won their condominium from the RSL. So, it had to be you that the poor girl told Cru about."

"What poor girl?" Joseph demanded.

"Cru-Ellah's daughter….Josephine".

The magnitude of horror that erupted in Joseph was immeasurable because it was so high. Josephine had blabbed to Cru-Ellah about what had happened and what she had seen in the shower. She must be under the impression that his body is nothing short of hideous and that his penis is ultra-small. Without realising the volume of his own voice, and definitely without thinking through what he was about to say, Joseph blurted out his defence for all to hear.

"DAD. I DON'T HAVE A SMALL PENIS!"

The overly loud announcement brought the entire party to a halt. Shocked guests turned to look at Joseph so quickly that they nearly hurt their necks. Acutely aware that he had said something entirely inappropriate for the setting, Joseph turned his gaze slowly over the room to see if anyone had noticed his words. The wide-eyed looks of his guests left him in no doubt that everyone had.

There really was no recovering from this one. Cru-Ellah and Harrington weren't offering any lifeline for the beleaguered party host. Looking around desperately for something to diffuse the situation Joseph's eyes fell upon Isabella.

"Isabella, may I please have a martini, make it a double".

Grateful that Joseph hadn't asked for affirmation of his statement from her in front of the crowd, Isabella moved quietly to prepare the drink for Joseph.

And that was the tipping point for the party. Although conversation managed to get started again, guests began to leave in their droves. Joseph could feel the minor piece of credibility that he had manufactured by suddenly becoming a textile artist, dissipate into thin air.

Ultimately, he felt it an exercise in futility to try and explain to Cru-Ellah and his father what had precipitated the shower incident. So, Joseph didn't even try. Instead, he did his best to not look horribly embarrassed as he bid goodbye to the party attendees as they left. Then after a while it was just Barry, Tymon and himself.

They cleaned up the aftermath of the gathering without saying very much. Much later when Joseph recovered Pussy and her paraphernalia from Millicent, he discovered the open packets of cat food in the laundry bin.

Joseph's mouth fell open as he realised that the 'pâté' being served by his father to the guests was in fact Pussy's kitty food. But he had received so many compliments about it? The stuff must be better than he would have thought.

It was the effects of excessive alcohol that demanded that Joseph retire early for the evening. Pussy snuggled up beside him and soon he was fast asleep. It would have been a lovely night's rest too had it not been for a repeat of the disembodied vagina's dream. Except this time, instead of female genitals chasing him, it was Tsarine Champagne bottles.

In his subconscious, Joseph knew that he was going to pay a hefty financial price for the party. All he could do was hope that it would not be as bad as he imagined.

Chapter 39

Self-Help Gurus Seldom Help Others

The party was fading from memory the following day. Joseph felt obliged to take the 'art' Versace outfit over to the gallery in the neighbouring retail centre. The owner that greeted him was helpful and encouraging. Joseph indicated that the outfit be displayed as if it were on a person and put behind glass to protect the many threads that were hanging off it.

Once his wishes were established, the owner let Joseph know that it would take a few days for the mounting and framing to be finished. He would give Joseph a phone call when it was ready for viewing and subsequent sale by consignment.

Satisfied that his day was already looking up, Joseph spent the rest of the morning going over his notes. The practical exam for his marine license was imminent. Joseph was not nervous, having done so well in the written part of the test. But he thought it safe to be as prepared as possible.

He was by now back in his condominium and looking for some words of encouragement online for his forthcoming exam. He used the usual search engine to see if it would pay some dividends. It directed him to a video sharing site and a video from a self-help guru.

This one had millions of views and centred around a middle-aged man who had let his salt and pepper hair grow long and put it into the obligatory ponytail. It screamed midlife crisis to Joseph, but he decided to watch it through anyway.

"Not fulfilling your full potential. Unsure of the direction that your life should take. Then you need my sage words of advice. The most successful people in the world use these motivation principles to remove any doubt that they can do whatever they want. And they will work for you too!"

The introductory spin from the fellow certainly did its job well. Joseph was now hooked on finding out exactly what those sage words of advice would be. He imagined that the message would be something simple and spoken many times before. Like, seize the day, or words to that effect. Nevertheless, he really wanted to know what the ultimate message was that the fellow as peddling.

"You can benefit from the same motivational messages that many of the top earners, the biggest stars, the most admired people in the world use every day".

Joseph was getting impatient with the build-up and wanted the payoff.

"Get to it would you!?" He said to screen.

However, the point that the guru wanted to get to was not the one that Joseph wanted.

"Subscribe to my daily, weekly, fortnightly or monthly videos and you too will find a new resilience and zest for the everyday humdrum that bogs you down now. I have something that will suit any budget. And remember, the more that you spend the more motivation you will get".

With the 'punchline' revealed, Joseph was not just deflated he felt somehow betrayed by this free video. It was meant to give him the new outlook on life that he needed. Or, at least, thought that he needed. A message on the overall costings of the various plans were then shown on screen. The man was explaining them, but Joseph had switched off and was now simply irritated that he had not received the motivational message for free. It was then that Pussy made an appearance and asked in passing what Joseph was watching. He responded by reading the title of the video to her. Pussy's reply was a bit of surprise to Joseph. She seemed to know more about the man than he did.

"Oh, Steven Summersmore; the motivational speaker. Although, Pussy has heard him called Steven wants-more and Steven gets-more."

Joseph was genuinely surprised. He didn't contemplate that Pussy took notice of such things. And he chuckled at the play on the man's surname. It certainly did paint a picture of a self-help guru that was only really helping himself to more subscribers and more money.

"That's funny Pussy. I love it."

However, the hilarity that Pussy was referring to was not what Joseph thought. Her next words confirmed that she was indeed referring to something else entirely.

"Yes. Humans having surnames. What a funny lot you are. Cats of course never use them. What would be the point?"

Pussy's minor revelation caused Joseph to shake his head. He needed to readjust his thinking of exactly what Pussy was referring to.

"I'd assumed that you had my surname?" Said Joseph with a hint of offence.

"Why would Pussy have your surname. Pussy doesn't even know what it is?"

This irritated Joseph far more than he would have thought possible.

"What do you mean you DON'T know what my surname is? You must have heard it countless times over the last few years?"

Pussy looked up at the ceiling and then at Joseph before answering in her droll way.

"No. Not a clue".

"It's WHYNEE!" Joseph snapped at her.

Pussy looked for the world like she had never before heard the name and then managed to further inflame Joseph by misrepresenting it back to him for confirmation.

"*Why-me?*"

"No! Why. NEE!"

Pussy's tone reflected that she thought that the whole discussion was a waste of her valuable time. But she did impress upon Joseph that she had her own ideas when it came to such things. And taking Whynee as her second name was definitely not part of her thinking.

"*If Pussy was to take on a surname, in the cat-world, the surname would be used first and then the first name. Pussy has always liked the name of that company that primary servant used to work for. Big Lips*".

Joseph frowned at the very mention of the company that had so casually discarded him after years of loyal service. Pussy clarified the feline viewpoint on the matter.

"*It would be Big Lips Pussy to the cats of the world. Or Pussy Big Lips to the humans*".

Neither of the names had any appeal to Joseph in the slightest. Nevertheless, Pussy continued to elaborate on the nomenclature.

"And you could be called, Jedediah Big Lips, or Big Lips Jedediah".

Pussy concluded with a self-satisfied licking of one of her front paws.

"My name is Joseph!"

"*Tom-arto; to-may-toe. Nobody cares*".

Deciding that it was best to end this conversation as quickly as possible Joseph conceded that perhaps adopting a surname was not the direction that Pussy should be taking.

"You know what Pussy; forget the surname. You can continue to be one of those single name identities that are known by just one. Like Cher".

"*Who?*"

"Forget it Pussy. It's not important".

"*That is what Pussy has been telling you all along*!"

Joseph groaned audibly and decided to wait for the examiner for his practical sailing exam at the security entrance to the marina. Closing the lid to his laptop he let his petulant cat know that he had the exam pending and that he would be gone for the entire afternoon.

***

Even without any motivational messages to take with him in the exam, Joseph felt that he completely nailed the practical. There wasn't a manoeuvre that the examiner could ask for that Joseph could not fulfil with aplomb. Even before they made it back to the marina and 'Beat The Odds' berth, the examiner let Joseph know that he had passed the exam.

There was nothing standing in the way of Joseph taking paying passengers on leisure cruises around the waterways of the Gold Coast. Everything was going exactly as Joseph had planned. The license would be approved, and he could get it in his hand by the end of the week. It would mean queuing at the local maritime services office. But Joseph didn't mind.

After gratuitously shaking the examiners hand and thanking him profusely, Joseph bade him farewell. He decided that the best way for him to celebrate was to post an advertisement on one of the local community noticeboards about his new service. He hurried home to log on and do just that.

It wasn't long before he had posted notification about his service online. Now all he had to do was sit back and wait for the first of his paying passengers to take up his offer.

Chapter 40

Sometimes You Succeed; Despite Yourself

Joseph was walking around on a cloud of success. He had endured the crowds at the local Maritime Services office, and he had in his hand his marine license. Every time he looked at it, he imagined what his new life would be like. Sailing all of his cares away and at the same time earning money. It was too good to be true.

Not that he had ever engaged in such things, not even as a youth; but this is what it must feel like to be high on an illegal narcotic. Such feelings though are usually short lived as Joseph was about to find out.

Upon returning to his condominium, he decided to check for mail and found two letters in his post box. Curiously, neither of them had a postage stamp on them. They would therefore have been placed there in person. Also, both simply had his name on them rather than the full postal address, confirming his assumption. The writing was different on both though. Clearly, each was from a different person.

Returning to the condo before opening them, Joseph was more than a little shocked at the first one. It was the bill for Charles Carver's repaired dental work.

"EIGHT GRAND!" Joseph shouted as he read the abnormally expensive figure.

All sense of joy and contentment dissipated from Joseph, like a drop of water in a sandy desert. He sank into one of the tub chairs and once more looked at the cost of Charles' tooth repairs that he would have to pay for.

"Why me?" He said with forlorn melancholy.

It was then that he realised that there was another letter that he had not opened. Fearing the worst (wisely), he opened it and read the contents. It was from Ismail and was the bill for supplying actual Tsarine champagne to the party.

"THREE GRAND!"

This was a double kick in the guts for him. He was aghast. How could they have consumed three thousand dollars' worth of champagne? What a thirsty hoard the attendees turned out to be. Joseph would have spent much longer feeling sorry for himself, but his mobile phone interrupted him.

"What now!" He asked suspiciously.

Answering the call, he found himself talking to the gallery owner that had his 'art work' on sale.

"I'm so glad that I caught you. Is it at all possible for you to drop by soon? I have the most exciting news".

In spite of the double whammy that Joseph had just endured, he couldn't help but feel enthused by the man's tone.

"Yes, sure. I can come over right now. See you soon".

He hung up and deposited both of the expenses on the coffee table. Then he put his hands on his waist and glared at the table in a rather hostile way.

"*What is primary servant doing?*"

Pussy had appeared from somewhere and was observing him. One of her favourite things to do. Joseph responded to her query.

"I'm waiting for the legs of the coffee table to fly off in all directions".

Accustomed to nonsensical answers from her domestic staff, Pussy pressed for more details.

"*Why would that happen?*"

Joseph snapped back his reply.

"Because it would surprise me if they didn't!"

Pussy decided that it was not worth pursuing this bizarre topic of conversation and moved towards the patio without any further word. Joseph made to leave the condo but not before giving the coffee table one more glare of suspicion. Surely those two bills wouldn't be the only bad thing to happen to him today. But he was wrong. He just didn't know it yet.

***

The gallery owner came forward to greet Joseph as he entered Dalozzo. The expression on his face gave away that he was indeed very excited.

"Thank you for coming so quickly Mister Whynee. I think that you'll be very pleased with the news I have for you".

It was infectious. The man's enthusiasm helped to jolt Joseph out of his depressed mood. Mr Dalozzo led Joseph over to where his newly framed textile artwork was being displayed. It looked absolutely fantastic. Finished in dark wood, with a fetching grey background and a thin orange line around it. The entire effect was somehow more than the sum of its parts.

Joseph was somewhat stunned that it turned out so nicely. But then that thought faded when he realised that the framing would come at a cost. He was about to ask for the bad news on the price that he had to pay for it, when Mr Dalazzo pointed to a small orange sticker placed on the top right-hand corner of the glass covering the outfit.

Joseph didn't understand. He indicated as such to the man with a simple shake of his head. Mr Dalazzo responded with an ebullient exclamation.

"It's sold mister Whynee. You are now a fully fledged outsider artist. Congratulations!".

Joseph's world stopped momentarily. He hadn't really contemplated that the destroyed clothes 'artwork' would actually sell.

"What?" Was all that Joseph could think of to say under the circumstances.

Mister Dalozzo was more than happy to explain the entire situation to him in explicit detail.

"As is always the case with an emerging artist such as yourself. It was not just the raw power of the artwork that you have created that helped it to sell so quickly. It was the provenance that the piece came with".

This confused Joseph somewhat. He was unsure what French geography had to do with his Italian clothing artwork.

"I don't see how a place in France has a connection to my artwork mister Dalozzo?"

Too refined to show his surprise and frustration with Joseph, the man explained the misapprehension that had occurred.

"Not Provence in France. Provenance of the artwork. The history and the story surrounding it. It all helps to give the piece more . .... credibility".

This was something that Joseph understood. Nevertheless, he was still confused as to exactly what history his newly created artwork could possibly possess.

"I don't suppose you could spell it out for me please. Just so that we are on the same page. You understand?"

Joseph's plea was responded to with delight by Mister Dalozzo.

"Certainly. Well, where to begin? As you know, a number of the residents from Palazzo Versace frequent my gallery. They have told me of the shock that your artwork provoked at your recent party when it was shown for the first time. This alone could be considered the beginning of the provenance of your piece. But it is the back story that they were able to relay to me that really piqued the interest of the purchaser. She listened with keen interest to that part of the story".

Joseph indicated with a rolling motion of his hand that mister Dalozzo should continue.

"It was the reason that you decided to create the artwork. It really captures the angst that you must feel. Spending that money on the clothes, just to dismember them in the hope that you can create an artwork to sell and pay for your penile augmentation surgery".

Joseph's mouth fell open in absolute shock. He was still formulating in his mind the defence that he intended to put up against such an absurd assertion, when mister Dalozzo let Joseph know the sale price of his artwork.

“I like to tailor each artwork’s price to the potential purchaser, and to reflect the amount of effort and emotion that the artist has imbued the piece with. So, I think that you will be very happy with the sale price of thirty-two thousand dollars!”

The incredible sum of money gained for the accidental artwork shocked Joseph more than the thought that his fellow residents think that he needed penis enlargement surgery. He felt a warm feeling coming over him. At first, he was unsure what it was. But eventually he was able to prescribe a word to it, satisfaction.

For the first time in what felt like ages, things had worked out perfectly for him. This was a feeling at least equal to that of winning the RSL lottery prize at the beginning of summer. Pussy’s misdemeanour had resulted in him coming out on top for a change. That was more than enough money to pay for Charles Carver’s dental work. The huge champagne bill from the party. And the original payment price for the clothes. And there would still be money left over!

Shaking his head in amazement Joseph realised that mister Dalozzo was shaking his hand vigorously.

“Congratulations on the sale of your very fist artwork. An original Joseph Whynee! I’ll deduct the one-thousand dollars it cost to mount and frame the piece. The buyer pays the gallery’s premium. Therefore, I will write you a cheque for thirty-one thousand dollars right now”.

True to his word within a couple of minutes mister Dalozzo had retreated to his office, and then reappeared with the magical piece of paper. Joseph was still walking on a cloud as he left and took the foot bridge back over the main road to Palazzo Versace.

He was greeted by the doorman as he entered the building. Then as he was crossing the lobby, Joseph realised that he needed to celebrate somehow. Or rather, reward Pussy for her serendipitous help with his finances. He glided over to the concierge. The man looked up with a smile.

"May I please have a serving of foie gras delivered to my condo?"

"Certainly, mister Whynee. I'll have the kitchen get right on that for you".

"Thanks"

***

When Joseph arrived back home, Pussy was lying on the dining room table. She looked up as he entered.

"Pussy. I have a little surprise treat for you coming from the kitchen. It will be here soon".

This pleased the Queen of the household immensely.

"*Pussy loves surprises*".

"It's just my way of trying to be the best primary servant for you that I can".

"*Oh, that's just lovely Joseph*"

Joseph picked up on the reference immediately. Finally, she had got his name right. After all this time. It was a sign that everything was finally going his way. It must be.

"You remembered my name!"

Pussy was less than impressed at the inference that she had every miscalled him in the first place.

"*I've been calling you that all along numskull*".

It wasn't long before the doorbell rang. Careful to answer it in such a way as to obscure the view behind him, Joseph took the plate from the fellow and closed the door. He delivered it to the cat, placing it directly in front of her.

"Foie Gras. Only the best for my Pussy".

The cat was delighted and began to demolish it with gusto.

Chapter 41

Appropriately Named

Tymon and Barry had initiated a Saturday morning ritual whereby they would all gather for breakfast out on the patio. Barry said it was because they never got to enjoy breakfast together during the week. But Joseph suspected that Barry was just so enamoured at living in such luxury that he wanted to enjoy every bit of it. And a leisurely breakfast of pastries and coffee overlooking the plunge pool and the water garden, seemed appropriately snobbish.

Joseph had organised a bottle of Nicolas Feuillatte Palmes d'or 1998 vintage champagne to accompany the breakfast. The boys were delighted at the news of Joseph's artwork sale. They wanted to know more about the purchaser. But in the shock of discovering the amount that he had earned for it, Joseph had forgotten to ask. So, for now the new owner would remain something of a mystery. Joseph promised to find out what he could from the gallery soon.

It was then that his mobile phone rang. Barry took on the duty of opening the champagne, whilst he and Tymon listened to the conversation that Joseph was having with the caller. It consisted of "Of course I'm available", "That would be perfect" and "I'll meet you at the entrance to the marina".

When he hung up, he stopped Barry, who was about to pour him a flute of champagne.

"Not for me. I have to keep a zero, blood-alcohol level for taking out my first passengers on a site seeing cruise of the waterway this afternoon."

He smiled triumphantly. Brandishing the mobile phone in the air in a gesture of success. Barry and Tymon were overjoyed for him. They both gave a chorus of praise.

"That's fantastic. The first of many I hope"

"Excellent news. I'm sure it will go well".

The remainder of the breakfast felt like a perfect way to celebrate his new direction in life. The glimmer of an idea that he had had when first discovering he had won the condominium and the sailing boat, was about to start becoming reality.

***

Joseph had spent the rest of the morning on cloud nine. He put on a pair of dark-blue shorts and a white polo t-shirt. He felt that it imbued him with a nautical look. One befitting the captain of 'Beat the Odds'.

When it was the time to meet his paying customers, he stood waiting for them at the security entrance to the marina. True to their word a man and woman and a small dog approached him. They would have been in their sixties. Both a little rotund. And both wearing rather garish coloured clothing. The man was carrying a picnic basket in his left hand. The woman holding the dog's leash in hers.

"You must be my passengers for this afternoon?"

Joseph thought that he had better start the face-to-face introductions. He held out his hand to shake the gentleman's then the lady's.

"Samuel Smythe. And this is my wife, Stephanie".

It was Stephanie Smythe that introduced the smallest member of the party.

"And this is Fluffy Toffee Pooh-Pooh".

Joseph was a little taken aback. He wasn't expecting a dog as a passenger along with the Smythes. The furry thing seemed to have a lot of attitude, for a diminutive canine.

"It's not a problem to bring him along, is it? We go everywhere together. Don't we precious?"

Stephanie really wasn't giving Joseph an opportunity to object. And even if he did, who would look after the dog whilst they went sailing through the waterways. And besides, he did not want to sour the very first paying passenger trip that he took on his boat. So, he gestured that everything was fine by him.

"All good missus Smythe. I'm sure that Fluffy Toffee Pooh-Pooh will love an afternoon's sailing as much as we will".

"Excellent. Thank you so very much. And please call me Stephanie".

Joseph even reached down to attempt a pat on the head of Fluffy Toffee Pooh-Pooh, but the little dog growled menacingly at him.

With the pleasantries now out of the way, Joseph gave a wave to one of the security guards behind the tall gate. Recognising Joseph, the guard let him and his party through. He was a big burly fellow that looked intimidating simply because of his physical size.

"Good afternoon mister Whynee. Taking her out for sail on this lovely day?"

"Sure am. It's a perfect day for it".

As they filed down the marina toward Joseph's yacht, Samuel juggled the picnic basket.

"I've everything here to make this a splendid occasion".

Joseph helped the trio to board. They exchanged further small talk about being seasoned veterans when it came to cruising the waterways of the Gold Coast. They were both keen to go out to the open sea and try to spot a pod of dolphins or even some whales. Joseph let them know that it was a bit late in the season for whale watching, but they could get lucky.

With a newfound confidence, Joseph made the casting off of the boat look easy. Before long they were moving under motorised power down the waterway and heading for the open sea.

***

The afternoon was going splendidly. As luck would have it, they had in fact spotted a whale at close quarters. It's massive fin waving above the water in apparent hello to all close by. Joseph had 'Beat the Odds' now under sail and the entire experience was almost surreal, it was so beautiful. The Smythe's had enjoyed the contents of their hamper. Joseph refused all offerings of food and drink as he was determined to stick to his marine licence stipulations to the letter.

About two hours into the journey, Joseph suggested that they pull in the sails and use the fold-down swimming deck to put their feet into the water. Samuel and Stephanie thought that this was a great idea.

Joseph had just set it up when Fluffy Toffee Pooh Pooh jumped down from the main deck onto the platform.

"Looks like he is keen to get closer to the water". Said Joseph.

But the reality was far removed. The annoying little dog was about to prove that he could elevate his stature from nuisance to major problem maker in the flick of a tail. No sooner had Joseph returned to the main deck to ensure that all of the sails were secured when Stephanie let out a cry.

"Oh No! Fluffy Toffee Pooh Pooh. How could you?"

The admonishment in rhyme caught Joseph's attention. He turned to see what the fuss was about. There on the middle of the swimming platform, the small dog had deposited a rather large doggy poo. Joseph recoiled in horror. His sparkling clean boat swimming deck had been soiled by dog poop. Maybe that is why in the olden days it was called a poop deck, thought Joseph

[Editor] You are not funny, you know?

[Author] Mind your own business.

"Oh Joseph, I'm so very sorry. He's never done this sort of thing before. He knows that there is no doing any poopie-doops until we get back to shore".

Samuel tried to explain the abhorrent behaviour of the lilliputian animal. Stephanie too was mortified. But, not wanting anything to sully his first paid outing, Joseph decided that he would not make a fuss about it.

"I'll clean that up in just a jiffy!"

Joseph went below and retrieved some sanitary cloths and pair of gloves. Thankfully Samuel was able to produce a dog sanitary bag for Joseph to use.

"He certainly lived up to his name, eh?" Joked Joseph hoping to lighten the mood.

Unfortunately, the joke (such as it was), fell completely flat with Samuel and Stephanie.

"What do you mean?" Asked Samuel.

He seemed to be completely oblivious to the play on words that Joseph was referring to. His wife was no better. With a perplexed look on her face, she blinked a few times in bewilderment at the humorous jibe.

"I'll get rid of this straight away."

Joseph felt that if he needed to explain why Fluffy Toffee Pooh-Pooh's name related to his action on the swimming deck, then it wouldn't be funny anymore. Feeling that discretion was the better part of valour, he hurriedly went about cleaning up the mess without a further word.

It was then that they all noticed an odd whirring sound. Each of them, the dog included, looked up and around to find out where the sound was coming from. Stephanie was the first to spot it.

"It's a drone of some kind" She said, pointing to the noisy interloper.

They all looked up. It was a drone. Four propellers and quite a significant camera hanging from the underbelly of the artificial oversized insect. It seemed to be pointing at them for some reason.

Joseph completed his cleaning duties and stowed the bagged poo and cleaning utensils below. When he reappeared, Samuel and Stephanie were looking over the bow of 'Beat the Odds". Joseph joined them. A power boat was close by. But not close enough to read the decals on her side.

"That must be where the drone is from". Concluded Samuel.

"I wonder what they are shooting?" Asked Stephanie.

Joseph added his voice to the minor mystery.

"That symbol on the side of the boat. I can't quite make it out. But it looks familiar".

Both Samuel and Stephanie nodded in agreement. It was Stephanie who came up with the solution.

"Oh, of course. It is one of those twenty-four-hour news channels. That's what it is!"

The moment that she said it, it made perfect sense. The drone with the camera, and the powerboat. Samuel elaborated on the potential reason for it being in the area.

"They must have heard about the whale and wanted some footage".

It all became clear. They were just after a story for their news channel. It was a pity that the drone was so incredibly irritating, otherwise none of them would have minded in the slightest. They were still watching the boat, the sound of Fluffy Toffee Pooh-Pooh growling and barking interrupted their observations.

As one, they all turned around. From their position on the deck, they all had a clear view down to the swimming platform. The dog could be seen barking and growling at the water. He ran this way and that very agitated at what he was fixated upon below the surface of the water.

Nobody even had the time to verbalise, 'what is he barking at', before the unthinkable happened. A huge white pointer shark emerged from the water, almost in slow motion. It reared up and snapped at the hapless dog grasping the small creature in its saw-toothed jaws.

There was a spurt of blood as Fluffy Toffee Pooh-Pooh's head was neatly detached from his body. Somehow in a fit of gymnastic prowess, the shark managed to flip both the head and body of the dog into the air. Both pieces of the animal did various athletic looking somersaults, before landing simultaneously in the mouth of the shark.

The shark, having successfully devoured its intended victim, sank slowly below the surface of the water. It disappeared below the choppy surface without a trace.

"AAAAAAAAAAAAAAAAAAAAAAAAAAAAAAAA AAAAAAAAAAGGGGGHHHHHH!!!"

The high-pitched scream broke Joseph out of his amazed stupor. He automatically turned to Stephanie to offer comfort. It was a human reaction. Only to find that t was Samuel that had emitted the piercing howl. Stephanie was frozen. The shock was so absolute that she either did not know how to react, or simply was incapable of doing so under the circumstances.

Joseph turned from one to the other unsure of what to do. It was then that Stephanie broke her silence with a similarly soprano scream of abject horror.

"OOOOOOOOOAAAAAAAAAAHHHHHHH – TOFFEEEEE FLUFFYYYYY POOOOH POOOH!"

Joseph decided in the heat of the moment, and not thinking logically, that he would race down to the swimming deck to see if the shark may have spat out the morsel. It was only when he arrived on the platform and was leaning over the side that he realised, what a precarious position he had put himself in.

He quickly retreated to the safety of the main deck of the boat. He offered the only consolation that he could think of.

"Oh No! I am SO SORRY for your loss!"

It was a well-meaning platitude. But it did nothing the alleviate the shock of what had just unfolded before their eyes. It was impossible to determine how much time went by. Joseph was doing his best to comfort both Samuel and Stephanie. But they were inconsolable.

At one point he grabbed the half-finished champagne from its ice bucket and offered the couple a swig directly from bottle. Both obliged without even thinking about it. Joseph wished desperately that he had something stronger onboard for them. But he did not.

The afternoon was whisking past them in a flurry of tears and moaning. Joseph exhausted his supply of tissues and had to resort to paper napkins for the bereaving couple. And even then, they were in danger of all being used up.

Eventually it was decided to get back to shore as quickly as possible. Joseph let them know that he would report the incident to the authorities. It would not bring back the dog, but it had the air of a plan of action. And somehow that helped matters a little.

***

The journey back to the marina berth was excruciating. The couple occasionally still bursting out in unbridled mourning for the loss of the yapping dog. Even though the tour had ended in tragedy, Joseph couldn't help pondering about collecting the fee for the boat charter. He thought about it and then dismissed the idea. Only to think about it again a few more times on the journey.

In the end he thought that it would be too difficult to bid goodbye to the couple and then hold out his hand for money. What would he say exactly?

'Hope you had a pleasant trip. Gratuities are accepted with a smile'

Common sense finally prevailed, and he resolved to instead, give them a hug each and spout something empathetic but bland. Like, 'who knows why these things happen'; or similar.

Chapter 42

Provenance is Cumulative

Joseph was doing his best to be the voice of consolation for Samuel and Stephanie. They were still sobbing when they left him. After the boat had been correctly tied up to its berth, Joseph's attention was caught by both of the security guards. They were in their little hut near the entrance to the marina. One of them was signalling to him to come over.

It must have been shift change over or something. There was normally only one security guard on at a time. Joseph approached and could see that they were watching one of the TV screens inside the hut. As he got closer, he could see that the majority of them were for CCTV camera surveillance of the surrounds. But one of them was a dedicated television.

As he approached, one of the big burly men turned around with a rather cheeky smile on his face.

"You're a celebrity mister Whynee".

It was probably the last thing that Joseph expected to hear under the circumstances. He moved forward to the entrance of the hut to see why the television was holding the attention of the security guards so totally.

On the screen, one of the news channels was showing footage of a whale.

“Turn it up, turn it up”. Said one guard to the other.

He reached for the remote control and pushed the volume up so that Joseph could hear the narrative. It was then that he noticed that the footage was focusing on ‘Beat the Odds’. Could this be the newfound celebrity that the guards were referring to? He recalled that there was a news boat and a camera drone nearby. He’d forgotten all about it during the Fluffy Toffee Pooh-Pooh crisis.

The narrator then broke through with his description of the events that were about to unfold.

“What you are about to see ladies and gentlemen is shocking. Please turn away now if you have a weak stomach. As you can see, there is a yacht nearby and our news boat camera operator decided to collect some random footage of what looks to be a lovely day out on the water. But then tragedy strikes!”

Joseph’s stomach sank and he suddenly found it hard to breathe. The narrator continued his excruciating explanation of the events unfolding on the television.

“A poor little dog, having fun out on the water with its owners, is suddenly the latest meal for a huge white pointer shark. Here it comes now!”

The camera operator had managed to zoom in on Fluffy Toffee Pooh-Pooh as he was barking at the shark below the surface of the water. From this elevated angle, the predator could be seen as a foreboding dark shadow approaching the dog.

And just as he recalled it only an hour or so ago, the shark reared up and snatched the dog from the swimming deck. However, that wasn’t the worst of it. As if the sight of the dog being made a meal of by a large shark wasn’t bad enough, the camera then zoomed in on the name of the boat. ‘Beat the Odds’ was now forever associated with the demise of the furry little noisemaker.

Joseph actually screamed when he saw the footage. Both security guards looked at him.

The narrator continued his running commentary.

“It really is the most horrendous thing that I’ve seen in many years. And no doubt quite a shock for the captain and others aboard ‘Beat the Odds’. Let’s see that again, shall we? But this time in slow motion”.

Joseph couldn’t bear to hear anymore. He put his hands up to his ears. But both of the security guards wanted to talk to him.

“That has been shown on high rotation for the last hour and a bit”, Said one.

“Yeah, and the video has been seen on their website over a million times already. Isn’t that incredible?” Said the other.

“This is terrible!” Joseph shouted in reply.

He turned without a further word and marched away. The world felt like it was crumbling around him. Either he had become paranoid, or on his journey back to his condominium, he could have sworn that there were people pointing at him and whispering to each other as he passed them by.

Serving to confirm his fears that the news item had become the latest ‘must see’ video on the internet, Isabella phoned him.

“Have you seen the news?” She said without going through the usual pleasantries.

“Unfortunately; yes!” Joseph replied tersely.

“The news channel has shared that story with their overseas branches, and it is now being viewed throughout the United States and the United Kingdom and wider Europe.”

Isabella’s news was as welcome as haemorrhoids. And just as painful. Joseph groaned and rolled his eyes so far back into his head that it hurt. There was more to the conversation, but Joseph was barely responding to Isabella. By the time he made it back to his condo, Isabella was attempting to be as sympathetic as she could, via phone.

"You mustn't blame yourself. Nobody could have foreseen this happening. It's just plain bad luck. For the dog mostly. And for the owners. But for you too darling."

Joseph was quite beyond comfort though. A beeping alerted him to another incoming call. He looked at the display of his phone. It was the art gallery.

"I've got a call from the gallery. They're probably calling to tell me that the sale as fallen through".

Joseph was predicting the worst. However, Isabella had not yet heard of the sale, so was confused by his reference. She told him so, and he promised to fill her in at a later date. Then flicking the answer button on his phone, he tried to sound upbeat with his greeting.

"Hello"

"Joseph, this is Daniel Dalozzo from the gallery. I have the most exciting news!"

Then there was a pause. Perhaps mister Dalozzo had been a little too enthusiastic about the news and had failed express the usual sentiments under the circumstances. He made amends.

"By the way, horrible business this. It wasn't your dog, was it? No, of course it couldn't have been. No pets allowed where you live. However, every cloud has a silver lining. At least I hope that you think so when I tell you the news".

Joseph could really do with some cheering up at this point.

"I'll take ANY good news that I can get mister Dalozzo".

"Your artwork has just left the gallery for its new home. However, it is not going to the original buyer. She has managed to on-sell it because of the celebrity that you have acquired with that terrible mishap on your boat this afternoon. You know that it's all over the news, don't you?"

Daniel Dalozzo's hurried explanation was not having the effect that Joseph had hoped. He waited patiently for the punch line.

"Well, of course you and I will never see any of the re-sale money, that has all gone to the original buyer. But she has managed to on-sell it for sixty-four thousand dollars! TWICE the price that she paid for it. Isn't that absolutely fantastic?"

"What!?" Joseph was genuinely shocked.

"It's all about the provenance of the artwork Joseph. And Josephine has managed to add to the provenance by letting the new buyer know the history of the artwork, how she came to purchase it and your subsequent ghastly afternoon boat voyage. And now its value has increased by one hundred percent. Incredible. I've never seen an outsider-artist like yourself be so celebrated so early in their career. It is simply fabulous".

However, Joseph had stopped listening to mister Dalozzo when he heard a very familiar name. He sought immediate clarification on exactly who the original purchaser was.

"Josephine, you say. Is she a retired financial adviser?" Joseph asked with trepidation.

"Why yes, I believe that she is. Don't tell me that you know her?" Daniel Dalozzo answered.

Joseph simultaneously groaned and used his free hand to slap it on his forehead and then drag it down the length of his face. He could only imagine the 'provenance' that Josephine had attached to the artwork. It was bad enough that a poor defenceless little dog died so dreadfully on his boat therefore adding more to the story surrounding the artwork. But now, that mangled Versace outfit would forever hold the inside gossip from a would-be lover, that had gone atrociously wrong.

There were further sympathies from mister Dalozzo, but mostly surrounding the inability to collect any commission on the new re-sale price, rather than the fate of Joseph's yacht hire business. By the time that he hung up there were text messages from Karalee and Austin. Both wanting to know whose dog had so publicly been eaten off the back of his boat.

Standing in the middle of the living room, Joseph felt like he was sinking through the inlaid marble floor. Pussy appeared from somewhere and queried his general demeanour.

"*What's wrong with primary servant*?"

Joseph tried to answer without sounding like the weight of the world was crushing him. He failed.

"I've had a bad day out on the water Pussy".

Pussy was, for once, a little sympathetic.

"*Pussy saw what happened on the news. One less noise-making dog in the world is not a bad thing, Joseph*".

Pussy's reference to watching the news jolted Joseph out of his malaise.

"You can operate the television?"

"*Of course, Pussy can operate the television. It's not rocket-science, Poindexter*!'

Clearly insulted by Joseph, Pussy turned her back on him and sat looking out into the private courtyard. Joseph did another groan-sigh combination and pondered how much worse the day could get. But thinking about such things is the quickest way to ensure that they happen.

***

Millicent Williams stood at the door looking accusingly at Joseph. He had answered the doorbell and was delighted to find his neighbour standing there.

“Millicent. I could really do with a friendly face right about now”. He gushed.

“I don’t believe that Fluffy Toffee Pooh-Pooh had ever been onboard a boat before today”.

Millicent’s tone was stern. Joseph could not understand where the tension was coming from.

“How do you know that?” He asked.

“That was MY dog. The one that I had to GIVE UP thanks to Charles complaining about me keeping it here!”.

Joseph’s bad day just got worse. Millicent continued.

“Stephanie and Samuel Smythe were the couple that adopted Fluffy Toffee Pooh-Pooh from me! Who knew that his first outing aboard a boat would be his last?”

Joseph could not think of a single thing to say. The sound of the television permeated the icy coldness that was dripping from Millicent toward Joseph. Eventually he tweaked. He had not put the television on. And he thought that he could hear Stephanie Smythe’s voice. Millicent verbalised the discovery as well.

“Is that Stephanie’s voice I can hear on the television.?”

They both hurried into the living room. There seated on the sofa with the TV remote control beside her was Pussy. The news channel was on screen. Stephanie and Samuel Smythe were being interviewed. This caught their attention immediately.

"It was beyond ghastly. Horrifying. Our poor little dog chomped up like a meatball in an Italian restaurant".

The interviewer asked the grieving woman a pertinent but impossible to answer question.

"Did the captain of 'Beat the Odds' offer to do anything. Chase the shark down maybe. See if it could be given something to make it vomit up the remains of your poor little dog. Just so that it could get a decent burial?"

Joseph could not believe his ears. The fantastic courses of action suggested, had no basis in reality whatsoever. But Stephanie seemed to be influenced by the line of questioning.

"You know, he did not offer to do a thing!" she said accusingly.

"We'll see if we can get an interview the captain to find out what was going through his head. Thank you for speaking with us under such difficult circumstances".

The interviewer concluded with the usual sign-off and threw back to the studio. It was the first time in Joseph's life that he actually wished for a disaster of some kind to happen nearby. Or a huge financial institution to collapse. Anything to break the slow-news day that was focusing completely on his upsetting mishap.

Millicent gave Joseph one final glare and exited without a further word.

Joseph spent the rest of the day dodging phone calls form the news broadcaster. He complained that he was far too upset to be interviewed about the incident. And when not trying to shake off the press, he was dealing with people that he knew messaging or phoning him about the news article.

When they returned from wherever they had been for the day, Barry and Tymon were a comfort, thankfully. They were the only true source of sympathy that he received over the entire sorry incident. Eventually his phone stopped ringing and the day finally came to a close.

Chapter 43

Fame is Fleeting; Notoriety is Eternal

The following day had begun with further phone calls from the news agency wanting to interview Joseph. Again, he declined. Joseph contemplated hiding in his condominium all day, but Barry and Tymon convinced him to go out for a jog with them around the boardwalk and then up the Main Beach peninsula and back again. Exercise would improve his mood, they told him.

The three of them were at the boardwalk, ready to begin their jog when the security guards on duty, the same ones from yesterday, beckoned him over. The three of them obliged.

"What's up?" asked Joseph with more than a hint of pending doom.

"You'd better take a look at Beat the Odds mister Whynee". Said one.

Suspiciously, the other almost burst out laughing as the first was still speaking. Puzzled but compliant they were buzzed through the security gate and all five proceeded to where Joseph's yacht was berthed.

It looked fine upon approach. But Joseph was looking at the obvious, rather than the subtle. It was only when they were almost upon the boat that Tymon pointed out the name of the yacht had been vandalised, with what looked like black marker pen.

The ‘B’ had been scribbled out altogether. And the ‘O’ and been turned into a capital ‘D’. The ‘dd’ had been redescribed into an ‘o’ and a ‘g’. And the ‘s’ and similarly been scribbled out. The name of the boat had been effectively altered to “Eat the Dog”.

“EAT THE DOG!” screamed Joseph.

“OH WHYYYYYYY MEEEEEEEEE!!” he bellowed.

The security guards were absolutely chocking themselves with laughter at Joseph’s agony. Unfortunately, even Barry and Tymon were busy attempting to stifle their laughs. There was a mariner from a few boats down that also had a very loud laugh at the transformed name.

Joseph was aghast. The security team were supposed to prevent anything untoward from happening to the expensive sail and motorboats moored in the marina. He was perplexed at why they thought that it was so funny.

“Cheer up” one of them eventually managed to say.

“It’s only whiteboard magic marker, it will rub straight off”. Said the other.

This did nothing to alleviate the confusion that Joseph was feeling about the entire situation.

“How do you know?” He asked suspiciously.

“We lent it to the kids that did it”. Confessed one of the guards, continuing to snicker.

So that was it! They were part of the conspiracy to rebrand ‘Beat the Odds’ to ‘Eat the Dog’. Joseph could only surmise that the ‘kids’ referred to were the offspring of one of the other wealthy owners of a boat somewhere in the marina. And instead of discouraging such vandalism, the security guards were party to it.

Joseph's utter refusal to find the joke funny in any way, was out of step with the rest of the crowd. Seeing that he was not onboard with the humour, one of the guards offered to remove it himself.

"I'll clean it off and polish it up good as new"

Unable to see the funny side, Joseph bade his jogging buddies to get going. All of a sudden, he had a lot of energy that he could put into the planned exercise. They began their run from a standing start, only slowing down to get egress through the security gate of the marina.

***

When they arrived back at the condominium, things had not actually improved. Tymon and Barry had found on their social media feeds, a photo of the altered boat name. Apparently the 'kids' who had committed the vandalism had photographed it and it had gone viral.

Joseph elected to have a shower and see if that could help improve his day any. When he finally emerged from his bedroom, Tymon and Barry were showered and changed and sitting in the living room.

"You know, we are almost out of cat food for some reason. That soft stuff in the foil packets. I thought that we had a lot, but it seems to have disappeared".

Tymon's observation only helped to stick another shard of dissatisfaction into Joseph. He had not let on to the guys that his father had been serving it up as a foie gras substitute at the party. He was about to shrug it off when the phone rang. 'Saved by the bell', Joseph thought.

Answering it he found Ismail on the other end.

"Oh good, I've caught you. We are having an impromptu immediate meeting of the residents in the ballroom. You're the last one that I needed to get hold of. Can you come across right away? There is an announcement that the press has made that the residents need to be aware of".

Joseph expected the absolute worst. This simply had to be about the demise of Fluffy Toffee Pooh-Pooh and somehow, he was going to the get the full blame for it. But what alternative did he have? There was no avoiding the meeting. He was part of this community now, for better or worse. He simply had to attend. With a resigned-to-his-fate note in his voice he accepted the invitation and let Ismail know that he would come straight away.

Joseph gave a farewell wave of his fingers as if ii were the last that he would give anyone. He felt like a man going to be hanged by the neck until dead. Seeing that Joseph had something to contend with, neither Tymon nor Barry asked for further details.

When he was gone, the guys sat in the living room quietly. There was an air between them that something should be said but was not. The moments of silence turned into an uncomfortably long pause. Eventually Barry felt compelled to verbalise what he knew they were both thinking.

"Should we say anything about the talking cat?"

Tymon looked to the ceiling as if he was contemplating a brain twisting equation. After a while he returned his gaze to Barry and gave his reply.

"I don't want to jeopardise our position here. We are on a really good wicket you know".

"I know" confirmed Barry. Tymon continued.

“My grandmother in Zakopane used to say that her cat could talk to her. But we all just thought that she was old and crazy. Who knew that she these things could actually happen?”

There was another momentary pause as both contemplated how they both came to be in the exact situation as Tymon’s grandmother. Barry chipped in with his take on the subject.

“It’s getting harder to ignore her. When she told Joseph; if foie gras weren’t meant to be eaten they wouldn’t be so tasty; I nearly blurted out with laughter”.

Tymon agreed.

“Yes. I had to bite my tongue from laughing too”.

As if sensing that she was being spoken about, Pussy ambled into the living room.

“*What are Pussy’s two new supplementary servants talking about*?”

There was nothing to it, they simply had to answer a direct question. Barry obliged.

“We were saying that we need to get you some more food. We’re almost out”.

This pleased Pussy immensely. Not in the least bit surprised that they could hear her, she proceeded to put in an order for additions to the usual fare that was served-up on a regular basis.

“*Excellent. Pussy will have some double-cream Camembert, and some of that foie gras, and definitely some of that caviar too*!”

The overly expensive and exclusive food items brought a roll of eyes from both Tymon and Barry. Tymon tried (without success) to convince Pussy that such items were rather expensive.

"Pussy, those are very high-priced foods. I'm sure that you can get by on your usual kitty food only. Can't you?"

Pussy was having none of it.

"*Expensive? Money and finance are a human construct. Felines don't get concerned over such trivial matters. Don't bother Pussy with these pointless details in future*".

Satisfied that she had settled the matter to her satisfaction, Pussy yawned and settled down on the cool marble floor for a nap.

Tymon and Barry exchanged rolled-eyes expressions. It looks like their Sunday shopping trip was about to get pricier than originally anticipated.

***

Joseph marched toward the ball room as if he was walking from a prison cell to his execution. When he eventually arrived, he found the residents all gathered in groups talking amongst themselves. Joseph's entry caused a few knowing looks. No doubt everyone was now familiar with the demise of Millicent's former pet dog aboard his yacht.

Ismail was the only one that seemed genuinely pleased to see him.

"Ah good you're here. We can begin".

Ismail had a head set on, with a microphone coming from it to just in front of his mouth. There must have been a remote unit hooked to the back of his belt, because he reached around and an audible switching-on of the system could be heard through the ball room speakers. Ismail called the meeting to order.

"Thank you everybody for coming at such short notice. When you hear the news, I'm sure that you will understand why we needed to make you aware of the facts".

The crowd had now stopped their casual conversations and were paying close attention to Ismail. He continued with a little of the background behind why the meeting was called.

"When our latest resident, Joseph, took possession of condominium number four, there was a great deal of rumour and misunderstanding about who he was and what we should expect when he arrived".

The crowd murmured its understanding and acceptance of the premise. Ismail continued.

"However, we've come to accept our latest resident with all of his unique quirks with open arms".

Joseph's spirits lifted momentarily. Until the absolute silence of the crown beat them down once more. Unperturbed, Ismail went on speaking.

"A press release is being made today about Glam-Metal band SSIK. You may remember that they had a string of hits back in the nineteen-eighties. You may also remember that they were notorious for trashing hotel rooms and in general some pretty deplorable behaviour."

This garnered a sound of remembrance and recognition from the crowd. Joseph could see people nodding and affirming their recollection of the rockers from the last century.

"They are doing a farewell world tour and will be playing one show only at the convention centre here on the Gold Coast. And I wanted to let you know that they will be staying here at Palazzo Versace in four of our best hotel suites."

There was clearly alarm from the residents at the very thought. Seeing and hearing the mood of the residents Ismail acted quickly to quell their fears.

"I assure you that they will not have access to the residential areas of the complex. And that the hotel management will not put up with any bad behaviour from them. Regardless of their status as celebrities".

Joseph could feel the general discontentment of the residents ease up a little bit. Ismail concluded his speech to the crowd.

"We can look forward to them being out guests early in the new year. Are there any questions at this time?"

As it turned out there were none. Therefore, Ismail thanked everyone for coming and moved over to Joseph to talk to him. Firstly, though he ensured that he had switched off his microphone. The crowd did not dissipate at all, instead they all remained talking in small groups, availing themselves of the opportunity to catch up on other matters.

"Nasty business about Millicent's former dog. I saw it on the news". Ismail said.

"I imagine that everybody has seen the whole sorry thing" Lamented Joseph.

"There you are!"

The voice behind them belonged to Harrington Whynee. He approached Joseph and Ismail.

"They told me that I'd find everybody here". Harrington said looking somewhat concerned.

"Dad what are you doing here?" Asked Joseph.

“I wanted to ensure that you were ok, after the incident, you know. The one on the news. Everybody is talking about it. And of course, this!”

Harrington held up his phone. On the screen, Ismail and Joseph could see a social media photographic post of the name of ‘Beat the Odds” twisted into ‘Eat the Dog’.

Joseph groaned audibly. Ismail gasped in shock. Overall though it was a lovely gesture for Harrington to come and check up on his son. Joseph thanked his father for his consideration. He let him know that it was just as hard dodging the news reporters that wanted to interview him over the matter as it was to watch the poor dog get consumed off the back of his boat.

“It looks like it will be just as hard dodging the social media fallout too!” Joseph concluded.

Harrington looked around at the gathered residents. Some of which he recognised from the party.

“What’s the gathering all about Ismail?” Harrington asked

“Just an information session about some VIP’s coming to the hotel early next year. I wanted to circumvent the rumour mill from inventing anything that would alarm the residents”.

Ismail’s explanation seemed to relieve Harrington much more than it should. He audibly sighed. Standing behind Ismail were Mister Ari and Missus Tia Nanaia. It was just at that moment that Tia’s large handbag gently nudged the toggle switch to the ‘on’ position of Ismail’s microphone headset.

Harrington felt that he owed Ismail and Joseph an explanation of his concern about the gathered residents. He blurted out his words.

“I thought that you’d found out that I served cat food as pâté at Joseph’s party”.

Harrington's voice was picked up nicely by Ismail's microphone and it echoed through the large room resounding clearly from the hidden speakers in the ceiling. A deathly silence filled the room. If there is an adjective for a group of people all simultaneously widening then narrowing their eyes in shock and disapproval, then it would be 'whyneed'.

And everybody's eyes whyneed as they regarded Harrington in the cold light of his confession. Acutely aware that everybody was staring at him, Harrington made a quick exit.

"Glad you're well son. Got to go!"

And he scampered from the room at a speed not befitting a man of his years. The accusatory stares of his fellow residents moved to Joseph. Acutely aware that he had all whyneed eyes upon him, Joseph blushed with embarrassment. Then, feeling that he had to say something, anything, to address the awkward confession, Joseph addressed them all.

"It looks like things are about to get a whole lot more interesting around here".

***

So, this is where we are going to leave Joseph's story for the time being. His formerly ordinary life has been turned completely around to become a most extraordinary life indeed. He doesn't know it yet, but the visiting glam-metal band SSIK are going to resonate with him in ways that he could never had expected. Pussy the cat will expand her tastes for expensive foods. And the other residents that Joseph holds in such high esteem, may yet prove themselves to be as foible as the rest of us.

THE END

The sequel:

Divorced, Dog Owner Too

www.ingramcontent.com/pod-product-compliance
Lightning Source LLC
LaVergne TN
LVHW010559100826
845148LV00014B/2772